Remember

Rainee

By

Lexi Pierce

DEDICATION

This book is dedicated to the many people who have brought love
and joy to Rainee's life:

Grandma Inez who faithfully taught that Jesus loves all children
The kumquat people
Reverend Teston
Avis and Delos
Len and Dorine
Tom and Ruth

And to my family:

Calvin, faithful husband and best friend
My daughters, my heroes

Main characters in the book

Rainee: childhood self character

Lorraine: adult self character

Jenna: Rainee's oldest sister

Eileen: Rainee's second oldest sister

Marta: Rainee's sister one year younger

Crystal: Rainee's baby sister

Autumn: Lorraine's oldest daughter

Ariana: Lorraine's middle daughter

Allison: Lorraine's youngest daughter

Justin: Lorraine's first husband

Derrick: Lorraine's current spouse

Mrs. Washington: art teacher who rescued Rainee

Dell: husband of art teacher who

               rescued Rainee

Pastor & Mrs. Stevens : Rainee's guardians

Chapter 1: Rainee's Life in the Swamps

It was hot, dripping hot, as only Florida days could be in the swampland. Tiny Rainee combed back her ragged chin length limp white blonde hair with her tiny, bony pale hands and sighed as if she were breathing her last breath.

Rainee's small, perfectly formed ears no longer acknowledged the noise of the constant buzz of insects at work. The flies trying to land on her translucent skin kept her moving constantly as she stood in the patch of grass among the wild palmettos and thick undergrowth. A few swamp cedars among the growth gave off a sweet smell that mixed with the wet, overwhelming perfume of the millions of tropical blossoms. The smells made her feel a bit light-headed.

Rainee wriggled her well-formed nose. A purplish knob now stuck out between her eyes. The purple bump's constant painful throb reminded her why she stood here in the swamp.

She supposed she should at least look for one of her sisters. It was not really safe to be here in the swamp alone. Her dad constantly told her that poisonous snakes lurked everywhere. And the alligators that fascinated her were really dangerous to children.

Rainee's dirty face looked white despite a spot of sunburn on each cheek. The skin was drawn tightly over sharp bones. She began to feel the sunburn and thought now was a good time to move. She looked around with large gray eyes staring out from sockets too old for her age. She poked at the hole in her dirty t-shirt and adjusted her too-big shorts. Then scuffing her small bare feet in the sand, she started out of the grassy patch and through the palmettos. The sharp fronds caught at her too-big shorts and made scratchy sounds. She stepped lightly away to prevent skin scratches.

Just as she stepped onto the dirt track, Rainee

remembered Jenna, her oldest sister, told her this morning that today was her, Rainee's, fifth birthday. She wished someone would remember but knew the likelihood was small. Sometimes she wondered if her Momma even realized she was her child, because she never talked to her...only if Rainee demanded an answer. Maybe she should ask her if she remembered it was her birthday.

Maybe Crystal would be playing outside with her stick? Crystal was always hollering as if in pain, and Mama was screaming for someone to just make her stop. Then she would set her outside and seem to forget her. Rainee didn't know how old Crystal was; just that she was still in diapers and stank a lot because Momma forgot to change them.

Most times when Rainee found Crystal alone outside, she tried to play with her, worried she might hurt herself. Crystal never cried when Rainee played with her. Rainee smiled. Maybe Crystal liked her? Maybe she could tell Crystal it was her birthday? Would she understand? Probably not, but at least she would have someone to tell!

Wandering down the sandy dirt track, Rainee headed back to the half-built deserted house that had tar paper walls. This was what they called their home. Inside there were no walls. Someone forgot to finish the house, she thought quite often. They had moved in when just a frame existed. Daddy covered the frame with tar paper. It would have been a nice house if someone had finished it...but then her family would not be living there. Arriving in the yard, Rainee saw that Crystal was nowhere to be seen; so, she turned to the house.

Rainee opened an old-fashioned screen door and heard a bang as the spring pulled it tight shut behind her. It was easy to see who was in the house anyway, because of the lack of walls! The two by fours had been set to make walls, but then the walls were not made. From the door Rainee could see the wood planks they slept on and called beds. Crystal was asleep where Momma usually slept.

Turning to the kitchen area, Rainee saw Momma cooking greens and beans. The smell of cornbread filled the air. Hmmmm. She liked beans and cornbread…the greens, ugh, but Momma made her eat them anyway. If she didn't, she slapped her face hard, and it really hurt. Absent-mindedly she felt her nose…yes, the lump was still there. Momma had recently slapped so hard her nose broke…Momma told her it was broken. That was why breathing was so hard, but no one took her to the doctor. She did not know what a doctor looked like; so, she did not question why no one took her.

"I'm hungry," she told Momma defiantly. She slowly inched into the kitchen area, as if afraid to go there.

Momma looked at her middle daughter with a look on her face sour enough to turn milk. Her dark brown hair was cut chin length but had been permed. The straggly curled mess hung limp in the humidity. Momma wiped a dirty hand across her bony face, too wrinkled for her thirty five years. "Can eat in about an hour," was all she said as she turned to stir the greens again. Her shoulders were permanently hunched forward as if she always carried a heavy stone. Her large gray eyes, also sunken in their sockets, looked lifeless as she stared into her cooking.

"Momma," Rainee whispered hopefully.

"Yes," Momma replied impatiently and poked at the pinto beans.

"Do you remember what today is?" she whispered.

"I can't hear you," Momma answered in an irritated tone, snapping her emaciated jaw open and shut as if catching flies. "Speak up girl if you want me to hear you!"

Rainee cringed as she stood about three feet from her mother, anticipating yet another blow to her face. Suddenly she decided she needed to be brave even if she got hurt. Raising her voice slightly, she spoke clearly in her light musical voice, "Momma, today is my birthday. Jenna says I am five now."

"Hmmmm," Momma almost grunted in a low snarl-y voice, shaking her damp curls as she put the wooden spoon next to the stove on the unfinished plywood counter. She turned toward Rainee and looked her up and down thoroughly, still snarling. "Yup, January 28. My mother's birthday. That makes it yours, too. Well, happy birthday, gal. Now go play or something and get out of my way!" She turned back to the stove and pulled open the oven door to check the cornbread. Rainee jumped backwards to avoid being burned by the oven door, tripping on a rag rug behind her.

Catching her balance as her bony, right knee touched the kitchen floor; Rainee felt a tear escape down her cheek. Righting herself, she turned back toward the kitchen door. Outside once again, Rainee went in search of Jenna. Jenna was two years older than Rainee and wise, so Rainee thought. She would know what to do.

Rainee soon found Jenna playing down the road at a real house. The house had painted yellow wooden sides and green shutters at the windows. The roof had those red clay half circle tiles instead of tar paper, too. The yard was covered with real, soft grass except for part of the backyard. That was made of raked sand. Play equipment was set up in the sand---a swing set and a merry-go-round.

Jenna was friends with the little girl, Brenda, who lived at this house. Her parents did not seem to mind that the dirty child showed up every day after school. In fact, when Rainee had tagged along recently, she discovered why Jenna went there every day.

Blonde, with beautiful skin and clothes, Brenda fascinated Rainee. And her mother was amazing. She was tall, with shoulder length dark brown hair that swung back and forth and was shiny...but best of all was her smile. She was always smiling at Brenda...and any children Brenda brought home. Rainee liked her smile. And if they came right when school was out, Brenda's mom always gave them a cookie or banana. That was why Jenna came every day--food.

Rainee and her sisters were always hungry. Beans and greens and cornbread were good, but often they only got that once a day. In the morning they might get a piece of bread and coffee. Jenna told her at school they got free lunch and she liked that. But Rainee did not go to school, so she never got lunch. She rubbed her tummy, as it hurt when she thought about food. Today she was lucky. Brenda's mom had a cookie for her. When Brenda's mom held out the cookie in her beautiful, red-tipped hand, the child smiled her best smile and told her thank you, like Jenna told her. Brenda's mom seemed pleased with Rainee, and told her she had good manners. Rainee blushed and thanked her again as she took the cookie.

Grasping the large cookie in her right hand, Rainee joined Jenna on the wide, white porch swing with Brenda. The swing was so wide it could hold several Rainees. She like swinging here as the painted green floor of the porch slid back and forth under her until she got dizzy. But best of all was getting to eat the cookie that had pieces of chocolate in it! Rainee loved chocolate.

Jenna had brown hair like Momma. It was short and permed and looked all frizzy in the heat. Jenna's face did not look like Rainee's at all. Jenna's face looked kind of flat with a knobby nose sticking out of the middle of it. Her forehead looked too big, because someone cut her bangs almost up to the roots of her hair, giving her pale blue eyes a frightened look. She did not care. She told Rainee she knew she was homely, and Rainee was pretty. It did not matter as she loved Rainee anyway. Jenna was not as thin as Rainee, but neither realized this was because of the lunches Jenna got at school. Rainee snuggled down next to her big sister in the swing and quietly listened as the two other girls chattered.

Talking about school, Jenna burst out unexpectedly that it was Rainee's fifth birthday. For no reason Rainee could understand, pretty Brenda started shouting to her mother in the house, "Momma, it is Rainee's fifth birthday! Do we have a present for her?" Brenda jumped down from the swing and skipped toward the kitchen door. This was a shiny metal door and had a perfect, unbroken screen.

Brenda's mom came to the screen door and opened it about a foot. She looked at the crumpled up little tow-headed blond child in the swing and smiled. "Yes, I think I do," she said. "Rainee, why don't you come inside and get your presents?" Rainee looked up surprised at first, and then hopeful. Jenna grinned and pushed her off the swing. Nimble as a cat, Rainee landed on her feet. Both girls followed Brenda eagerly into the house.

"What did you get for presents at home?" Brenda asked Rainee rather innocently when they stood inside the shiny new 1950's chrome, black and white kitchen.

Embarrassed, Rainee rubbed her bare toe against the shiny, black and white checked linoleum floor. Jenna spoke for her when Rainee said nothing. "Rainee can be kinda shy," she said. "Rainee never gets birthday presents. Momma said she was born on Grandma's birthday, so she wished she was never born. Our mama hates Grandma. We never celebrate Rainee's birthday."

Brenda's mother stood listening to this innocent report in horror on the other side of the swinging door that separated the kitchen from the dining room. Her blue eyes round, and her lips pressed tightly together, she pushed open the swing door a little too forcefully. "Well, today, Rainee, you are having a birthday party!" she exclaimed as she got down the cookie jar and filled a plate with cookies. Then she drew a pitcher of milk from the small ice box. She asked the children to wash their hands and faces at the sink while calling outside for her other daughter to come into the house.

"Today is Rainee's birthday!" Brenda's mother announced to Lanny, her older, brown-haired daughter, "And she is five. That makes her a big girl! And she is a nice girl, too. So today, we are all going to eat as many cookies as we want, and drink all this milk until it is gone!" She set the cookies and milk on the table, bringing out small Tupperware glasses for the milk and napkins for the cookies.

The girls all giggled and started to reach but Brenda's momma cried, "No, not yet, we have to sing happy birthday to Rainee!" Soon all the children's voices joined hers to sing happy birthday to Rainee for the very first time in her life. Rainee felt her heart begin to glow and a smile come onto her face like it would never leave. She knew they would have to eat all the greens and beans when she got home, but she took three cookies anyway. Today was her birthday, and she felt good.

Treats over, Brenda's mom announced present time. She told Rainee to close her eyes. Bending over, she looked at the tiny face with eyes squished shut and saw the ugly purple lump on Rainee's nose. A look of anger quickly passed her face and left. She was glad she could do something nice for this tiny, sweet little girl no one seemed to want.

Soon Brenda's mom placed a box in front of Rainee and draped something soft across her arm. Rainee opened her eyes when Brenda's mom told her she could. Her eyes widened with delight, for inside the box she found a whole bunch of cookies just for her. And across her arm was a pretty yellow cotton dress Brenda had outgrown. It still looked new to Rainee. Rainee started to cry. "For me?" She asked in wonder as she touched the lace on the yellow frock. "Yes, Rainee, I think it will fit. You go home and wash up and try it on, OK? And hide the cookies…they are just for you. OK?"

Then Brenda's mother did something Rainee had never felt before. She knelt down and kissed Rainee on her dirty cheek and hugged the fragile child. "God made you a special little girl, Rainee. Don't ever forget it." Rainee looked into Brenda's mother's smiling eyes and knew she meant what she was saying.

"I am special," she whispered and smiled back. "Thank you."

Gathering her prizes, Rainee took Jenna's hand to walk home for supper. It did not seem so miserably hot anymore. Although the swamp grew up on both sides of the road with palmettos closing in to scratch their legs, she did not notice. Today she turned five and found out she was special. And she had a brand new dress to prove it.

Chapter 2: Of Kumquats and Lemonade

Rainee stood in awe. Her mouth was shaped in an 0, showing where her two front teeth fell out just after her sixth birthday. Her always uncombed blonde hair had been divided and the top half pulled into a tight pony tail with a rubber band. The pony tail was so short, it stood straight up to the ends of the hair, where it curved slightly. Her usual attire of a dirty white t-shirt and shorts several sizes too big showed several holes today, but she paid no mind. Rather, her gray eyes stared wide open ahead of her, where, as far as she could see, were rows and rows of citrus fruit trees—oranges, grapefruits, lemons and limes.

The sandy, carefully tilled soil beneath her feet showed no weeds between the trees on the ground, just the white sand, with an occasional dropped fruit marring its surface. Between Rainee and the trees stood a crude split log fence, easily negotiated by the agile legs of the little girl as she scrambled into the orchard.

Jenna, now eight, discovered the orchard yesterday; so, today she did not bother to stop and admire the view. Rather, she scrambled through the fence as soon as they arrived. She now sat under the nearest orange tree rapidly peeling an orange, her gangly legs crossed. Her knobby knees poked through her ill-fitted beige shorts. Jenna's hair had grown some and most of the perm had been sheared away, leaving straight brown hair. Her bangs were still un-naturally short, leaving her smudged face looking startled. She seemed to not realize her looks, as she tore away at the fruit in her hands.

Rainee joined Jenna on the ground and held out her hands expectantly as Jenna peeled. Rainee had difficulties with her hands; so, completing tasks like peeling oranges was hard for the tiny child. Jenna often helped her with such chores. School in the coming fall would be really hard, Jenna thought, because Rainee could not tie her shoes or hold a pencil right. By then they would be expecting her to wear shoes and write. Rainee had never owned a pair of shoes before....what would she do?

Jenna peeled off a generous section of the orange and handed it to the waiting younger sister. Rainee began to munch, allowing the liquid gold of juice to slither down her already dirty chin. "Hmmmmmm," was all she said as she finished her part of the fruit. Jenna finished hers and then stood to retrieve another orange globe.

"Don't you think we might get caught?" Rainee suddenly asked fearfully. "Don't kids who steal get sent to jail?" She looked around the two of them furtively and then up at Jenna, expecting Jenna to once again care for her.

"Don't worry, you ninny," Jenna scoffed with a crooked smiled that showed her crossed front teeth. "The people that own this place live in a house way on the other side of the orchard. They won't miss the little fruit we eat." Jenna proceeded to pick the second orange and sat down to peel it. "Sides, we are hungry. God put the fruit here for us hungry kids to eat. That's how I sees it." Then she handed Rainee her share of the second orange. They stayed in the orchard and munched on fruit until the sun set. Then they slipped quietly home through the night with only a full moon to guide them.

Each day they returned to the far end of the orchard to fill themselves with fruit for several weeks. Rainee's skin began to take on a healthier color, no longer pale and almost see-through. Her dull, sunken eyes began to sparkle, and she felt herself beginning to like herself more. She had no idea the fruit was the reason, only that now she felt as if she was not just a shadow anymore.

Rainee's once guilty conscience had abated, and now she joyfully joined Jenna each day to steal as much fruit as both of them could eat. They even became so brave as to venture into the middle of the orchard and eat a few grapefruit, because Jenna knew Rainee had a real taste for sour things. Still, no one seemed to notice or care that the two dirty, homeless waifs took up residence among the fruit trees.

Fall arrived and with it school for Jenna. Having repeated first grade twice, she was finally moved into the second grade along with sister, Eileen. Rainee, however, remained home despite being six years old. Their mother saw no sense in sending Rainee to first grade....she might catch up with the older two, she reasoned, and two in the same grade was hard enough.

So Rainee continued to play in the swamps alone much of the day, chasing butterflies, and watching the nest of alligators by the old cedar log creek bridge when she felt brave. There were big alligators there. Much bigger than Rainee, and they scared her a bit, but if she did not get too close, they did not seem to mind. And if she got brave and got on the bridge itself, they paid her little heed. Looking closer, you could see little kid alligators, and closer still, baby ones. These she liked to watch. Once a rabbit got too close and she watched a huge alligator grab the rabbit and eat it whole. Yuck, she thought as she watched the alligator toss the torn animal and then gulp. Yuck. But she came back anyway, almost every day.

No one knew she visited the alligators. Why would they? No one knew where she was most of her life. Mother never asked her where she was going, and she never asked where she had been when she would appear at the house hungry. No. She was a tiny soul set free on the natural world without anyone caring what would become of her, but she did not care. Away from the house it was peaceful. Nature was so interesting! And always making pretty musical sounds....and no one hit her.

Almost by instinct, Rainee headed home when Jenna was due from school. She would wait in the yard for her big sister, who would tell her about that magical world of school. They would then go to Brenda's for their snack...and after playing hard, would excuse themselves for dinner...only mother never had dinner ready before dark. So, they would sneak down to the very end of their palmetto-lined road to the orange orchard and have their fruit feast for the day. Rainee thought her life pretty good about then. She even felt happy…that was until a day shortly before Christmas, when her world would change forever.

Jenna and Rainee, dirty as usual, were sitting among all the old orange rinds from their last gorge eating new oranges, when Rainee heard the snap of a twig very close by. Thinking of the wild bobcat she once saw in the swamp, she braced to run.

Then another twig snapped, but this time a voice accompanied the noise, "Hmmm, I see our little thieves are at it again," an old man's voice chuckled.

Rainee could see no one yet, but she knew their secret feasting had come to an end and was terrified. Found out… "What will jail be like?" She cried out to Jenna.

"Hush," Jenna whispered hoarsely, "Down here maybe they don't see us yet."

The old man's voice chuckled again as he stepped from behind a tree only a few feet from them. Dressed in denim overalls and an old cotton plaid shirt, the man called softly, "Oh, but I do see the two of you." As Rainee crouched to run, the kind old voice continued, "No need to run, my dear. We will not hurt you, will we, Martha?"

The old man was tall and stood straight. He had a ring of white hair around a bald head and a wide white mustache over his smiling lips. In his knarled right hand he held two large paper pokes (a poke, for those of you who are not from the South, is a grocery bag). He handed one poke to the old lady with him and shook open the one left in his hand.

The woman looked at the two girls with smiling blue eyes and the kindest look Rainee had ever seen. She also shook the poke open in her withered hands. "Tell you what, girls. We have been watching you steal our fruit for weeks now….and we have watched you get better...My, the little one has color in her cheeks now, Samuel, isn't that lovely?" The old woman smiled widely. Her smile seemed to reach her eyes, now faded blue, but dancing. She shook her short, permed white hair as she continued to shake out the poke.

Rainee self-consciously touched her own dirty face and stared unblinking at the kind lady's face. "I think they are afraid of us," the lady sighed, clicking her tongue against what were obviously still her own teeth, as they were old and stained. "There is no need to be afraid, little ones. We won't hurt you. We can tell how hungry you girls have been, so we have said nothing all these weeks. God gave us this orchard of fruit and it is much too much fruit for two old people to pick anymore."

The old man called Samuel held the poke in his hand out to Jenna. "Here, take this," he suggested softly as he shook the poke slightly. "Fill it up completely. We go by where you girls live quite often and wonder how you stay alive! SO, fill up these two bags clear to the top....we can see several other children at that place...and that they are hungry, too. When we are finished picking, we want you to come to the house. We have some other things for you."

Rainee, mouth agape, took the oranges as Jenna picked them and placed them carefully into the poke. The woman named Martha and the man named Samuel began to pick fruit and add it to the poke, too, but Samuel wandered over to the grapefruit trees and brought a few grapefruit back to add to the oranges. They noticed the grapefruit peels on the ground, too, and knew one of the girls was fond of that sour fruit.

When Rainee's poke was almost too heavy to carry, and Jenna's, too, the lady named Martha took Rainee's poke. She then, took her hand, "Come up to the house. I have made a lunch of sandwiches and lemonade for you to finish your meal today!"

In disbelief Rainee followed the lady with Jenna close

behind. She furtively looked from side to side to plan her escape with each step, but finally realized the two old people were probably too frail to hurt her.

For the first time Rainee caught sight of the old white Florida homestead as they cleared the grove. A wide veranda graced two sides of the house where several swings and summer chairs sat beckoning invitingly. Rainee ran up the porch steps and flung herself onto the closest swing as Jenna joined her. They pumped the swing for a moment and chattered, quite forgetting their hosts.

Martha and Samuel sat the fruit on the edge of the porch and disappeared into the house. Soon Martha reappeared with frosty glasses of freshly made lemonade. Bits of lemon pulp floated in them. Samuel was close behind with large plates of sandwiches and pale, glittering sugar cookies. Rainee looked in astonishment as Samuel produced tiny plates and filled two for Rainee and Jenna.

The porch swing swung to a squeaky halt as he offered the two plates of food to the children. Shyly each reached out and took a plate. Rainee looked at Samuel with tears in her eyes and said, "Thank you," as Jenna had taught her. Then Martha offered her a glass of lemonade.

They sat listening to the old couple talk about their own grandchildren who now lived far away in a place called Georgia. They munched the food and drank lemonade until the sun slipped behind the trees.

"Oh, my," Martha seemed to suddenly sense the lateness of the day, "Samuel, you walk the girls home, OK?" She picked up a poke of fruit and gave it to Jenna. Samuel picked up the second poke, "You tell your mama this fruit is from their friends, Martha and Samuel, and your family is welcome to all the fruit they can eat so long as you live in that place." She smiled and looked at Samuel. "There is only one condition."

Rainee knew it was too good to be true! Now they would send them to jail. She started to look scared again, which made Samuel laugh. "It is nothing bad," Samuel reassured her. "It is just we think you girls should know something about God. SO, in exchange for the fruit, we want you to agree to go to Sunday School with us at the Baptist Church across from your school come Sunday morning!"

"Sunday School?" Rainee asked innocently, "What is Sunday School? You mean there is really a school on Sunday I can go to?"

Martha laughed rather incredulously. Poor girls, she thought. "Do you know who God is?" She asked.

Rainee nodded her head hesitantly. "Yes, it is a word Dad uses before he hits me. Jenna says, though, that God made things like your oranges."

Martha gasped a little under her breath, then reached out and gently stroked the tow-headed child. "My dear, hitting you is a bad thing. God does not want us to harm his little children. You see, Rainee, God is a spirit. You cannot see Him, but He is alive. He created everything you see including you, his child, his most special creation.

Suddenly Rainee remembered something someone else said to her so long ago. Brenda's mother told her she was special. Was this why?

Curious, Rainee's quivering mouth opened to speak and then closed. Finally, she swallowed bravely and asked, "How do we get to know this God who made us special?" She asked.

"That is why we want you to come to Sunday School," Samuel explained patiently as he shifted the fruit to his other arm. "You see, in Sunday School we learn all about God and His Son, Jesus."

"He has a Son?" Jenna asked in a rather amazed voice. "All we have is girls in our family." Her face looked hopeful, as she always wanted a brother.

Martha laughed out loud then, her mouth opening wide to show her stained teeth. Her soft white curls shook as she threw her head back. "Yes, my dears. God has a Son. SO, shall we pick you up at 9:30 Sunday morning?"

Rainee looked dartingly at Jenna who was staring at the pokes of fruit. She could tell all Jenna wanted was free fruit, but Rainee's mind had wandered now, and the fruit did not seem so important. God. There was a God who thought she was special, and she would find out who He was on Sunday!

Before the bolder Jenna could speak, shy Rainee almost shouted, "Yes, I want to go with you and learn about God." Jenna seemed to grudgingly add her ascent as she adjusted her fruit and then started down the well-worn steps of the old farmhouse. Today was a most remarkable day, but what would Sunday bring?

Two days later, Rainee stood before the piece of broken mirror by her mother's "bed." Jenna was impatiently combing Rainee's hair up into that stick-up pony tail Rainee seemed to always want to wear these days. Rainee peered into the dark glass, looking wonderingly at her clean face and the pretty yellow dress Brenda's mom had given her.

She finally had a reason to wear the perfect cotton and lace confection that now fit her. Jenna jerked hard on Rainee's hair, secretly jealous of the dress. Below the dress Rainee had on Eileen's well-worn pair of KID'S tennis shoes, because she owned no shoes. The tennis shoes were too big and red, but she did not seem to care. Shoes and a dress all the same day! It was certainly a special day.

Just as Jenna twisted the rubber band one last time around the irksome pony tail, a deep car horn sounded outside. "Thanks for getting us into this!" she hissed at Rainee as she stooped to tie Rainee's too-big shoes.

"Quick!" Rainee shouted impatiently, "Hurry or they might forget us!"

Jenna finished the tying and then adjusted her own shoes' ties. Straightening to her own height, she realized Rainee, two years younger, was taller than she was now. She looked despairingly at herself in the mirror and sighed heavily. Patting her own hair, she buttoned the last button on the one good red plaid blouse she owned. This and a blue A-line skirt made up her outfit to wear to Sunday School. She again stared at the pretty, yellow-bedecked Rainee and scowled. Some days she wished she could be pretty, too!

Rainee ran out the loud kitchen screen door with a shout good bye to her other sisters. Jenna followed closely. Then Rainee stopped in her tracks. Beside their shelter was parked the most giant of a car. It was green and looked brand new with curved fenders, round head lights and a big C ornament on the hood. Mouth wide open, Rainee gingerly touched the car before hearing a loud, deep laugh from the driver's side window.

"It won't break, Rainee, if you get in," Samuel called to the tiny girl. (They had found out the girls names while drinking lemonade). He then opened his door and stepped out of the car. Shutting his door, he opened the passenger door. "Here, girls, the whole back seat is yours!"

Rainee crawled onto the mammoth seat and slid over so that Jenna could join her. Never in her whole life had Rainee been in a real car. They had an old truck. Dad, Mom and Crystal rode in the seat of the truck. The back of the truck was a flat bed without sides Dad said he used to haul things for the farmers he worked for sometimes, for he was a farm migrant worker. Rainee did not know the truck did not really belong to her dad, but to the farmers group. She just knew that it scared her to sit with Eileen and Jenna behind the ugly, rusted black cab on the open bed whenever they had to go anywhere. She was sure the wind would suck her off that flatbed one day, as she often felt it tugging at her. But today she sat royally on a wide green upholstered seat, sharing the space with Jenna.

It was only a few blocks to the church. The girls could have walked, but it was obvious this kind elderly couple felt it their responsibility to see the children safely to the church door. When they arrived at the side of Citrus Park Baptist Church, Samuel slowed and parked. Turning off the ignition, he slowly opened his door and got out of the car. Standing tall, he reached over and opened the back door for the girls. "Martha will take you to your Sunday School classes," Samuel smiled at them.

Martha, who had disembarked from the front door on the passenger's side of the car, scurried around the front end of the new Cadillac to take a hand of each girl in her hands. "Today I will introduce you to your teachers!" she chirped joyfully. "They will be so glad to have two new students for their classes!"

Rainee watched in amazement as she saw Brenda's family walking up to the church from their house. So this is why Brenda's mom knew she was special, she thought with a smile. She must know what Martha knows! Jenna shouted at Brenda and soon the pretty girl joined her friend, excited to see her at her Sunday School. Martha consented to letting Brenda, all dressed up in pink and lace today, lead Jenna off to her class since they were in the same grade.

For a split moment Rainee hesitated at the side door of the one story white and red brick building that stood in an L shape with the rest of the church (later she would learn the rest was called the sanctuary). What if she was not wanted? She thought. No one ever wanted her before...but Martha seemed to sense what Rainee was thinking, for she took her free hand and petted the child's blond head. "It will be all right, Rainee, my dear," she smiled. "I told Mrs. Clauson you were coming and she is so excited to meet you!"

Rainee obediently followed the elderly lady into the building where other children swarmed around. Already she could see that half the children she saw around their shelter were there. Soon Martha stood in front of the door to a small room. On the door was written "first graders."

"But I am not in first grade," she told Martha, rather embarrassed. "I am six but Momma has not let me go to school yet. So I am not in any grade."

Martha smiled and told her she talked to her mother the night before when Rainee was asleep. She had found out her age. Her mother had agreed she should go to the first grade Sunday School class.

"But," Rainee whispered as if in a conspiracy, "No one knows I can read."

Martha looked at the child's face wonderingly for a moment. "You can read?" she asked, for if the child had not been to school, how could she read?

"Yes," Rainee whispered back, "but no one must know. Momma would be angry because I read Jenna's books to Jenna so she can pass her tests."

Martha looked startled for a moment and then grinned. "Well, my dear, no one here is going to tell your Momma and get you in trouble. You just go ahead and read anything Mrs. Clausen asks you to read, OK?"

At that moment a tall lady with almost black short permed hair and black glasses strode up purposefully to the pair. "Is this Rainee?" the lady asked in a rather soft; almost cotton candy kind of voice.

"Yes, my dear," Martha answered, for she seemed to call everyone my dear, Rainee noted. "This is Rainee. She will be coming to Sunday School with me each week and will be in your class." With this announcement, Martha took Rainee's hand and placed it in the outstretched hand of Mrs. Clauson, who was smiling at her with a wide, closed-mouth smile.

"What a pretty name!" she told Rainee as she led her to a small, lavender painted, child's chair at one end of a small table. "I have never heard it before."

"It's not my real name," Rainee answered with an open, honest face. "It is the name everyone calls me, though, cause my real name is too big for my sisters to spell."

"Can you tell me your real name?" Mrs. Clauson asked as she proceeded to the other end of the table and picked up what looked like a brown notebook bound on the left side. "I like to keep a list of all my children's names, their ages, birthdays, and addresses. So I will write it in here with the others." She turned the book around so Rainee could see the list of children's names.

"My name is Lorraine Deanna Perkins but called Rainee. I was born on January 28, 1952. I am six years old...what is an address? I don't really know what an address is." She gasped a little, for she had said all of this information in one breath but with a small smile on her face.

"Rainee, an address is the street name and number on the house where you live," Mrs. Clausen told her in a low, patient, polite voice.

"Oh, there are no numbers where we live, Mrs. Clausen," Rainee said honestly. We live on Palmetto Street two houses down from Brenda Larson."

"That is good enough," Mrs. Clausen smiled. Scratching something into her notebook, she then put it down. Soon other children filtered into the classroom and Mrs. Clausen began a Sunday School lesson. It was about God's son, Jesus, and how he used a little boy's lunch to feed many, many people.

Rainee was amazed and sat listening quietly as teacher told the story. Then she gave each of them some pictures to color and cut out to take home. She said the picture of the man with long, flowing robes was Jesus. In the hands of the little boy were two small baskets, one with fishes in it, and the other with what Rainee thought looked like bread rolls. She quietly colored neatly and listened to the teacher go over the lesson one more time before a buzzer sounded to dismiss Sunday School.

Soon Martha appeared at the classroom door to retrieve Rainee. Jenna, she was told, had been asked to sit with Brenda's family for church. Would she like to join them? Rainee nodded yes. Martha led her into the sanctuary and up to the front where Brenda and Jenna sat whispering in a long, long, polished wood seat Rainee would come to be told was a pew. Rainee sat down gingerly beside Jenna and carefully stowed her colored pictures next to her so as not to muss them.

Just as Jenna began asking Rainee how she liked Sunday School, a man stood up and asked everyone to stand. Rainee obeyed. Someone handed Jenna a book of songs but Jenna handed it to Rainee. "Turn to page 48," the man said in a booming voice coming from too stiff a starched collar above a dark blue suit. His graying, receding hair looked wet and was slicked back. His nose was large and looked like a triangle to Rainee.

Rainee took the songbook and obediently turned to page 48, then held it so that Jenna could see. Soon she heard the congregation singing the words, "Onward Christian soldiers, marching as to war, with the cross of Jesus going on before...." She did not understand the words, but she loved to sing. After a line or two she understood the tune and joined in with the singing. Jenna gave her a long, strange look and did not sing.

One song followed another while Rainee continued to sing. Then a rather heavy man in a gray suit stood and asked everyone to stand for prayer. He had brown hair that was also greased and parted to one side. The top stood up in a nice peak, which Rainee thought made the large face look nice. The man's collar did not look as tight as the man's who led the singing, but when he began to pray, Rainee suddenly felt as if someone she had never met before was in the room...someone kind and gentle who already knew that Rainee was special.

As the prayer ended, everyone noisily sat down and the man in the gray suit began to preach. Brenda leaned over and quietly whispered, "That's Pastor Teston, he's our preacher. He tells us all about God. I like him. He is nice." Then she straightened up again when her mother poked her to be quiet.

Rainee sat eyes glued to this new man's large face, listening to every word he had to say while Jenna stirred restlessly at her side. "God, he told her, loved her...he loved her enough to send his Son to earth as a baby. It is his birthday we celebrate at Christmas. But sending Him was not enough...no, for people had sinned so badly, the world was a dark and black place.....and still is today....no. He had to ask that Son to die before he made him alive again and took him back to Heaven to live with Him, so that we could become the beloved members of His family."

"Each of you, from small to old, is one of those people He is asking today....will you come....will you decide today to follow Jesus and become a special member of His family, his beloved child? If you will meet me here at the altar..." and he pointed to a dark polished rail in front of him. "Come, and I will pray with you and welcome you into the Family of God." The church full of people began to sing: "I have decided to follow Jesus, ... no turning back. Should no one join me, Yet I will follow....."

Rainee, never taking her round gray eyes from Pastor Teston's face, found herself walking to the front of the church and in front of that altar. Soon others followed, but it was her eyes that the pastor met. A big smile had spread across his face as he came over to where Rainee stood. "What is your name, child?" he asked in a low, gentle voice as he took her hands in his.

"Rainee, sir," she answered, "My name is Rainee Perkins."

"Rainee, child," Pastor Teston spoke, "Would you like to become God's special child today, accept Jesus as your Savior, and become forever a member of His family?"

Rainee's eyes shown with joy....to belong to a family who called her special. How could she not join? "Yes," she nodded. "I want to be a part of God's family."

In the next few moments Pastor Teston told Rainee how to accept Jesus into her heart. When he released her hands, Rainee smiled up at him, "Today I have met God and Jesus and I can tell they are with me...right here in this room! Because I can feel their love. Because I have decided to follow Jesus!"

Chapter 3: He Took Her Where She Would Not Go...

Thirty six years later:

Whispering and restless feet punctuated the late afternoon classroom lecture. Dust particles danced in the shafts of sunlight shining through the high west windows. Someone sneezed, and a wave of giggles passed through the large lecture hall. Lorraine continued to talk, but the student noise drowned her out. With great difficulty, Lorraine, the professor, raised her eyes to gaze out at the 200 undergraduate students before her.

In the past a number of students had told her that her deep gray eyes startled them when she caught their eye in class. Most of the students seated in the stadium-type seats of the auditorium, and even the few who opted to sit on the stairs because the classroom was overcrowded, however, were not even looking at her now. How was she to catch any wandering eyes?

These days, Lorraine thought, her classes always seemed to be overcrowded. Ever since she received that best teacher of the year award the previous year, she battled students to keep classes within do-able limits. Lorraine, though, loved the students. She sighed because the heavy work schedule demanded control of class size. Chatter reminded her that her thoughts were also wandering. She needed to make another effort to get the students' attention.

Even the dimmed lights and the overhead projector, however, seemed to burn into her eyes. How could she keep their attention on such a lovely day? She wondered to herself.

Lorraine silently confessed that she certainly did not feel up to daring the students to meet her on the college green out under the blue September sky. She had done that in the past few years. She knew the students loved being out in the mild weather. Today, though, she felt such an effort was more than she could give to them.

The room began to suddenly spin before her. Disconcerted, she grabbed for the microphone stand and shook her head. She could not keep their attention at all today, she concluded, let alone do anything to make the class interestingly different. There was no energy to even put forth the effort to teach. She overwhelmingly realized she was failing to teach anything this day.

Lorraine tried to refocus her eyes on her overhead and notes. It was of no use. She could no longer see them. Instead, blackness hovered in front of her bleary eyes. She reached up and brushed her hair from her pretty face. Just last week a curious student had commented how shiny and hip her long blonde hair looked and guessed her to be 32 years old. She smiled at this stray thought. She would turn 43 in January. Today, though, she felt like 82 going on one hundred.

Lorraine rubbed her eyes desperately with the back of her hand, but the blackness still did not move. It was useless. She could not see. Her attempt at teaching was pointless. Sighing, she attempted to raise her voice to get the students' attention. "I am rather ill. I am, therefore, going to dismiss class early today," Lorraine explained. "Please call the department to see if class will be held tomorrow. The way I feel right now, I don't think I will ever see you again!" The students chuckled, thinking she was joking. They began to quickly file out of the room in a noisy mass, though, when Lorraine motioned for them to leave.

She mechanically slid her hand up the microphone stand and turned the mike off. Then she reached to her right where she always kept the overhead projector. Lorraine flipped off the overhead's light. Her movement, however, caused her to brush the podium and dislodge her notes. She heard them softly slip in protest to the chalky lecture room floor. Frightened, Lorraine tried to lean over to pick them up, but once again, the room began to spin. Finally, she dropped to her knees in order to retrieve them. All 200 students had left the room. An aerie quiet permeated the once noisy auditorium. Managing to shove the rest of her notes into their folder, she attempted to rise, but a cold, heavy weight seemed to be on top of her. "God," she prayed, "I need help."

Leaving her materials where they lay, Lorraine began a long, arduous crawl uphill to what she knew was the back of the room and the door. (The front of the class was one story lower than the back of the class.) Thank goodness no class was scheduled to come in for another hour. She was afraid no one would see her and she would be trampled.

After some minutes, she reached the door and clawed it open. Once in the hall, Lorraine was able to drag herself up onto a bench and collapsed against the wall. The end of classes signaled. She could hear students pouring from all of the large auditoriums in this newly constructed classroom center. With its state of the art equipment, stadium-type seats, real microphone systems and visual aides to be dreamed of, rooms here were coveted by most teachers. She was so glad she had landed a class in this mammoth building—until now.

Lorraine tried to get someone's attention. Seeing nothing, however, she could not target a single student. No one seemed to hear her feeble cry for help from the bench. As quickly as it began, the flood of students stopped. New classes must be starting, she thought. Then, she could hear no one remaining in the hall. Lorraine attempted to stand but her legs would not hold her light weight. Again, she was reduced to crawling. She inched her way to where the door should be at a snail's pace. Blackness and nothingness then completely claimed her.

"I am cold," Lorraine thought, "and why am I laying on something so hard?" Whispers floated above her head. She felt so heavy, so very, very heavy. "Where am I? Why does everything look so distorted? How did I get here?" she hurled at herself in panic. Suddenly a face appeared inches from her own hurting face. It was the kind, bespectacled face of her medical Doctor, Michael Danson. "Hello, Lorraine," she heard him say. "Can you hear me?"

Lorraine blinked her eyes at the bright overhead light. The black gradually receded enough so she could see her surroundings somewhat.

"What am I doing here?" She asked anxiously, gazing into the doctor's blue eyes.

"Funny," she randomly thought, "I never noticed the color of his eyes before. I failed to previously realize that his nice brown hair was disappearing. Why would I notice such details now?"

The doctor attempted to get her attention again. "You drove yourself here. Another patient saw you collapsed against your steering wheel and came to get the nurses. They brought you into the office. Are you feeling like you can talk for a few minutes?" His carefully professional voice sounded worried.

"Yes, yes, I feel like I am in reality for the moment. How long have I been here? What is wrong with me, Doctor?" Lorraine heard panic in her own whisper-soft voice.

"First things first, dear. You have been in the clinic about an hour. Your legs are very swollen, Lorraine. So are your face and arms. Can you tell me if you have been sick lately?"

Lorraine blinked and shook her head to clear it. "I noticed I started feeling poorly a couple of days ago. I asked my supervisor for a sick day but she refused because the semester has just started. It just seemed like I had a little virus, so I went to work."

"I am afraid it is not just a virus, Lorraine. We are running some preliminary tests. I am guessing you are in kidney failure. That would explain all the swelling, faintness, and high blood pressure. You may have also had a stroke. We are planning to send you on to the hospital in Rockwood as soon as we are sure you can be moved."

"I'm not going to any hospital. I can't! Kidney failure? I was fine last week! I ran two miles yesterday! I can't have something that drastic all of a sudden, can I? I mean, I haven't felt that sick until today!" Lorraine's eyes enlarged with pleading, as fear of such a drastic possibility overtook her. "I am supposed to pick up my daughters at three o'clock. Tomorrow I am scheduled to give two tests and turn in my research grant proposal. This can't be right! I can't miss my children! I can't miss work!"

"Lorraine, I don't think you understand. You aren't going back to work tomorrow. Unless we hospitalize you immediately, you will not live to pick up your daughters ever again. Can you understand? You are gravely ill. The specialists in Rockwood need to treat you. They might be able to turn your kidneys around. I just don't know enough about these things. All I do know is you are retaining so much fluid, you could go into congestive heart failure at any moment."

"But doctor, I am only 42 years old. Women my age don't have heart failure. I eat right. I exercise five times a week. I don't smoke. I don't drink. I simply have no risk for what you are telling me! I felt fine until today. Surely I just need to doctor my virus?" Lorraine reasoned to convince herself that the doctor just did not understand.

"I don't know why your kidneys aren't working, Lorraine. They just aren't. Sometimes even the healthy have serious life-threatening problems we can't explain. The specialists can figure the puzzle out. Just try to rest quietly. I am giving you a sedative to force you to rest. I am glad you have regained consciousness. It is a good sign that your body is not giving up on life. We have to get the swelling under control before we send you to the hospital though, because that is what puts you at risk for congestive heart failure. I don't want to risk that with a fifty-mile ambulance ride ahead. So, please, take the sedative and try to relax. We will take care of you."

"But my daughters!" She started to cry as she thought of the fear her children would feel in not being picked up, only to find out their Mommy was in the hospital.

"Don't worry. We were able to get hold of your husband. He has already gone for the children. They will meet you here and go to the hospital with you," Dr. Danson patted her arm reassuringly. "Dr. Semdka, the kidney specialist, teaches at the medical school. You will be in the best hands in the area. Just try to rest." He turned to the white capped, young nurse who stood discretely behind him. "I think Lorraine needs some company. Can you stay with her for a few minutes while I finish with my last patient?"

The nurse, cap bobbing over her dark curls, stepped over and took her hand. "You are in good hands," She confidently smiled. "We have an IV and catheter started to remove some of the swelling. That will make you feel a little better. Just rest. Please."

"But I can't breathe," Lorraine whispered so softly the nurse did not hear her frightened cry. Dutifully she took the water and pill the nurse held out to her and slowly swallowed the medicine. Dr. Danson held a reputation for never being wrong. Surely, this was a first time. She sighed.

She was so tired. So very tired. Maybe it did not matter if she did not talk anymore. She could not believe she drove herself to the doctor. Something inside told her that she needed to go there, but she did not remember the drive at all. Lorraine could not remember anything after that bench in the hallway. Maybe if she slept a while she would find out she was just having a nightmare.

Ever so quietly, the world slipped away, while the nurse stroked her hand and murmured reassuring words. Her last thoughts became restless dreams: "I am very sick. So sick I could die. But I will not! I still have small children who need their Mommy. I will fight this. I will fight it for them." Somewhere, deep inside in a place she had never touched before, she knew that she would have to fight, and it would not be an easy battle.

Lorraine felt herself slipping into a place of peace, only the peace frightened her inner soul. It asked her to let go of life. She turned further and further inward to face her new, ugly enemy in spite of her will to run away. The battle for her life raged on within Lorraine's body. Then she soon noticed a soft, beckoning light flickering at the edge of her dream world. No, she told herself, no, she could not let that wonderful beckoning win. It was not her time. It was not her time.

A long time seemed to pass. Slowly, Lorraine felt her heavy body awakening. Someone was calling to her. As she gallantly struggled to focus on the voice, a feeling of not wanting to come back surrounded her. Then Lorraine jerked her gray eyes open and met those of her trusted Doctor Danson. He smiled at her. "The IV is working. We have drained about twelve pounds of fluid from you! I want you to try to sit up now. It is important we try to give you back some strength. Your heart is out of danger for the time being. The nurse is bringing a little snack to boost your blood sugar. It is running quite low. After that, the ambulance will be ready to take you to Rockwood. Do you want to see your children? They are in the waiting room!"

"What time is it?" Lorraine asked groggily.

"About eleven PM. You have been asleep for several hours. I called your husband and told him to bring the children," he replied.

"It is too late for them to come to this office. They should be in bed," She stated flatly. It once again struck her how serious her illness must be for the doctor to approve such a late visit. Fighting her sleepiness, she whispered, "Please, oh, yes, please, bring them in now."

Tears fell unbidden down her cheeks as the doctor helped Lorraine into a sitting position. Dizziness engulfed her, but the blackness did not return. She could hear her five year old chattering in the hall. Sweet, sweet, Allison. Oh, how she wanted

31

to hold her! She could hear eleven-year-old Ariana trying to hush her baby sister. Bright, dark haired and skinned like her father, Ariana never seized to amaze her. She was born with multiple medical problems but never failed to overcome with her optimistic, matter-of-fact personality.

It was the oldest, fourteen-year-old Autumn, who sounded too worried, as she also tried to quiet her baby sister. Autumn was a freshman in high school and teenager through and through. Her curly blonde hair was cropped short because she had no time to "do it up constantly." The curl was her father's, but the color Lorraine's. She momentarily asked herself if her oldest could survive her tortured adolescence without a mother and felt another wave of panic. Of the three girls, Autumn exhibited the most fragile personality. Oh, she fretted, this threat of losing her mother could indeed destroy that fragile child. A prayer escaped her cracked lips, "Please, God, please, don't let even this oldest child suffer the loss of her mother. Surely, you know she would suffer greatly from such a loss. Please, don't let it happen."

The Doctor finished checking her vital signs and seemed satisfied. He gave her an encouraging smile and turned to let the girls into the room. Allison bounded in and jumped up onto the examining table with her mom. "Hey, why they got that thing in your hand?" She blurted out, "It's making a sore!" She reached for the IV.

Maternal Ariana stepped up and whispered loudly to Allison to not ask questions! "Mommy is really sick! Leave her alone!" Ariana pulled the small hand away from the IV needle and tubing.

Autumn also tried to quiet the smallest girl. Lorraine smiled at her two oldest children. Must not let on how serious things were—not yet, not yet. No need to scare them prematurely. She held out her free hand to Allison and pulled her into her arms. "Hello, sweetheart," She murmured into the child's hair. "Aren't you grown up to get to stay up so late?"

"Can you read me my story?" Allison asked as she pulled a book in front of Lorraine.

Ariana stepped forward. "I can read, Mom," She said, and Lorraine nodded in agreement. "Alli likes me to act out the voices of this story." With that, Ariana began to read, as Allison nestled closer to her Mom. Autumn reached over and brushed Lorraine's hair from her face, smiling bravely.

"My girls," Lorraine whispered, "Oh, how I love my girls."

Autumn smiled and nodded. "We know, Mom, we know. Just rest, OK?" Already, Lorraine could sense that Autumn was feeling the weight of being the most grown up of the children. With mother in the hospital, Lorraine thought, she will have to help take care of Ariana and Allison. Lorraine did not know if she could. How many fourteen year olds could cope? Autumn gave her a brave smile, but stark fear reflected from her dark blue eyes. Momma must not die, her heart seemed to cry out. She could not bear it!

Lorraine reached up and stroked Autumn's cheek. "It will be OK, sweetheart. The doctors are taking care of me. I know you can be a big sister to the other girls. Ariana is quite grown up for her age. Alli will just need a little more of your attention. Surely your dad can take some time off from his part time job if needed."

Lorraine looked fretfully toward the door. Justin was not a man who liked to have demands put on him. It seemed to her that children were only a necessary nuisance for him. How would he react to this crisis?

Ariana began to cry quietly and Allison, whom Ariana nicknamed Alli when she was a baby, joined her. "I don't want to stay alone with Dad," Ariana stated. "He is mean when you aren't there."

"What do you mean?" Lorraine asked. She had never

heard any of the girls complain of this before. A new fear began to edge its way into her frenzied mind. Was there something she did not know about that went on when she was at work? If so, this was no time to go to the hospital!

Autumn unconsciously edged herself closer to Lorraine. "It's OK, Mom, I will take care of them," She spoke in a too-grown up voice.

"What is Ariana talking about?" Lorraine asked Autumn.

"Nothing. It's nothing," Autumn responded encouragingly.

Just then, the door opened. The doctor and her husband, Justin, came into the examining room. The unbearable smell of fear permeated the atmosphere. Justin pulled on Autumn's shoulder and told her to go out into the waiting room. He repeated his action with Ariana, but when he reached for Allison, Lorraine pulled her closer.

"It's OK," Dr. Danson said, "Allison can go with me and Lorraine in the ambulance. You take Ariana and Autumn and meet us at the Rockwood Teaching Hospital Admitting office."

"I'm not taking no three kids to a hospital," Justin replied hotly. "I am taking them home. It is way past their time for bed. Lorraine is fine. She is just faking being ill so she won't have to go to work! We're going!" With that, Justin pulled both of the older girls out the door with him. Lorraine heard them burst into tears as the door to the parking lot slammed behind them with the loud cracking noise of metal hitting heavy metal.

"Oh, dear God," Lorraine prayed, "What is going on? Why is he angry? Why did he hurt the girls?" She turned to Dr. Danson whose face showed obvious signs of concern. "Will they be OK?" She demanded.

Dr. Danson released a long breath. "Sometimes men react strangely to crisis. I don't think he will intentionally hurt his kids.

We'll have to keep an eye on that, too. In the meantime, you, me, and Allison are going on that ambulance ride, because he is wrong. This is not a fake illness. It is very serious. I know you do not want to go to the hospital, but you must! I will tell the ambulance driver we are ready to load up."

Minutes later Allison and Lorraine were secured into the back of the ambulance. Dr. Danson hopped into the front seat beside the driver. He told Lorraine he wanted to be sure she was OK on the way. As the ambulance left the parking lot, the siren wound into an incessant whine. The driver silenced the siren when he gained the freeway, but the high speed continued. Lorraine cuddled Allison close as the turning wheels gradually sang the child to sleep. It was good she slept, she thought. Moments later Lorraine, too, drifted off into a sleep of fears and nightmares.

Chapter 4: He Asked of Her What She
Could Not Give

In the ambulance Lorraine felt overwhelmed by her dream, the familiar dream of facing a big steel door. It was thick, tall and wide. She could not reach the door handle. She was safe, though, she heard someone say, because it was closed.

This old nightmare, she heard herself saying. Why again? She had had this dream many times as an adult. Always the nagging questions came. "What is beyond that door that requires it to stay closed? Why is it dangerous to open the door?" The questions echoed throughout her dream, but she never heard an answer. She pounded on the door, but some great hand pulled her back saying quietly, "Not yet. Someday, dear, but not yet." Exhausted, dreamless sleep finally settled over Lorraine. It was not time to open the door. It was OK to walk away. She slept on as the ambulance driver pushed the speed limit to reach the Rockwood hospital.

Dr. Danson checked Lorraine's vital signs every few minutes and seemed satisfied. Beside him rested blood and urine samples he would turn over to the kidney doctor. This lady was one of the most gifted teachers he had ever met, a friend and a long time patient. He was not going to let her slip away without a fight!

Dr. Danson also knew Lorraine was a dedicated mother whose kids needed her. He glanced over at sleeping Allison. She was in his wife's kindergarten Sunday School class. His wife often commented on how obvious it was that the child had a good mother. Still, the doubts raised by Justin's behavior were of concern for the children. There was a shadow in that man's life that had always made his behavior a bit hard to understand. Tonight that shadow took on a monster's face. No, that man could not be trusted to parent the girls on his own. The safety of the girls would have to be ensured soon. Now, however, he could not let Lorraine know how serious his misgivings were. Lorraine needed to concentrate on surviving a very dangerous medical condition. "Dear God," Dr. Danson prayed softly, "Give us the knowledge to bring her back to her children! They need their mother so much!"

Lorraine was jarred awake by the sudden replaying of the ambulance siren. For a moment, she could not remember where she was, or why the ambulance siren was so loud. "We should be at the hospital in another five minutes. Your vital signs are good. I think we have averted a heart attack for the moment. The ambulance driver says Dr. Semdka has arrived at the hospital and is waiting for us. He is a gifted doctor and has the best chance of getting this thing turned around," Dr. Danson smiled over at Lorraine.

She looked down at her daughter. "What will I do with Allison while they are working on me?" She worried out loud.

"Oh, I think Justin was just talking. I am betting he will be here soon. Then he can watch Allison, along with the other girls, while they are running tests on you."

Soon the siren was turned off as the ambulance made its approach to the hospital emergency room doors. Dr. Danson reached over, unstrapped Allison, and gathered her into his careful arms. "I can look after one sleepy little girl for a few hours," he smiled.

The paramedics soon had Lorraine installed in the emergency room department. Nurses came to take over her care. Someone from admitting came in and completed paperwork. She could hear Dr. Semdka being called over the P.A. system. She wondered what he would be like. The IV and catheter bags were exchanged. A kind nurse with dark red hair asked if Lorraine would like a heated blanket. Realizing she was hot one minute and shivering the next, and she nodded her answer. The heated blanket did feel good next to her skin.

A technician took more samples of blood. Then he took the samples of blood and urine that Dr. Danson had brought with them. How much blood could they take before they had it all? she drowsily wondered.

Minutes later the new doctor walked into the emergency cubicle. He was gray-haired but obviously well-built. Must exercise a lot, was her first impression, as Lorraine was introduced to Dr. Semdka. He let a shadow of a smile cross his face. "I know about you!" he stated. "Teacher of Excellence for Philadelphia State last year. Let's see what we can do to get you back on your feet!"

Dr. Danson settled Allison on the narrow bed with Lorraine. He then joined Dr. Semdka in the consulting area. Dr. Danson painstakingly went over everything he knew about Lorraine's medical history and current symptoms. Satisfied with his report, he brought up his concern about Justin. He felt that Justin could do some real harm in this situation with just his harsh words. They discussed Dr. Danson's suspicions. Dr. Semdka agreed he would keep Justin under observation. Soon the laboratory work they ordered STAT was handed to them.

"I think we are going to need a kidney biopsy to diagnose this thing," Dr. Semdka stated. "There are too many possibilities to guess a cause and to determine a treatment. I will set that up for first thing in the morning. In the meantime, I will admit her to the fourth floor, the nephrology (kidney) unit. They will keep close watch on her there. She is stable right now. I would like to make sure her heart is OK before I attempt the biopsy. It can be tricky."

Dr. Semdka and Dr. Danson returned to the cubicle where Lorraine had once again fallen asleep. Dr. Danson gently touched her forehead. "Dr. Semdka says you are stable. I am going to go ahead and go home, as my wife is here to pick me up. He will take over your care. He is a great doctor, and I truly believe he will give you the best care possible. I will stay in close touch with him, OK?"

Lorraine nodded slowly and watched Dr. Danson until he disappeared down the white hallway. Suddenly she felt completely alone, and it frightened her.

Dr. Semdka took Lorraine's hand to get her attention. He quietly explained the tests they had done so far, what they had found, and what they needed to do next. He then informed Lorraine of the need to observe her overnight to be sure her heart remained stable. Tomorrow he could do a procedure called a kidney biopsy. For tonight, she was to concentrate on getting a good rest.

Lorraine nodded her dark blond head briefly, releasing herself into this new doctor's care. Everything sounded so unreal. Finally, she asked, "Where is Justin? He was supposed to meet Allison and me here."

"He isn't here yet. I am going to go ahead and send you up to the nephrology floor so you can rest," Dr. Semdka stated.

"But what about Allison?" She asked anxiously as she glanced over at her youngest daughter.

"Oh, that problem has been solved, Doctor. Dr. Danson has explained to the nurses that the little girl needs to stay with you, so they have special permission to put a cot in your room for her to use. We allow family in patient rooms here."

Relieved, Lorraine rested back against the raised head of the hard bed. Tomorrow she could face her diagnosis. Tonight Allison needed to sleep. She needed to sleep. Lorraine adjusted Allison beside her, smiling into the soft childish face. Somehow, someway, she had to get through this—her girls needed her more than she knew.

Chapter 5: He Showed Her What She Would Not See

It was early morning when Lorraine woke again. Sunlight filtered into the stark white hospital room through thin curtains. An IV pole beside her bed showed she had two IV's going at once. A heart monitor was also beeping next to her bed. A stabbing pain in her right side began to rapidly increase in intensity, and then wrapped its way around to her back. She caught her breath and moaned. The pain brought back memories of her appendicitis attack ten years ago. Suddenly Lorraine sat up. The events of that day played in full color before her eyes as if she were watching a movie.

Lorraine felt herself slipping back to the tiny town of Potterville in upper Indiana. She lay on the couch, crying and asking Justin to take her to the hospital. He refused, accusing her of pretending illness. Autumn, then four, was curled up on the floor beside the couch, and baby Ariana was asleep in her arms. She felt so weak. She could not even get up to put the children to bed. Instead, they had fallen asleep close to her. The pain seemed to get better for a while. Lorraine slipped away from the room, it seemed, and it no longer mattered if no one would get help. Caught between life and death, she hovered at the sight of her sleeping children.

Night passed and Justin finally went to the phone when he could not arouse Lorraine. He dialed the family doctor and told him his wife was faking appendicitis. Thankfully, the doctor suggested he bring Lorraine to the emergency room for a checkup—just to be sure it was not all psychosomatic. Appendicitis could be deadly, so he, the doctor, should rule it out, not Justin, who had no medical training, he told Justin.

A neighbor friend agreed to come over and watch the children. Justin somehow managed to drag Lorraine into the car. The thirteen miles to the hospital were to forever hang in a forgotten haze. At the hospital, the doctor barely aroused Lorraine to ask where she felt pain. How bad was it? Lorraine remembered responding, "It is better," and drifting away again. There was a bright light beckoning to her at the edge of consciousness. Oh, she wanted to go to it. It was so nice to have the pain gone.

The doctor told Lorraine he was checking her temperature and panicked. It was raised slightly—a common symptom of appendicitis. He told Justin he thought his wife was not faking and ordered an emergency appendectomy—as fast as they could get Lorraine into surgery—and it had better be fast. He suspected the appendix had burst, explaining the pain relief. Minutes later, Lorraine came to enough to see the bright surgery lights and doctors in surgery garb. Her doctor told her they were going to put her to sleep. Sure this was her last moment in this life; she whispered that they must get Justin. She must tell him she forgave him for letting her die. The Doctor reassured Lorraine that she would not die, and told her there was no time to get Justin.

Lorraine's next memory was of waking up in intensive care with Justin talking to the doctor in the doorway. Lorraine moaned as they turned to her. The doctor came over, laid his hand on her shoulder and smiled. "We got it out and mopped up most of the poison. Another couple of hours and we would have lost you!" he told her. "You have to stay here for a while on massive antibiotics to counter any poison left in your body. Do you understand?"

Lorraine had realized at that time just how dangerous Justin's refusal to get help had been. Why, she asked God, Why? There seemed to be no answer back then, just as there was no explanation for Justin's behavior when he arrived at Dr. Danson's office.

Now, ten years since that surgery, Justin was risking her life once more! With this thought, the present reasserted itself as the pain continued to mount in Lorraine's right side. She tried not to cry. She must not waken sleeping Allison. Her tears, though, would not stop. Finally, she turned her back to her daughter and gave in to the sobs. That her husband did not care if she died echoed over and over in her mind. Why did he want to get rid of her? This was more frightening than her illness. A sense of complete abandonment overwhelmed her as she continued to cry quietly.

What seemed hours later, Lorraine heard the cush, cush of nurses' shoes as they entered her room. "Good morning!" A cheery voice spoke softly. She turned over to meet the brown eyes of one of her graduate students and friend—a counseling major who was doing an internship in the kidney unit. Lorraine did not realize that Karen would be here. "They told me you were up here, so I did not wait for my regular rounds. I think you will like Dr. Semdka. He is the kindest man I ever met. He told me to cheer you up so you would do better during the biopsy. Well, I can tell you, he also said he appreciated getting a patient who obviously took care of herself. Said that really increased the odds that you would come through this crisis better than most."

Karen went over and touched Allison's hair. "In case you are wondering, I have been put in charge of Allison, should Justin not show up. I do not understand his current weird behavior."

"That makes both of us," Lorraine sighed. "But I sure am glad to see a friendly face! Are you enjoying your hospital internship?"

"It has been harder than I thought it would be. Partly because if I get called in on most cases, it means the patient is very, very ill, and that has been a little scary. It is also extremely rewarding, though, as I find families so grateful that I am willing to listen to their fears and concerns. That is why I am here for you, too, you know. You are not my professor today. You are my client. And I want to again reassure you that the doctor says you should do just fine with today's procedure, OK?"

The nurse walked in and traded Lorraine's IV bags. The doctor came in shortly thereafter with that shadow of a smile on his face. "Good morning!" He boomed. "Glad to see Karen got in here. Understand you already know each other! The IV the nurse put up has a sedative in it. Once that takes, we will have you rolled down to surgery, where we will perform the kidney biopsy. Your heart seems to be handling your physical condition remarkably well. I can tell you exercise a lot. That is really what has saved your life in this situation. A person in average condition would not have been here for me to work on by now. I think, however, that you will do just fine. Keep in mind I cannot put you under full anesthesia because of your condition, so you are going to have to be very strong for me." With that, the doctor walked out of the room with crisp, purposeful steps.

Justin came shuffling in through the door at that moment, a single rose clutched in his left hand. "Gonna go through with this, huh?" He mumbled. Justin stiffly held the flower out to Lorraine. "Guess I thought you might like this," He continued. Lorraine accepted the flower with a sense of bewilderment. Flowers did not go with the attitude he had shown thus far. Things just were not making much sense! Justin sat down in the beige recliner under the window, turning his eyes to the view outside.

"Where are Autumn and Ariana?" she asked.

"At school, where else?" Justin suddenly snapped. "You do not think I want them here so you can show them how good a hypochondriac you are, do you?" Lorraine's eyes wandered to the flower. Seeing her eyes on the flower, Justin grudgingly said, "Oh, that. Dr. Danson suggested it might make you feel better when he called me this morning and told me of the biopsy."

Lorraine shuttered within and closed her eyes. A tremendous dread overwhelmed her. When she opened her eyes again, Dr. Semdka was back in the room talking to Justin. "I am glad you are here, Mr. Hawkins. Your wife needs all the support you can give her. A kidney biopsy is a surgical procedure. We make a four-inch opening in her back over her kidney and then go into the kidney. Once in the kidney, we remove a piece of tissue for testing. Since kidneys are so interconnected, we only need to biopsy one of them to diagnose the disorder in most cases. We will have to keep her here for a day or two at least, to make sure she is stable."

He turned to me. "After the surgery, you will be brought back to this room on your back. A sand bag will be placed under your kidney wound. This will help to stop the internal bleeding. Kidneys have more blood in them than any other organ, so messing with them is rather touchy. Excessive bleeding is a real possibility. One in one hundred people have to have a transfusion after this procedure. One in 1,000 dies from blood loss. I have to tell you these odds so you can understand how important it is to follow my instructions one hundred per cent. Once back in the room you will be asked to lie absolutely still for twenty-four hours. I know that is hard, but the more still you are, the less likely you will bleed. Do you understand?"

Dr. Semdka then turned back to Justin. "While she is in surgery, Mr. Hawkins, I want to have you tested for possible tissue donation. In all likelihood, your wife is going to need an emergency transplant. Anonymous kidneys that match are hard to get with such short notice; so we normally ask family members to be tested as potential donors."

A look of horror crossed Justin's face as the doctor continued to make eye contact with him. "Not on your life am I giving that woman one of my kidneys! There is nothing wrong with her—she just wants more attention! So pack her up so I can take her home!"

Dr. Semdka carefully observed the nonverbal messages dark haired Justin shot at Lorraine. What he saw turned his stomach. This man was going to let his wife, the mother of his young children, die!

"You are wrong, Mr. Hawkins. Your wife is gravely ill, and she needs your help."

"No! No!" Justin ranted. "If she is that sick, then let her

die! It is her turn to die. She won't get a kidney from me, and I am not asking anyone else for one either. It's just her turn to die, so let her!"

The noise had awakened Allison and she began to cry. Karen scooped the frightened child up into her arms and took her to the staff break room, where she talked the child into eating some candy corn. What a jerk Mr. Hawkins turned out to be. How could such a nice professor be married to someone like him? She seethed.

Back in the room, Justin was once again screaming at the doctor, only Lorraine could no longer hear. Faintly, as if in slow motion, she saw and heard as the doctor slammed her husband against the wall, and growled orders into his face, but she could not make out what the growls meant.

Instead, the room was fading, fading, and in its place stood the great metal door of her nightmares. "No, God, no!" she cried. "It is daytime. That belongs in my dreams, not in daytime! Please don't ask me to open that door. Please!"

A great hand, however, was reaching down in front of her. "It is time," She heard God say; "It is time."

"Time for what?" she whimpered.

"Time for Rainee to come home," the Voice answered.

"Rainee, who is Rainee?" she asked.

"Rainee is you," The Voice answered, "and she wants to come home."

"I don't know any Rainees," Lorraine inhaled sharply, but the Voice did not seem to hear. Instead, a great hand reached out and, little by little, as if with great effort, opened the great metal door.

"Go," The Voice commanded, as the Hand pulled her

through the doorway.

"No, I can't. I can't. I'm afraid!" she cried, but the hand continued to push her until she fell through the door and into a great black abyss.

The abyss seemed bottomless, and she tumbled down, down, for what seemed like forever. Falling, falling, Lorraine began to scream. Then she heard someone else scream, too. Only the other person screamed in the voice of a little girl. Lorraine began to look around and saw a little blond girl with old-fashioned clothes on, who was also falling and screaming. Abruptly, ground rose up below her and she saw that they were both running, running, through a dark cedar woods, tripping over boggy spots. Suddenly she knew. The little girl was Rainee....and so was she...this was her little girl self. Lorraine knew she must run, run, run, and never stop, as she became, once again, the small child her parents had long ago nicknamed, "Rainee," after her grandmother.

Just as she thought she heard a noise behind her, someone from far away started calling to her. She did not want to leave, but as suddenly as it had come, the abyss disappeared, and Dr. Semdka's face appeared before her. Justin was no longer in the room.

"Are you all right?" the doctor asked as he patted her shoulder.

"I don't know," she cried.

"Don't worry. Lots of men get scared when their wives get sick. I think Justin will be OK in the long run. In any case, we will find you a kidney if we need to fine one. Do not worry. I have no intention of losing that precious little girl's mother! The sedative should start taking effect soon, so they are coming to take you to surgery. I will see you there, OK?" Dr. Semdka gave Lorraine a brief smile and quietly left the room.

Lorraine once again nodded at the doctor and fell back against her pillow. Yes, her precious girls. She needed to live for her girls, she begged of God, as tears streamed down her puffy face. Gradually the sedative took effect and Lorraine regained a sense of calm. Lorraine knew deep in her soul that God had not abandoned her. He was right there, and he would go with her through her night.

Karen came back in with Allison and handed the little girl to her mother. Allison proceeded to tell Lorraine that Karen had given her candy for breakfast, and that was great! Unwillingly, Lorraine laughed. "This once," she smiled and gave her child a hug. As she became sleepier from the sedative, Karen picked Allison up to take to a playroom, leaving directions for the nurse so Justin could find them. Not that he would want to help, she thought, but the doctor said it was Justin's responsibility to look after his daughter in the end.

Lorraine counted seven people when she was wheeled into the operating room. How could she be so conscious that she could count bodies? she mused. Oh, yeah, Dr. Semdka said they could not put her under because of possible danger. Goodie. Fear rippled through her swollen body. "Well, here goes," she told herself, as the orderlies moved her onto the operating table. Someone turned Lorraine onto her stomach. Others arranged lights and checked her vital signs.

Finally, Lorraine heard Dr. Semdka's voice, "We are about to start. The anesthesiologist will monitor your sedative drip and apply a local anesthetic to your back. A technician, Steve, is going to sit below your face, so you can see him. I want you to carry on a conversation with him until I tell you that you can stop. Do you understand?"

Lorraine shivered. "I think so," she murmured. "OK, people," the doctor addressed his surgery team, "Let's get the biopsy on the road."

Someone pumped up the table to raise it into the air. Steve, a thin, brown-haired young man, slid onto a stool directly between the floor and her face. "Hi, I'm Steve," he told her. "I want you to look me in the eye at all times and just keep talking to me, OK? I've gotten lots of patients through this, so everything will be OK. Just concentrate on me."

"OK," Lorraine whispered. In the next moment, she felt a needle enter her back, then another and another. Finally, the doctor announced he thought the local had had time to take and they should start. Steve was talking non-stop, asking Lorraine questions about her work. He knew Dr. Hawkins' reputation. He asked her what classes she liked to teach. On and on he chattered, making her answer his questions.

Pain seared through Lorraine's body and she gasped. Steve, without breaking conversational stride, stated that she needed more local. More needles entered her back. Then the searing pain intensified greatly. Still, Steve talked on earnestly. He asked Lorraine questions about her kids. Once more, he said the patient needed additional local anesthesia, and then the doctor announced she was at maximum dosage and they would just have to finish. At this statement, Lorraine flinched. "Look at me," Steve crooned. "Just keep looking into my eyes. It's almost over."

Steve asked Lorraine where she grew up. Out of the blue, the present began to disappear again. Oh, no, not here. "Not now, please, God," she prayed, but could not answer Steve's question. Where had she grown up? She had a hard time picturing it. At last, she said the first thing she could think of, "Florida."

"Florida?" Steve seemed surprised. "That's a long ways from Minnesota. And you sure don't have a Southern accent."

"Been too long in the Midwest, I guess," she lied. Why did she not have a Southern accent if she grew up in Florida? That question never came up in her daily life. Lorraine now knew, though, that she wanted to know the answer to that question.

"We're done, "Dr. Semdka announced victoriously. "Are you OK, Dr. Hawkins? You did a great job of staying still. We are going to move you back to your room and put you on the sand bag. You cannot move for twenty-four hours, OK?

Orderlies turned Lorraine's gurney around and pulled it through the operating room swinging doors. Dr. Semdka kept pace with her as she went down the hall. "I told Karen to be sure Justin and Allison were back in your room by now."

"Oh, yes," she giggled senselessly, "I want to see them. Why am I giggling?" she asked, and then answered her own question. It must be an after-effect of the sedative. Lorraine watched the walls scroll by her in a blur. A fast elevator soon took her to the fourth floor with Dr. Semdka beside her.

As they approached the room, Allison came tearing down the hall with Justin in pursuit. "Mommy!" Allison called and grabbed her Momma's hand that dangled over the side of the portable bed. Lorraine smiled. "Momma's fine, Allison," she whispered. "Momma's fine."

"Can I sit on your lap?" Allison demanded.

"Not right away, young lady," the doctor smiled. "We have to let your Momma have some time to get better, OK? Karen said you bought your Momma a present in the gift shop. Maybe after we get her in her own bed, you can give it to her."

"I'd like that," Allison smiled at the doctor.

Knife-splitting pain ripped through Lorraine as the orderlies moved her into her bed. Next, the sandbag was placed under her right side where the biopsied kidney was throbbing.

"I have ordered some morphine. That will help with the

pain," Dr. Semdka stated. "You must be immune to the canine drugs, because the local anesthesia seemed to have no effect."

Lorraine startled as she remembered what dentists used to tell her. They used gas because giving shots was like giving her nothing at all. Why had she not remembered this earlier? After that, she remembered something else, too. "I am deathly allergic to morphine, Doctor. They gave me morphine with my C-section with Allison. I almost died. I can use codeine, though."

The doctor turned and stopped the nurse from turning on a new IV she had just added to the IV pole. "Better replace that one with codeine," he told the nurse. Next, he turned to Justin, who was sitting once more in the recliner. "Your wife will sleep most of the next twenty-four hours, so I suggest you take Allison home and get some rest, too. Tomorrow you can bring the other girls and we will see what we need to do to get your wife back on her feet!"

"First, though, I think Allison has something for her Mom." He smiled at the little girl, who reached over to the counter and picked up a gift-wrapped package. Smiling from ear to ear, she held the brightly wrapped package out to her Mom. Still feeling very bleary, Lorraine took the package with another giggle. Oh, boy, she thought.

Her hands shook too bad to unwrap the gift, so Justin took it and finished the job. There, in a tiny box, was a child's troll, all dressed in pink, with bright pink hair. "The lady in the store said she could help you get better," Allison smiled.

"She already has," Lorraine held the gift to her heart. Allison had given her one of her favorite toys, a true gift to not keep it for herself. Justin held Allison up to kiss her mother carefully and then told Lorraine he would see her the next day.

As they disappeared out the door, the nurse came in with the codeine. Tomorrow was forever in the future. She was glad she could sleep.

Chapter 6: He Told Her What She Would Not Hear

Searing pain awoke Lorraine at first light. A tug of restraints reminded her that she must stay still for a little longer. She began to whimper. The pain from her old back injury began creeping down both of her legs. She had not slept on her back for ten years because of this injury. The biopsy, however, forced her to lie flat. The pain medication seemed to control the pain from the biopsy, but her back pain was unaffected.

Lorraine's moaning caught the attention of the intensive care staff, and a nurse scurried into her cubicle. "Is your pain much worse?" The kind nurse asked as she leaned over and plumped her pillow.

"It is not my kidney. It's an old back injury that the surgery has aggravated. The pain is going down both of my legs. Is there no way I can move?" Lorraine begged with tears on her cheeks.

"I will call the doctor to see if we can increase your pain med. No, orders are you are to be still until ten when Dr. Semdka comes to see you." The nurse gently touched Lorraine's arm with a sympathetic smile.

Lorraine sighed and then opened her gray eyes wide. "Find a focal point, she told herself, and find one now." After a minute, she noticed the rose that Justin brought. She zeroed in on the flower. Concentrate, she scolded herself when her mind wandered. The smell of roses is so beautiful. She loved her rose garden. She mentally took herself to that place. One at a time, she imagined the scent of her many rose bushes. Gratefully, she gave in as sleepiness caused her body to relax. Peacefully, Lorraine floated among her roses in her dreams.

Dr. Semdka's strong voice woke her. The nurses removed the restraints. Someone told Lorraine that she had slept through breakfast, so a nurse ordered something to eat. She had to admit she was hungry. How long had it been since she had last eaten? She looked up at her IV pole. No doubt, one of those bags had some type of feeding in it, or she would be even hungrier!

Dr. Semdka soon appeared at her right side. Justin followed close behind him. The three girls shadowed him. Oh, Lorraine was so glad to see her girls. Even before the biopsy, she wondered if she would ever see Ariana and Autumn even one more time. Relief brought on tears, and Lorraine began to cry softly. Dr. Semdka took her hand and smiled his faint smile. "Well, Doctor, I am pleased you can follow orders. There are no complications from the biopsy."

"What did it show?" she quizzed, as she held out her left hand to the girls.

"Definite damage. There is severe damage in the filters of your kidneys. Your right kidney is shriveled and almost nonfunctional. In looking at the kidney, I was surprised you have had kidney function all these years, because I date that kidney's damage to around the age of twelve." For some reason, his statement sent her once more to the great door in her mind. Suddenly, Dr. Semdka's voice sounded far away.

"No, God, not again," Lorraine pleaded, as she fell through the great door. Only this time when she saw Rainee, the child was screaming. Her family lived in a broken down, condemned house when she was twelve. With little electricity or running water, an iron potbelly stove was their only source of heat, even in the 1960's, in northern Indiana. Her child self, Rainee, stood with the stove just inches from her back. It was cold. She was cuddled up to the stove to get warm. Lorraine heard a faceless man swearing at Rainee and punching her. Rainee ducked behind the stove to escape. The child pleaded for the man to stop—just to stop, but he started viciously kicking her.

"Mommy, Mommy, Mommy," Lorraine heard Rainee scream, "Stop him! Stop him! Please stop him!" In the background she heard that eerie, guttural female laugh she had heard in so many of her dreams.

The sound of that laugh jerked Lorraine back, back, even further into her past as she left the beating behind the stove and the pain that had destroyed her kidney.

That same guttural voice now cried, "Go away, and leave me alone!"

Lorraine saw Rainee again. She was tugging at her sleeping mother's sleeve, trying to wake her.

"Mommy, please help me. Please, wake up! Wake up!" Why did she need her to wake up so desperately?

Then Lorraine saw Rainee sitting, staring out of the bare living room window of the tar paper house they lived in while in Florida. Rain slashed at the fragile house and constant violent lightning filled the sky. She had never heard a storm roar like a lion before, but this one did, and it frightened her until she shook. Rainee obviously needed someone to comfort her. An especially deep clap of thunder followed by another blinding bolt of lightning sent her scampering to her mother's side with more pleading.

Momma and baby Crystal laid on the wide board shelving with a single dirty cotton blanket covering them. "Momma, Momma," Rainee continued to cry, "Please help me!"

Jenna appeared at Rainee's side first, followed by Eileen and Marta.

"Momma," Jenna poked viciously at her mother, "You must wake up. We are in a hurricane and the neighbor's garage just blew by!"

Mother groaned and turned over, waking baby Crystal. Crystal began to cry in fright as she saw the fear in her sisters' four faces. Angrily Momma pulled the blanket off Crystal and closer around herself, "It is just thunder. Now go away! And take Crystal with you!"

"But Momma," Eileen now tried pleading, "We are hungry!"

Momma turned over to glare at her five girls, all looking at her in terror. "Oh, for goodness sakes!" She cried, "I am sleeping. Now go to the kitchen and get something to eat. Just leave me alone!" She promptly turned over and feigned returning to sleep. Soon the children could hear consistent snoring.

As the storm continued to roar, a lightning flash showed a smile on Eileen's broad face, making her look a bit ridiculous in the weird day-night light. "Momma's cake!" She whispered with satisfaction.

Looking out toward the kitchen, Rainee saw a beautiful two-layer chocolate cake on the table. Momma loved chocolate cake and made one every Sunday even if there was nothing else to eat. Each girl got one piece of cake, and then Momma ate the rest. But there on the table sat her newest cake she had finished before the storm started.

Eileen, determined to eat, dashed out into the kitchen after one brilliant lightning flash, but another flash hit before she could reach the cake. Screaming, she scampered back to her sisters, who smirked at her terror, forgetting their own.

"Eileen is chicken, chicken, chicken," someone started, and soon all the girls were quietly joining her. Eileen's face reddened in anger as she turned back to the kitchen. No one was going to call her chicken!

This time she managed to grab the cake with both hands and return to the other girls before lightning struck again. Setting the cake on the floor, she proceeded to dip into its top with her fingers. Licking them clean, she dove again, forgetting Momma was inches away. Soon all the girls were eating cake with sticky fingers and giggling.

As the storm lessened, Jenna ran for glasses of water. Soon only crumbs were left of the cake. It was then that Momma turned over and opened her eyes. "My cake!" She roared as she bolted into a sitting position, "My cake!" Leaning over to retrieve the plate covered with only crumbs, a slow roar began to rumble from her throat. Her eyes bulged and her face turned red.

"Run!" Jenna ordered to her sisters as she dashed for the safety of the outdoors with Crystal clutched to her small body. Rainee obeyed and followed, as did Marta. Eileen, however, was caught in her mother's harsh grasp.

"You little pig!" They heard Momma scream in pace with the whack of her metal brush against Eileen's skin. Eileen cried in pain but Momma did not stop. Over and over she hit her with the brush until the metal handle broke off the brush.

Eileen later told Rainee Momma threw the broken brush on the floor screaming that she had ruined her brush, too, and continued to slap her face with her large hands.

Rainee ran as fast and far as she could into the swampland despite the flooding from the storm. Jenna, still holding Crystal, soon found her, "I hope Eileen is OK. That was awful."

"Maybe we shouldn't have eaten the cake?" Rainee asked.

"Probably not. But there was nothing else to eat, and we were hungry. Listen, the swamp is all flooded and not safe; we had better try to get back to the house. Oh, look! There is the neighbor's garage!" She pointed to a crumpled up building close by. They turned back to the house to help Eileen with her wounds.

Dr. Semdka's gentle hand on her forehead brought Lorraine back to the present. "I only know of one thing that will cause one kidney to die, while the other lives. Someone had to have kicked the Haites out of you. That's what you are remembering, isn't it?"

Lorraine looked around at her children, "Autumn, could you take Ariana and Allison to the gift shop?" she pleaded with her oldest.

"I will take them on home," Justin stated. He moved the girls out of the room. He loudly grumbled that he had always known Lorraine was not right in the head as he and the older girls disappeared out of sight.

Dr. Semdka took her hand, "You are not crazy, Lorraine. I don't want you to listen to what Justin says. He is very mad at you for getting sick, and wants to use his words to punish you. You've had to deal with more than one kind of abuse in your life, haven't you?"

Her startled look told Dr. Semdka he was right. Her sobs confirmed it. "Now, tell me. What happened when you were twelve? What were you remembering?"

Between sobs, Lorraine told someone for the first time of an incident she had totally blocked out, but could remember vividly now. "I can remember him kicking and kicking me, Doctor, but I can't remember his face. I see his hands grabbing for me. I see his feet kicking me. I hear his voice tearing my soul to pieces, but I can't remember his face! Why? Why? I have not been able to remember what my parents looked like for as long as I can remember. Why?"

Dr. Semdka squeezed her hand. "Sometimes, when a body experiences extreme pain or trauma, the mind copes by blocking the incident out. Literally, it is as if the event never happened. Then, sometimes years later, another traumatic event or illness unlocks that block, and the patient remembers the blocked event. For some reason, you still have a partial block. I suspect it will come down soon, because your body is too sick to spend any more energy on mental blocks. When that happens, you will remember their faces."

Lorraine shuttered. She was not sure she wanted to

remember. Her last two trips into that abyss had been frightening enough. How much did God think He could ask of her? Why did she have to remember at all? She had long ago dedicated her life to helping others. Somehow, she had always felt as if she needed to pay something back.

Dr. Semdka squeezed her hand again. "What was left of your kidney tissues showed you to have what we call minimal change syndrome. That means the filters in your kidneys aren't working. In your case, I would guess, your right kidney was simply reflecting what was going on in your good, left kidney. The damage appears to be extensive, but we have a treatment short of a transplant we can try. You may still need one of those, but we can buy some time by putting you on steroids. That will help your kidney to heal enough to allow for some kidney function. I will warn you not to be too optimistic. I still want you to be looking for possible donors. In the meantime, I will get the steroids started. If the left kidney begins to produce enough urine on its own, we can stop your diuretics and send you home for a time. How does that sound?"

"Oh, I would love to be home!" Lorraine smiled. "When can we start?"

"Whoa. Let's slow down for a moment. I do have to tell you there are often some severe side effects to long-term steroid treatment. What we will start you on is called prednisone. Lots of people take small doses of this stuff to handle their asthma. Your adrenal gland naturally produces a hormone that mocks prednisone, but in very small doses. We are talking of giving you ten to twenty times the average dosage, so you will have all the possible side effects."

Lorraine began to look scared again, "Like what?" she cringed.

"First of all, you will begin to shake a lot. Your memory will become confused, and short-term memory will be difficult. You will probably have hot flashes. As the treatment progresses, you could gain a lot of weight. That can't be helped. If we have to keep you on steroids for very long, your joints may begin to lock up. Since we will need to have you on such high doses over a longer-than-usual time, I suspect you will experience this. High blood pressure and anemia become problems. We will monitor all these physical side effects and treat them one by one. Many people also become diabetic on this long-term treatment, and I expect you will not escape this effect. Last, and perhaps most serious, people on this high, long-term dosage level tend to become suicidal. Even without your PTSD, I would expect you to have suicidal thoughts, so we will have a therapist check on you every day."

Lorraine held up her loose, left hand. "First, is it absolutely necessary I do this? Couldn't I just get better?" she pleaded.

Dr. Semdka smiled a sad little smile and stated, "This particular disease is a childhood-onset disease. What I am saying is you have had it your whole life. Different things cause it. Frankly, I don't know what caused yours. You have unconsciously been battling this kidney problem most of your life. The kicking incident could have caused it. I just don't know. In all truthfulness, I am amazed God spared your life when you were twelve, because the damage to your kidney indicates that incident should have been fatal. All I can say is, God is not finished with your life. We have a fighting chance to give that life back to you and your girls with treatment. I just need your permission to get it started. I also need your permission to call your department head. I am afraid you will not be going back to work this semester."

Lorraine looked into Dr. Semdka's eyes. She sensed he was her only chance to stay alive. "Please, yes, go ahead with the treatment. However, I want to ask you two questions first."

"Most certainly," Dr. Semdka agreed.

"OK. First, why will I be suicidal? I have been through a lot and never contemplated taking my own life. Why now?"

"Good question. The steroid will make you feel emotionally out of balance, and very sick. For some reason it drives many people to despair. That is why we even have to watch our stronger patients. The emotional effects are just too unpredictable."

"Maybe I will be your exception," Lorraine prayed out loud.

"I hope so. Just in case, Karen is setting up student therapists to check on you every day."

Lorraine shuttered, but knowing the doctor had limited time, she pushed on with her questions, "Next, what does that PTS stuff stand for?"

"Oh, I am sorry. Since you are in the field, I thought you would know."

"No, I haven't dealt with that before," she responded.

"PTSD stands for Post-Traumatic Stress Disorder. It was a term applied to war veterans who came home traumatized so much by the war experience that they relive those events over and over. We used to think this reliving of trauma only happened to soldiers. Today we know child abuse and battering victims also experience such behavior."

"Children and adults who are abused or battered, however, may block the abusive events for years. Then, for some reason, those blocks come down and they begin reliving their abuse sessions in living color. Physical trauma sometimes destroys such blocks. I am afraid this is what you are experiencing. My suspicion is that you have blocked additional events from childhood and adulthood. Now that your mind can no longer maintain the blocks, you will experience these events again. It can't be helped. What I can do is make sure a good therapist is assigned to your case. This can be a healing process, not just a painful time. Does any of this make sense?"

"Yes, now that you have explained it, I do remember

learning about PTSD in conjunction with war crimes. I am not surprised it applies to abuse, too. I generally remember being abused as a child. A few incidents have always been clear to me. The one I remembered today, however, has been hidden from me all this time," Lorraine sighed, I wonder what else I blocked..."

A great dread overwhelmed her spirit as she remembered Rainee running through the woods. What had happened that time? She was not sure she wanted to know. She also vaguely remembered traumatic adulthood events with Justin. These faint echoes of memories invaded her mind, too. "Oh, God," Lorraine prayed silently, "Help me to find Rainee. I seem so lost, like I have never had a home."

Dr. Semdka squeezed her hand one last time, while telling her the nurses would be starting her on the steroids immediately. Lorraine rolled over on her side, and then sat up carefully. This gave her back relief for the first time since the biopsy.

She sighed gratefully. Work was over, at least for a while. How her family would make it without her full paycheck, their main living money, she had no clue. Justin had not held a steady full-time job in some time. She sighed. She could not worry about that. She must concentrate on getting through the treatment so she could avoid a transplant.

Chapter 7: He Made Her What She Would Not Be

It had been three months since Dr. Semdka started Lorraine on steroids for her kidneys. Today he told her that the kidney disease had actually gone into remission. They could start to withdraw her from the steroids very slowly. It would be another three months before her body was totally clear of the medications. Hope once again lived in her heart. The hardships of the last three months exhausted her, but she had endured them. Justin spent this time away from home as much as possible but failed to get a steadier job.

In that time Autumn became a second Mom, for there were days on end when Lorraine could not leave her bed. Ariana also grew up dramatically as she accepted a grown-up's share of home responsibility. Even little Allison lost the bloom of early childhood. She went about the house with a more serious, contemplative look. Yes, Lorraine's illness drastically changed them all.

The one it changed most, however, was Justin, who appeared more and more rigidly like his real self than he ever had before in their married life. Twice Lorraine caught him hurting the older girls, and twice she ordered counseling or a divorce. He opted for counseling. Being a charismatic male with female counselors, however, he convinced the counselors he was fine. His wife was crazy, he laughingly told Lorraine he had reported to these women, but he was fine and in no need of help.

In desperation, Autumn called social services to report the child abuse issue. The worker there just told her that Justin was well known in the community as a warm, caring person. She, the teen ager, must be lying about his behavior. No, they did not plan to look into possible abuse charges against him. They believed they were unfounded. Was Autumn sure she and the other kids were not making the stories up?

Lorraine finally began to call old friends. Some knew Justin before they were married. This was one avenue where people believed her. However, they also knew more about the abuse than she realized. One friend commented that she remembered when Justin punched her out when they were still a young couple. Did she not remember this? Lorraine immediately denied the charge, but that night a new part of her mental metal door opened—the part that protected her from the abuse she bore as an adult. Over and over, as she reached out to her friends, her adult life began to make sense. Slowly the marriage she once convinced herself she could endure, became a continuation of her childhood of nightmares.

One lady told Lorraine that she knew Justin was hurting the older girls when she had fallen down the basement stairs and spent two weeks in the hospital. Surely, she knew about this? Lorraine realized she knew nothing of these facts Everyone was in smiles when she came home from the hospital that time. Upon carefully quizzing the girls now, however, she discovered the smiles were cover ups for abuse.

In horror, Lorraine remembered Ariana and Allison's fears in the doctor's office the night before the ambulance ride to the hospital in Rockwood. This past episode probably made them afraid. The stories of a life hidden from her present self came out into the open, as one episode after another invaded her fragile mind. She began to wonder how she could have not seen any of this before. She began asking more questions. This time she focused on the girls' life with Dad while Mom was at work. This uncovered events she cringed to hear about, but knew she must.

Lorraine now realized her hard work to never have her children suffer harm in any way like she had as a child had been useless. Why did her children feel they could not tell her what was happening in her absence? She was forever helping other abuse victims to find themselves. Why could she not help herself and her own children?

Lorraine began to remember more and more of her childhood as her body functioned less and less. She often woke with memory episodes preventing sleep. The following days she began telling the children some of her childhood memories. Even her good memories had been blocked because of her childhood pain. She finally a few of these good times back and reveled in recalling them for her children. One such memory was when she, as Rainee, moved to Indiana from Florida.

Chapter 8: Rainee Moves to Indiana

Rainee sat in excitement on the double-decker Greyhound bus as it headed north on U.S. 27 out of Tampa, Florida. It was 1958 and she was almost seven years old. Gazing around, she realized all the passengers were Army soldiers except her Mom, three of her sisters, and herself. Jenna was not with them, as she would travel by car with their Dad to Indiana, Mom explained.

A young soldier leaned over and asked Rainee if she could play a game with him? Delighted, she told him yes, as several other soldiers turned to participate. Soon her sisters joined them. As the soldiers played games with the girls, or sang songs to them, the miles slipped by. Each time Rainee sat down with a different soldier, she badgered him with questions. Why was the soil red here? Why were the mountains blue? Did he live in Florida or Indiana? Often the answer was neither. Had she heard of Kansas? Or Arizona? No, but she would someday learn about those places and find out! Ahhhhh.....her interest in geography began here.......

Momma announced to the bus driver that this was their turn to get off the bus after more than a 24 hour ride. The bus driver pulled off the busy road and stopped. He helped Momma and the girls out of the bus. Then he reached into the huge baggage compartment and found their suitcases. Giving the largest one to Eileen, a smaller one to Marta, and one to Rainee, Momma grabbed the smallest case and threw baby Crystal onto her hip. As the driver pulled away, they began a long walk down a country road Rainee had never seen before.

Trees here looked odd....their leaves were all yellow, and red and orange. Rainee did not know about autumn colors. In Florida it was always green. The air seemed cold and crispy to her.

Just when Rainee was wondering where they were going, Momma turned into a dirt driveway to a tiny house. "This is your grandfather's house, your Dad's father. Go and knock on the door. He is expecting us."

Rainee ran ahead up the drive until she arrived at the house door. The tiny house was covered with what looked like brown tar paper. Stepping to the door, she realized it was open. She craned her long, slender neck forward to see into the house. Her nose picked up the scent of tobacco, mint, and sweat.

As her eyes became accustomed to the dim interior, she realized the house was made up of just a living room, a tiny kitchen and one door that led off to a bedroom. Looking through this door she could see that an unmade bed took up most of that room.

A woman as shriveled as the dried orange peels she had left behind on the ground in the orange orchard stepped out of the cluttered bedroom. Back straight as an arrow, she glared at Rainee with piercing blue eyes as she thumped to the front door in heavy boots. "Which one are you?" She asked in a raspy voice that hurt Rainee's ears.

"Rainee," Rainee stammered as she gazed nervously beyond the old woman.

"Rainee? Didn't know one of them thar kids had such a fool name!" The woman scoffed, waving a very arthritic finger in Rainee's face.

An old man, as grizzled and as white-haired as the woman, toddled through the kitchen door and up behind the old woman. He looked Rainee over from head to foot and then informed the woman, "Her name is Lorraine, Peter's middle child. Fool called her Rainee for some odd reason. Come in child!" He commanded as he turned even more startling blue eyes on Rainee. "Ah, here comes da rest o' 'is big family!" He pointed at her mother and sisters.

"I am your grandfather!" He continued to talk to Rainee,

including the other three children in his gaze, "and this is your step-grandmother, Mildred….ha, ha, ha……Your eighth step-grandmother! This is our house where you will be for now."

Rainee looked at the tiny space, and realized he was staring at the floor in the living room. It was obvious she and her family were expected to sleep on that floor. It looked hard, and the carpet was old and dirty. Rainee shuttered and turned away.

A metal thing in the middle of the room caught her eye. Her grandfather saw her look, and told her that was their heater…the house's only source of heat for the winter. "You'll be glad we got it when winter gets here!" he laughed. "You aren't used to winter after them thar balmy Florida days, are you?" He laughed almost gleefully at his own humor.

Mother stepped in front of Rainee and called out hello. Baby Crystal, now two, squirmed, and mother placed her on the dirty floor. She then placed her suitcase next to Crystal.

"Where is Pete?" Grandfather asked suspiciously.

"Well, me and these four girls came on the bus. Pete and the eldest is coming in a car he got for the trip, bringing the rest of our things." This speech seemed to wear Mother out as she collapsed on a rust-colored broken down old couch.

"Humph!" Grandfather emitted several uninterpretable sounds before he joined Mildred in the alley of a kitchen, "Suppose we have to feed you," he called out as he took a potato peeler in hand.

"Who is she?" Rainee whispered hoarsely to Mother on the couch. She knew Grandmother, her father's mother, was in Florida. That was why they had moved to Florida when Rainee was but a baby. Grandmother lived in a nice house and never had them over. Momma said her father's side of her family was from the South. Grandpa talked like her other relatives. How did he end up in Indiana?

Mother did not speak to her for a moment. This was not a clean house. It was not a nice house. Rainee wished she could go outdoors into the fresh sunshine!

"That is your step-grandmother," Mother explained. "Grandfather and she were married several years ago. Both of them are in their eighties. Grandfather and Grandmother were divorced forty years ago. Since then he has been married eight times. All the other step-grandmothers died except for Mildred.

"Why?" Rainee asked innocently, still staring into the unkempt kitchen.

"I don't know. Now quit asking questions!" Mother demanded, as she rubbed her chapped, worn hand across her frazzled, dirty face, "I need to rest."

Staring out the front door, Rainee's inquisitive eyes soon lighted on a beautiful red barn...The paint was obviously brand new. It was surrounded by trees turning orange and yellow...what a lovely sight. As she watched in glee, the sun began to paint the sky many colors as it set behind the barn. First the sky was streaked with pale pink, then orange and coral. Finally it turned a muted mauve and gray before darkness fell.

Caught inside the tiny house, Rainee felt panic enter her chest. She needed to get out... to be free...where could she go? The swamps that were her sanctuary were forever gone. She would have to find new places to run. New places to hide. For she sensed new dangers lurked here, and she must be able to run.

Rainee stood shivering in the noisy school playground. Only a few weeks ago they had moved to this place that was now so cold and snowy. She had never seen snow before yesterday when the storm started.

Today, children were laughing as they dropped to the snow to make "snow angels." Others were sliding on a large piece of ice in front of Rainee. A little boy ran over to the ice patch with a broom and began sweeping the light coating of snow that had fallen since the ice had been cleared. "Slide's better if the snow is gone," he shouted at Rainee. She timidly smiled back and then stared at her shoes. She would not have even known what "slide" meant yesterday!

Her teacher, Mrs. DeBall, came up beside Rainee. "Have you ever slid on ice before?" She asked Rainee. Rainee, continuing to look at the ground, shook her head no. "OK, everybody," Mrs. DeBall pointed at the children on the ice, "Let's clear off the ice. Rainee wants to try to slide for the first time, and I don't want anyone tripping her!"

With many shouts and giggles, the children melted into the sidelines around the patch of ice. Mrs. DeBall took Rainee by the hand and led her onto the ice. "Watch me and then do as I do, OK?" She said. With that, Mrs. DeBall ran a few steps and then stepped sideways, allowing her feet to stay on the ice. Swoosh; she made a perfect slide path across the ice patch. "See," she laughed, "It is easy enough even for your old teacher to do it!"

Rainee giggled at Mrs. DeBall's remark. Taking a deep breath she began to run, and then planted her feet as Mrs. DeBall had done. Swoosh; she went, all the way up to Mrs. DeBall. "I did it!" She cried unbelievingly. Everyone clapped. "Can I do it again?"

"You have to get in line now," several students yelled as they formed a line to take turns on the ice. She gladly joined the back of the line. The recess bell rang, but Mrs. DeBall motioned for her class to stay outside. "My first graders get the ice for the rest of the afternoon!" She cried happily.

The sun came out and turned the world into a mass of glittering jewels. Rainee no longer felt the cold. Banging her hands together as the other children did, she discovered she could warm them. Over and over she slid until she was exhausted. Then one of the other students showed her how to make snow angels.

Mrs. DeBall divided the class into two groups and challenged them to make a snow fort. After what seemed like a long day of work, Rainee found herself inside a small room made entirely of snowballs. Several windows had been left open facing the other team's fort. Soon the teacher yelled, "Snowball fight!" And snowballs rained down on her fort from the "enemy's fort." A pile of snow that had been built up in the corner soon disappeared as her team returned the snowballs. Just when she thought they were losing, the school bell rang for the end of the school day.

Mrs. DeBall led her class into the building where they quickly picked up their books and lunch boxes. One by one they raced for the door. Rainee grabbed her things and ran to catch the school bus that would take her to her grandfather's. Mrs. DeBall yelled behind her, "I am glad you have come to be in my class, little Rainee! You lend sunshine to my day!" With a warm, soft feeling inside her heart, Rainee stepped onto the bus.

What seemed like forever later, the bus pulled up in front of the house. A huge truck was pushing an old school bus up beside the trailer behind the house that her great-aunt and uncle occupied. A huge muddy trail was left where the truck had dragged the bus. Rainee's father ran out to the bus stop and hurried the children into the yard.

"Guess what?" Rainee's Dad cried, "I found us something to live in!"

Rainee stared at the empty, rusty bus. Dad led the children into the bus, patting the windows as he went, for the seats had been removed. "See?" Dad pointed at a small bench below the first two windows behind what used to be the driver's seat. "This is your new bed!"

Rainee touched the cold bench and shivered, "I am really cold," she began to cry.

"Oh, buck up," Rainee's Dad yelled, frustrated that Rainee was not excited. "You can always go into the house and get warm during the day. At night we have all those quilts your Step-Grandma made and had in the attic. They will keep you warm enough at night."

Rainee did not meet her father's eye. He turned away and pointed out similar benches to the other girls, telling them who would sleep where. A wide bench was built across the back of the bus. Dad told the girls he and Ma would sleep there. Rainee looked for her mother, but she was not in the bus. She backed down the stairs to the ground and ran for Grandpa's house.

Mom was sitting in front of the small gas heater Grandpa had in his living room chatting with Step-Grandma Mildred. Mildred seemed pleased about something. Grandpa came out of the bedroom, a pleased look on his face, too. "Guess we get to get you kids out of our hair, huh?" He shouted at Rainee.

Crystal toddled over to Mom crying, but Mom ignored her. "I guess it's a place to sleep anyway," she agreed.

"Don't you think we will freeze? It is so cold out there!" Rainee sighed. Mom was not listening to her either.

Mom soon stood and gathered several quilts to take to the old bus. Step-Grandma Mildred grumbled that she had better fix them all something to eat. Rainee sat down in the chair by the heater and pulled out a book Mrs. DeBall gave to her this morning to read. Happily, she was soon lost in its pages.

Christmas came and went uneventfully. Grandpa did not believe in Christmas, so there were no trees or presents. Rainee missed Christmas. Even the small presents she had received in the past meant a lot to her. And almost none of her things had survived the trip to Indiana from Florida. How she wished for her doll that she had slept with in that warm place. Mom told her she was too big to sleep with a doll anyway; so, she was glad it was lost.

The clothes Rainee wore that winter were all from a church's charity box. The coat, two sizes too big, at least kept her warm. She also received a pair of worn rubber boots from another church box to wear on her feet to keep out the snow. They were women's boots, which made it hard to walk, but she soon learned their slippery rubber bottoms made sliding even more fun. She never complained. There was no one to complain to, for mother seemed lost in her own world, and Dad was gone most of the time. Grandpa paid the most attention to her, but this scared her. Something about him reminded her of Bluebeard in a story the teacher read to the class in the fall.

Lorraine startled and came back to the present as the memory of Bluebeard came back to her mind. She looked up into the face of Allison, who was looking at her with a concerned look. "Did he ever hurt you?" She asked as Lorraine realized her daughter was referring to her story.

Lorraine shook her head. "No, I tried to stay away from him as much as possible. Mom told me before we came to Indiana that I had six other aunts and uncles, and seven more step-grandmothers. They all died while living with him. The children's biological mother ran away when my father was a baby. He was the last of nine children, including three sets of twins. Only two aunts and my father survived childhood."

Lorraine continued, "My real grandmother went to live with relatives in Florida, the same relatives we lived with sometimes when we lived there. I got to know my real Grandmother, who seemed nice but would not let us stay at her house. No one would tell us why all those children and women died, or why she left the children. It must have been awful for her. After I became an adult, I had to do a family history for one of my college classes, and I came to realize Grandfather had killed them. I knew then that my childhood fear of him, and re-labeling him, "Bluebeard," had a reason." Lorraine sighed. "I had forgotten writing that paper, too."

Allison shuttered. "Did anything else happen to you while you lived at your Grandpa's?"

Lorraine sighed and closed her eyes. "Grandpa's house..." she whispered and returned to the past.

Rainee stepped off the school bus in a bright winter day to discover Grandpa's yard was filled with relatives. It was her birthday, but no relatives had ever celebrated it before. Did all these people know it was her birthday? Grandma, Mom's mother, would, because she shared her birthday, but the rest?

Aunt Barbara, Dad's youngest sister, came out of the bus-house carrying a large cake. "Ah, there's my birthday girl!" She cried happily.

Aunt Barbara had three boys and no girls. She had visited Rainee and her sisters at least once a week since their arrival in September, and once in a while Rainee was asked to visit at her house. She loved these visits. Aunt Barbara worked at the hospital, and her husband, Uncle Ben, worked in a truck factory. They seemed rich to Rainee. Aunt Barbara was always dressed really pretty, and wore hats to match her dresses. Their house was the prettiest house Rainee had ever seen. They owned a small farm several miles from Grandpa's that Uncle Ben farmed "on weekends." He joked that he was a "gentleman farmer," whatever that meant.

Their house even smelled good, Rainee daydreamed, as Aunt Bessie caught her eye again. "Look!" She cried. "I made you a birthday cake! And my boys brought you presents!" She ushered Rainee into Grandpa's house and set the cake on the kitchen counter.

"You can't serve that thing in here," Step-grandma Mildred growled. "The kids will make one mess out of my house!"

"Don't worry," Aunt Barbara crooned. "After we sing happy birthday, I will chase them all outside to eat. We will have a winter picnic, shall we?" She seemed to laugh as she winked at Rainee.

Rainee liked Aunt Barbara, who seemed to really like her, too. Suddenly Rainee felt a shower of happiness falling on her head. Someone had remembered her birthday. She could not remember having a birthday party with family ever. Not ever!!! And presents, too!!!!

After the cake was gone, the children gathered in the bus-home to watch Rainee open her presents. To Rainee's delight, when she opened her presents, she discovered her cousins had bought her a small doll. Squealing with delight, Rainee cradled the doll in her arms until all the children had filed out of the bus. Carefully, so as not to muss the doll's hair, Rainee tucked her new doll into her bench-bed and gave her a kiss before following the other children outside to play in the snow.

The cousins brought different kinds of sleds with them. The next door neighbor's children also had sleds. Soon the whole tribe assembled at the top of a steep hill behind the neighbor's house. The cousins and neighbor kids began taking turns sliding down the hill on their sleds.

A little later her oldest cousin, Leroy, came over to Rainee. "Don't you want a sled ride?" He asked. Leroy was twelve, which seemed very grown up to seven-year-old Rainee. "Are you scared to ride?"

Rainee shook her head. "No, but I don't know how. It never snowed in Florida."

"Oh, yeah, I forgot," Leroy nodded. He hollered at one of his younger brothers to bring over their smaller sled. "Here, put one hand here," he pointed to a small rope handle on one side, "and the other hand here." Rainee sat down on the sled and grabbed the handles like he said. "Now, I am going to give you a little push and you will go down the hill. Just sit good and straight and you should make it to the bottom!"

Terrified, Rainee gripped the handles as Leroy pushed. A deep, cold winter wind smacked her face, as she rapidly descended the hill. Down, down she went, almost past everyone else who had gone at the same time. Finally she stopped at the edge of the orchard. Good thing she missed the trees, she thought, as she stood up and grabbed the rope to pull the sled back up the hill.

Just then Aunt Barbara called that the boys were to come. It was time to go home. Rainee ran back over to the bus-home, where Aunt Barbara stood. Aunt Barbara gave her a hug. "Thank you for the birthday party," she said.

"Where is your doll?" Aunt Barbara asked

"Oh, I tucked her in bed because the party made her tired," Rainee explained as she ran to get her. Inside the bus-home, Rainee threw back her quilt, but her doll was not there. In terror she cried out and began searching the bus-house. Finally, back on her parents' bed she saw her doll, ripped into pieces and the hair pulled out. Crystal sat next to the doll, looking pleased. "My doll," she gurgled as she held up the broken doll.

Rainee grabbed what was left of the doll and ran outside, holding the doll up to Aunt Barbara. "Crystal broke her!" She sobbed.

Aunt Barbara held Rainee and tried to console her, but she would not quit crying. Her first family birthday party was ruined. Aunt Barbara explained the terrible thing to Momma when she came out of Grandpa's house. "Oh, for goodness sakes, Rainee, it was just a doll. I thought someone had been killed!" With that she took the doll from Rainee and threw her into a snow bank. "You are too big for dolls, anyway!"

Rainee clung to Aunt Barbara until she could control her tears. Then she went into the bus-home and crawled under her quilt. Pulling the quilt over her head, she sobbed herself to sleep. All the relatives went home while she slept. She woke to a nightmare and began sobbing again.

Her Grandma on her mother's side was a Christian. Rainee asked her not long before what people at church meant by saying "Christ died for you." She wanted to know what Pastor Teston taught. Grandma seemed pleased by her question and told her God sent his Son to take the blame for everyone's sins and he had to die as a result. Later God made him alive again, but not before he went through all that pain and dying. That was why people could join God's family, like Pastor Teston told her. Tonight, Rainee dreamed that Christ was talking to her and telling her he died for her, too. "You love your little doll very much," He told her in her dream. "I love you very much, too, just like your Grandma said."

She was crying out, "But why did you have to die?" When Dad shook Rainee awake. Rainee pulled away from Dad and dug further into her quilt. Her sobbing continued. "Why are you still crying?" Momma demanded.

Rainee became afraid. Suddenly she knew that if she told her parents the real reason she cried, they would be very angry with her and might hurt her again. Even Aunt Barbara left when Momma told her to go. She was all alone and must tell no one why she cried. Rainee dug even deeper into her bed, wrapping her arms around her curled up legs.

"Oh, leave the crybaby alone," Momma told Dad. "She just likes the attention." Dad followed Momma to the back of the bus. The other girls were already asleep. Soon Rainee could hear her father snoring. She sat up and stared out of the bus window at the white winter world shimmering in moonlight.

"I'm glad you love me, God," she whispered. "I don't think Momma or Daddy love me. I'm afraid, God. How can I grow up without a real Momma and Daddy? I am glad you love me." In that moment a light fell onto her small bed. From the light she heard a gentle, soothing voice, "I am God's angel. He has sent me to watch over you. He has told me to tell you that He will be your Father. He will take care of you. Sleep now. You are safe." Rainee curled up under her quilt once more, and quickly fell into a restful sleep.

Ariana placed a hand on Lorraine's shoulder, bringing her back to her own children as she sat curled up in the one recliner in their house that relieved the pain her treatment brought. "Did you really understand that God would be your Father so young? How did you realize you had no parents despite both parents living with you?"

Tears trickled down her face as the sweet memory of realization brought Lorraine a little more peace. "Ariana, in the time before this event that I lived with my parents, no one ever told me they loved me. No one ever held my hand. I never sat on anyone's lap and listened to a story. My body was distorted from lack of food. My mother told me constantly that she wished I had died when I was born. She did not want me. It is not too hard for a child to feel totally unwanted when they are told so practically every day. My father often made fun of me to the other children and anyone listening. I lived for the rare moments when he would be in a good mood and call me his Rainee. He is the one who gave me my nickname. I came to believe if I could just be Rainee all the time, maybe he would love me all the time."

Lorraine continued, "As I got older, the abuse got worse and his hatred of me buried those warm 'Rainee moments.' I leaned more and more on the guidance of my Heavenly Father. That faith grew even in the dark years, when I had no church family and I was not allowed to even say God out loud. It was in one of those dark moments that I began to secretly read my Bible. Pastor Teston gave me a Bible before I left Florida. One day in Psalms I found a verse that confirmed my belief that God was very involved in making sure I grew up all right. The verse says, 'When my father and my mother forsake me, the Lord will take me up.' That reassurance was really needed at the time and He gave it."

Allison, wonder on her face, questioned, "Did you really see an angel? I mean, people say they do, but did you?"

"Yes, sweetie, I believe my faith as a little child allowed me to see God's messenger. He came back again in another time when I needed him, but that is a story for tomorrow," Lorraine smiled wistfully as she looked out the window at the setting sun. "I think you need to ask your Dad to take you out for some supper now."

Lorraine heard Allison's voice beside her whispering to Ariana, "Do you think you will ever see an angel? Do you think it is possible?" and Ariana's reply. "I don't know. I do know that Momma needed God to be extra close when she was little, and so God made it so. That's all we have to know."

"It's OK, Rainee," Lorraine spoke to her inner child in soothing tones. "It's all right. You are loved by God and your children. You are still OK."

Chapter 9:
He Carried Her When She Could Not Walk

One day in late spring a great anger began to eat at Lorraine as she listened to the doctor's explanation of her slow withdrawal from steroids and what to watch for in side effects. It was bad enough she had almost died and was in constant pain. Why did she have to suffer more side effects when she needed her strength to take care of her children? "Why will you allow this?" she shouted at God over and over again.

That same horrible day Lorraine remembered hearing Justin demand that the doctor, "Fix my wife. She can't even perform her wifely duties anymore, and I have needs she has to meet. Make her so she can be useful again. Look what you have done to her!"

Done to me? Lorraine wondered. The doctor saved her life. Was that wrong? Did Justin still think she should have died? Deep down Lorraine shrank from the answer to that question, for the answer, she knew, was, "Yes!"

The doctor explained to Justin that Lorraine's joints were beginning to freeze. As steroids were withdrawn, they would stiffen even more. There was a chance she would lose movement altogether, so how could he be worrying about whether he was getting his "duty," when they were trying to give him back his wife's life?

Obviously, Dr. Semdka had little use for Justin's attitude. As Justin continued to press the point, Dr. Semdka sighed, and handed him a business card. "Dr. Ward may be able to start working with Lorraine to help her regain some of her joint movement. I just don't know how effective the treatments are yet. They are experimental. I also know they are extremely painful. You'd better appreciate what your wife has to go through to become functional in any way again!"

The doctor's comment brought the cedar woods back to

Lorraine's mind. She was Rainee again, running, running, running, as if her life depended on it. Only for the first time she heard noise clearly from behind—it was the roar of a heavy hunting rifle. Terrified, Lorraine watched as Rainee jumped under the canopy of a very old cedar tree. Hidden from the path, the child tried to quiet her own breathing. Caught in terror, Lorraine, came back to the present when the doctor put his arm around her shoulders.

"We have to take things a day at a time, Lorraine," the doctor warned her.

"A day?" Her mind cried out. "I can't even take an hour at a time!" Wrapped in pain, Lorraine crawled back into their car for the fifty-mile drive home from Rockwood. It was the dead of winter. Winters in upper Minnesota are vicious. A strong wind buffeted the small car as she watched a blizzard building in the west. Lorraine prayed that they would make it home before the storm hit.

Being on the road in a prairie blizzard, she knew, was deadly because of white-outs coming up without notice. Too often, the news told stories of people driving off the road and dying, because the storm had totally blocked the travelers' view. Slowly they inched toward home, to arrive only minutes before the snow.

Gratefully Lorraine pulled herself from the car as the first wave of white-out began. The house, only two feet away, looked distant and gray. She reached out and grabbed the corner of the house while she could still see it. She could see Justin doing the same. Fighting the wind, Lorraine made the back door and fell into the back entry. Justin tripped over her and then righted himself. "Can't you even walk enough to get into the house?" He sneered.

Crying, Lorraine pulled herself to standing as Autumn came running upstairs from the basement. Autumn had just completed the laundry. "Are you OK?" she cried as she helped her Mom into the living room and her recliner.

Exhausted, Lorraine fell into her chair and let Autumn take her coat off. With one last tug, the snowy garment came free and Autumn went to hang it in the laundry room to dry. Lorraine curled into a ball, as the pain syndrome she was coming to live with spread quickly throughout her body. Justin came into the living room with a look of disgust on his face. "I suppose I have to cook supper tonight, too?" He barked.

Her cries became rasping sobs. Ariana came in from her room and knelt at her feet. "What do you need?" She asked anxiously.

"My pain pills and ice packs," she whispered as her hands and feet curled out of control. "And the heating pad might help between ice packs."

Ariana ran into the bathroom and returned with the medicine and heating pad, then into the kitchen for ice. (Lorraine developed an allergy to all pain medication as time passed. She would learn she had to live with the daily pain). For now, though, she quickly spilled out two pills and situated the pad over her hands. Putting the pills in her mouth, Ariana helped her with a drink of water.

Slowly the pills gave her a little relief. Lorraine fell into a light sleep, as she heard Justin slamming pots and pans in the kitchen. "Worthless kids," he screamed. "They could have had dinner ready, but chose to be bad instead!"

Her eyes fluttered open and Lorraine reached for Ariana's hands. "It's not you girls' fault," she whispered, "Try to ignore him, OK?"

Everyday Lorraine spent two hours with a chiropractor, whom the orthopedic surgeon Dr. Semdka recommended, was training with the new joint treatments. Traditional physical therapy would not help to release the frozen joints. The orthopedic surgeon's tests showed almost every joint in some stage of freezing. Something must be done! Otherwise, he was afraid that Lorraine would spend the rest of her days in bed, having to be fed and cared for by a nurse. Nursing home care became a real possibility over the next few weeks, but she begged to be allowed to stay home with her children, whom she feared to leave in Justin's full time care.

The chiropractor, Dr. Evans, worked her hands and her feet, cracking and breaking the joints. Then he manipulated the broken joints over and over. Gradually he succeeded in getting movement back into her extremities for longer periods of time. Then he assigned a wellness intern to teach her to exercise her atrophied muscles so that these joints did not return to the frozen state. Over the next few weeks, he worked on her legs, arms and neck, adding new exercises to assure continued movement in each part. After these joints were loose enough, the doctor told Lorraine she could return to work part-time. Her body was getting used to not having steroids.

Lorraine baby-stepped her way into her first class while still in excruciating pain. The doctor wrote her boss. He told her Professor Hawkins would have to begin work part-time, but the boss did not listen. Lorraine arrived at work to discover she was given a full teaching load. She was also reassigned to her old research project. Another professor had continued this project in her absence. Sighing, she swallowed one pain pill after another as she tried to sit through office hours, and stand through classes. Spring dragged on so very slowly. Would she never be pain-free again? One thing she was grateful for—the extra busy schedule kept her too tired to revisit her memories most of the time. Life with memory episodes seemed to shrink into a very small part of her present life. Nights became more restful as exhaustion chased the nightmares back into her subconscious.

Lorraine, however, consciously remembered Justin's recent treatment of the children. Unable to shake an overwhelming sense of guilt, she arranged for after school care for Ariana and daycare around Allison's school hours. Autumn signed up for after school activities at the high school.

Justin complained of the added expense but did not seem to mind the extra freedom. Lorraine hoped he would get the hint and start working full time again. He did not seem inclined to follow this hint. He would continue to work part time and go to school but no full time schedule.

Halfway through the semester, the chiropractor announced he was ready to start on Lorraine's hips, pelvis and back. He told her if they could get movement again in these parts, perhaps it would diminish her pain. Gladly she submitted to the torturous treatments, breaking a cold sweat when the pelvis/back joint finally was broken and released. Often, she wondered if she had made the right choice—the choice to live. As painful month followed painful month, Justin continued to nag Lorraine with comments that led her to believe he wished she was not alive. Then she would remember how much her girls needed her and go on with life.

One day, as spring finally arrived in mid-May in that cold north country, Lorraine had a whole day without pain pills as her allergies to them began to develop. Her movements were still guarded, slow, and painful but she began to hope for better health. She also began to believe life was the right choice. Justin had submitted to three more months of counseling when she threatened divorce; so, maybe they would be okay. Still, he chose another young, female counselor he bragged about manipulating.

Lorraine knew deep down that her husband suffered from some deep-seated problem his own past handed him. Fearful of what she would find, she refused to label the problem, but continued to seek help for herself and her children. Surely, if we got enough help, the problem will be resolved, she reasoned.

The semester ended and Lorraine looked forward to a

slower summer. The last thing to do before leaving work was her yearly evaluation. Despite missing so much of the year, the department head insisted she had to have an evaluation. Lorraine was not afraid of it. Her students gave her excellent evaluations. She published three articles that year. Thank God, she really finished them the previous year and they just needed to go through the red tape of publishing in time for this year's evaluation. She was, therefore, in a very positive mood as she swung into the small conference room. In shock, she realized the department head was not alone. The dean sat beside her, and another faculty member was on her other side. Suspicious of what was about to happen, she stopped at the door.

"I would like to postpone this evaluation for a day. Since administration feels they need such a strong front, I will need to consult the union to see if I need representation before we go further," Lorraine declared and walked away.

In the hallway, she met a fellow professor from another department who had become Lorraine's good friend. Concern was written all over his face. "Rumor has it that your department head is set to fry you," he noted.

"Fry me? But why? Just last year I was named teacher of the year and got that research award. This year I brought in a lot of grant money. Yes, I only worked part of the time, but I was approved for disability for the time I was off. What do you know that I don't know?" Lorraine asked him.

Dr. Brown held his hands behind his back as he gazed into her face. He was sure she did not have a clue about what went on in the college while she was gone. After some contemplation, he sighed and began, "Your department head teaches as well as administers. She expected that teaching award for herself. She also wants your grant money. She has one big ego problem and you are her current target. Her father bought her that position when he endowed the college with five million dollars. She is not really qualified for the position and she knows it. Anyone who makes her look bad, she gets rid of in nasty ways. She has decided she can get rid of you now because your illness makes you an easy target. "

"Get rid of me?" Lorraine choked, "How can a college get rid of a teacher just because they were sick?"

"I hate to tell you this, but you don't have tenure yet. Without tenure the department head can take your job easily."

"But isn't it illegal to get rid of someone due to illness?" Lorraine gasped.

"I'm sorry, Lorraine. If I had it my way, I would transfer you to my department. You are one of the best teachers on campus. But that is why you are in trouble. Professional jealousy is lethal. No, you have no legal repercussions. In this state, it is against the law for a state employee to sue the state, and we are state employees. There are no laws to protect the sick and handicapped yet. I am so sorry. My advice to you is when you go into that meeting, tell them first thing that you are resigning, so you are in no need of an evaluation. Then just walk out, OK?" He patted me on the back, "I will help you get another position."

Something had to be done to help Lorraine, but Dr. Brown knew the power of those above her, and how they loved to abuse it. Ten years at this college had taught him to steer clear of that department's administration. Why did the good teachers always have to pay for the vindictiveness of their administration?

"But we just bought a house last year because I was promised tenure!" Lorraine angrily stabbed at a mark on the hall wall. "The girls like it here. It would kill them to have to move on top of all the stress we've been through this year." Lorraine stumbled down the hall, leaving a concerned Dr. Brown staring after her.

The following day Lorraine walked into the conference room flanked by two union representatives. Sitting opposite her department head, she surprised everyone there by announcing her resignation. Broken, utterly broken, she stood and walked out as Dr. Brown had advised. She had lost her health. Her marriage was in shambles. Her career was lost. How much more could she stand?

Lorraine fearfully made her way home. She had yet to tell Justin she lost her job. She knew that could bring no support, only verbal abuse. She longed to run but to where? Dear God, what was she supposed to do? She cried out to Heaven. "I am going to carry you for now," she heard a still small voice respond as she felt her spirit enter a restful state. She was so glad she still had her faith in God. He would go with her through yet another night. She wondered how she had arrived at such a deep faith as a child?

After dinner that evening, Lorraine broke the news of her resignation to the family. As expected, Ariana became hysterical. She had a wonderful friendship group here, and the idea of moving would be most painful for her.

Autumn did not seem to care—high school had been tough this year. Maybe a new place would be better. Autumn would later tell me she had secretly hoped this change meant leaving her father at this time.

Allison was too young to really understand. She asked if they could live in the same house and became tearful when Ariana informed her that that was not likely. Through all the children's responses, Justin remained moodily silent.

Finally, Justin spoke in a deep angry voice, "Well, this is a fine fix you have put us in! I can't take care of you and the girls!"

"Why not?" I responded angrily, "Why not? I paid for a Bachelor's and Master's degree for you that you choose not to use. Don't you think this is a good time to put it to some use?"

"I will never do anything you tell me I need to do!" Justin

shouted back at her. "Well, I can think of only one thing to do—take you to my brother's until you can get another job!"

"No, that is not an option," Lorraine responded. "Daniel is not right in the head. It would not be safe to have the girls around him. Besides, he runs a freaky cult and commune! I do not want my girls raised that way!"

"Well, you don't have a choice, lady!" Justin shouted back, "We are going!"

Lorraine felt herself sinking into a deep pit of darkness. Her pain cycle came on stronger than it had in months. In terror, she collapsed in her chair as she watched her joints, one at a time, return to immobility in response to the stress. She laid there in her chair for the next week, only summoning the courage to crawl to the bathroom and back again. Her daughters applied heating pads and ice packs. At last, a little relief came, but she knew she had lost valuable ground. Why? Why? If she had a curable illness, why did she feel so sick again? Maybe it was all in her head. Maybe Justin was right.

More and more Rainee visited Lorraine as her illness reasserted itself, and she became frozen once more. She would hear Rainee's musical voice calling to her across time and asked her to remind her of more of her childhood. Where had her faith come from? She asked Rainee. This was a time of learning to understand her past in a way that would eventually give her the strength she needed to face the present. As an ill adult, she had turned more and more to faith to manage her life. When had it become so important to her that she could not see life without it, though? she asked herself. The answer came one night as she was thinking of her Grandmother who had died when she was eight years old.

Chapter 10: The Angel Visits Rainee

Rainee's Aunt and Uncle visited Rainee's family with their three children when Rainee was about seven years old.   Lorraine watched as if a spectator as Rainee walked over to her Dad and her Uncle, who were drinking beer and exchanging fishing stories.

Lorraine heard Rainee ask her dad, "Why do you drink that stuff? It smells bad!"

The men laughed at her. Then Dad held out his bottle to her. "I guess you are old enough for a little drink!" The men teased and chortled until Rainee took a sip. Gagging, Rainee told her father the beer was disgusting. This simply made them laugh more. Rainee ran off to play with the other children.

Weeks later these relatives returned. It was her eighth birthday. She loved being born on Grandma's birthday because Grandma told her that made her extra special to her. Special to Brenda's Mom and the kumquat people, too, she remembered as an adult now. Tears began to slide down Rainee's already tear-smudged face as she remembered Brenda's family and the kumquat people. She felt safe with them.

Aunt Barbara, though, had brought the boys for this birthday, too. Grandma, Momma's mom, gave Rainee a special present after everyone else was gone and told her, "I love you, little Rainee, more than the sun and the moon, and God loves you even more!" She remembered Grandma's withered arms around her shoulders hugging her so tight she could hardly breathe. But that was OK, too, because she had received so few hugs.

A few days passed, and then a day came when the fragile world she lived in once again crumbled.   Her Aunt and Uncle had come unexpected that day. The adults acted weird. What was wrong, she wondered?

When her aunt and uncle left, Rainee heard her Mom call her name. Coming inside as the sun was setting, Rainee looked surprised. Momma never asked for her.

"What is it?" older sister Jenna demanded of Momma, as she followed Rainee into the house.

"Grandma's dead. Heart attack. No more Grandma. Funeral day after tomorrow. You girls will go," she stated in a dull, flat voice, "She was only sixty..." she added as if to someone else.

"No, no, no!" Rainee screamed back, "She is fine. She can't be dead! I love her!" She broke into uncontrollable sobs.

Continuing in her dull, monotone voice, Momma added, "Grandma is dead. She was just talking to Aunt Mary, and dropped dead. Suppose it was a heart attack. Everyone in our family dies young of heart attacks." Then she began to mumble, "I don't understand. She just turned sixty. She was fine yesterday." Momma walked away from Rainee.

Horrified, Rainee stood frozen to her spot just inside the living room door. Then as if an injured animal was loosened from a trap, she screamed, "No, No, NO!" and ran out the door. Running as fast as her body would let her, Rainee found herself in a park by the river. She sank into a swing and numbly swung until the early March cold evening descended. Unable to feel her body anymore, she slowly rose and made her way back to the condemned house they now called home. Ignoring her mother's call for dinner, Rainee slipped up the attic stairs and dove under the hand-made quilt on her army cot bed.

Only then did the tears come--great big, hot tears of pain that racked her body and tore at her throat. In desperation, she began to pray. "God, is Grandma in Heaven with you? She said she would go to Heaven someday because she believed in you. She is with you, isn't she? Why couldn't you let her stay with me? Why?"

A lonely moon slipped above the horizon, sending eerie light into the bare, unfinished room. Dad had found them this place to live in after the police told them they could no longer live in the bus last summer. Rainee squatted under the pile of old quilts she called her bed and continued to cry quietly far into the moonlit night. Eventually she heard the soft breathing of her four sisters. The next-oldest, Eileen, began mumbling in her sleep, and then was quiet again.

Rainee pushed the broken window up to open it all the way. She could hear the icy river murmuring its song a few feet from her now as the ice broke up that day for spring. She liked to listen to the river's song most nights. Tonight it seemed too sad. The strong wind made her feel cold, but she did not close the window. Rather, she stared into the starry sky. "Grandma, Grandma," she whimpered, "Can you hear me? Grandma, I need you so much. Please, don't leave me. Please don't leave me here. Daddy and Momma hurt me. They don't love me. Please, Grandma, come and take me with you. I want to go to heaven with you!" Silent, dry sobs now wracked Rainee's undersized boney body and she rocked on her heels as she gripped the curtain-less windowsill, her knuckles as white as snow with the effort.

When there was no answer to her moans and cries, Rainee decided to talk to God again. Grandma must not be able to hear her in Heaven, she thought. But she knew God could, and maybe He could tell Grandma she loved her and wanted her back. Between mouthfuls of tears, Rainee prayed, "God, please tell Grandma to come home. I need her here. Do you really need her more than I do? Please, please, I need my Grandma. She is the only one who protected me."

Rainee sat down with crossed legs and thought for a few moments. Then she began to pray again. "God, if you need Grandma so much there, do you think you can let me come there to live now, too, so I can live with my Grandma? Please, God. She is the only person who loves me…. Please, God…."

Rainee collapsed face first onto her make-shift bed,

burying her body-wrenching sobs in the quilts so the others would not awaken. Just when she thought she could not bear another moment, she felt a warm, gentle hand stroking her straggled long blonde hair. "Rainee," a familiar voice whispered.

Rainee looked up to see the light she had seen on her sixth birthday, and the same angel shining from the light. "Rainee," the angel crooned lovingly, "God hears your prayers, but He cannot take you to live with your Grandma. You must stay here for now."

"But why, why?" Rainee cried as she pulled herself back up on her knees. "No one loves me here. I am afraid to stay here. Why do I have to stay here? I want my Grandma, please!"

"Your Grandma wants you to know she will always love you, Rainee. And God wants you to know He loves you more than you can understand. He needs you to stay here, Rainee. He knows how hard your life is, but He has some work that He needs you to do before you come to Heaven. You must grow up. Work hard to stay close to Jesus. You have been called for a special task, Rainee. He knows you are little and cannot really understand. But you will. And no matter how hard life is going to be, you will always have Him with you to love and care for you. In a very special time God will send you the helpers you need. Now rest, my child. Rest. Tell no one of my visit tonight, for your parents will get angry and hurt you, and God does not want you to be hurt. He will protect you in a way you will understand later. And He will send others who will love you. You can trust Him, Rainee, because He loves you. Now sleep, Child, you must have sleep to help you go on."

Rainee slipped down between the quilts, sleep overcoming her. In the morning she was still warm, and the open window had been closed. And in her heart she knew Grandma was watching over her, and so was Jesus.

Chapter 11:
He Kept Her Safe When She Dwelt in the Darkest Places

Just as Lorraine was barely beginning to move once more, she received a phone call that set her back more. Her mother died of unknown causes that morning. Could she come the many miles to her funeral? In great sadness, she told her sister the doctors would not allow her to travel that far. Her sister did not believe Lorraine and ridiculed her. Their mother never was much of a mother, true. However, she was mother, and she had better come to her funeral. In great grief, Lorraine hung up the phone, realizing that what little family connection she had with her siblings was in jeopardy, too. "God," she prayed, "How much more would you ask of me? I don't think I can take anymore."

Only days later, Justin came home and packed the house up. He had sold the house and made arrangements for them to live with his brother in South Carolina.

Still too frozen to be of much use, Lorraine watched as her things disappeared. Finally, she was roughly helped out to an over-stuffed car. The children were loaded. They began the 2,000-mile drive to South Carolina against the advice of her doctors.

They told Justin moving Lorraine could greatly increase her pain problems and might kill her. She would not tolerate such a move. In horrendous pain during those long days in the car, Lorraine retreated within herself and prayed whenever possible. Her daughters tried to cheer her up with songs and stories. Lorraine tried to remain a comfort to them. When would all this end? God, will it ever get better again? She prayed. Why must they go through so much, God? Why? Why?

What Lorraine did not know was that this was only the beginning—the beginning of learning to live a new life where little could be recognized as her own—where her children would become the stronghold she clasped to her heart when she would give up on life. Today, today contained enough evil without worrying about tomorrow, Jesus said. She knew what He had meant. Today she was being moved to the one place on earth she had vowed she would never expose her children to: her brother-in-law's strange cult. How could she stop it when she could not move? She was a prisoner inside her own body as Justin sped east on interstate 70, then south to pick up interstate 40, continuing eastward to the Carolinas.

Lorraine did not even know if she could stay alive. "Please, God, she prayed silently on that long trip, "Please, keep me alive! My children now need me more than ever! Please rescue us somehow. Please." Once more, she placed her hand in God's, and she knew peace in the middle of a great emotional storm.

Chapter 12: He Led Her Where She Would not Follow

Six weeks passed since Lorraine and her family arrived in South Carolina. Not too surprisingly, upon arriving they discovered that Daniel and his cult group were well hidden in the foothills of the Smoky Mountains. Seventy miles from Charlotte, North Carolina, Rainee soon realized she could easily die before anyone could get her to medical care. Out west, towns were far apart, but a helicopter trauma rescue service kept medical care within comfortable range. Not where Daniel lived. Each morning, as she awakened, took her medicine, and tried to do something of value, her doubts about the reason for being alive grew larger. Her determination to find meaning, however, grew, too.

After much searching, Rainee found a physical therapist that was familiar with the treatments she received in Minnesota. The physical therapist was, unfortunately, far away on the other side of Charlotte. Three afternoons a week, the children and Lorraine snaked their way out of the hills so that she could seek some kind of relief as Justin agreed to drive for something to occupy his time.

Under the careful hands of the therapist, though, Lorraine could feel her body slowly thawing from its medical freeze once more. The way back to their new home was full of switchbacks and bad roads; however, so often by the time the trip was over, much valuable physical progress was lost. Frustrated, Lorraine cried out to God for help and refused to quit. If she was meant to live, then she must fight to get her life back.

Justin spent the majority of his time with his brother, Daniel. Too far from any town of any size and employment related to his training, Justin seemed to relish in being excused from even attempting to support his family. Daniel continued to reassure him that the group would care for them, so Justin need not feel responsible.

In the short time Lorraine's family lived at the compound,

she could see that Daniel had pretty much taken mental control of Justin. Subtle though his brain washing techniques were, she was deeply aware of the imbalanced brother's attempts to also gain control over herself and the children. Lorraine thanked God daily for the professional training she spent years developing, as she felt herself fighting the devil himself to keep Daniel away from their minds and souls.

Lorraine soon discovered that cult members monitored any moves they made or phone calls attempted. Everyone in the group seemed to know what she had told her friends privately over the phone. Exasperated, Lorraine purchased a phone card on a trip to Charlotte after she began driving again because of improvements. She began making her long distance calls from pay phones at gas stations along the way into town. She also began to look at the job market. Every day she prayed that God would somehow rescue them. If this meant she needed to find work despite doctors' concerns, then let God open a door in a tight job market for her. Please, she often begged, please, let us find our way out as Moses and God's people found their way out of Egypt.

After eight weeks of life in the compound, Lorraine sensed that God was about to answer her prayers. She had no idea how. She only knew she must follow the quiet guidance God was placing in her heart.

The following week Justin failed to accompany her to Charlotte at all. She sensed this was really an answer to prayer. After her therapy appointment, she bought a fast food lunch for herself and the girls. Next, she purchased a newspaper. While the girls ate in a lovely park and tried out the swings, Lorraine combed the paper, looking for ads in her field.

Just as she was about to give up, a large print ad caught her attention. Mental health was looking for someone with a PhD. who could work with extremely troubled children and their families. Needed immediately. With hands trembling, Lorraine walked to

the pavilion in the park where she could see a pay phone booth.
she dialed the number given in the paper and waited impatiently.

Fear clutched her heart as she listened to a secretary
answer the phone. She had not done full time clinical work in a
long time. This might be a wild goose chase. Still, she forced a
calm voice and told the secretary she was calling about the
position in the paper asking for a PhD.

The secretary seemed a bit surprised. When Lorraine
asked her why she seemed surprised, she was told that the ad
had been placed in the paper just this morning as a departmental
joke. Last week the government demanded they get a PhD. on
staff. The facts were, however, that few PhDs existed in this part
of the country. Was Lorraine positive she had a PhD?

Lorraine took a deep breath and told her she did indeed
have a PhD. Could she come by and bring her resume? The
secretary gave her the address and directions and told her she
was looking forward to meeting a Doctor. Yes, Lorraine was
reassured; they had a psychiatrist on staff—had to have to
dispense meds by state law. The supervisor had a master's
degree.

Lorraine asked the children if they would like to stay in the
park, since Autumn was now fifteen and could watch the others.
All three, however, were fearful of letting Lorraine out of their
sight. The last two months had taught them even more anxiety.
Without a home, except two rooms in a compound, having to
leave their dog behind, and reading extreme fear in their mother,
the girls were becoming more and more guarded. They agreed
that they could ride over to the Center and wait for their mom in
the parking lot.

When Lorraine and the children arrived at the Center, they
discovered that there was another smaller park right across the
street from the office. Delighted, Allison had to be reined in until
times and expectations for the next short while could be made

clear to everyone. Then fifteen year old Autumn was put in charge of the younger children.

Seeing the children safely across the street, Lorraine slipped through the front door of the Center. A small crowd of children greeted her in a children's waiting room. Toys were strewn across the floor. In one corner, a table and chairs were provided, along with crayons, paper, clay, and many table toys.

A bubbly secretary greeted Lorraine from behind a safety grid. "May I help you?" The kind-looking, shorthaired, blond lady inquired.

"Hello," Lorraine said just loud enough to be heard over the din of children's noises. "I am Doctor Hawkins. I called a few minutes ago about bringing my resume by."

The secretary smiled broadly, "Oh, you are fast." She laughed lightly. "Well, I am faster. I have already told the supervisor you were coming. She wants to know if you could stick around for a little while for an interview."

Caught off guard, Lorraine blinked rapidly. She was not dressed for an interview. Although she had tried to dress in case she could pass out resumes, interviews usually required a professional suit. As she surveyed her appearance, she heard the secretary laugh softly.

"We aren't too formal here, if that is what you are worried about. Ms. Wright, the supervisor, knows you aren't expecting an interview. It is just that we are desperate to fill this position quickly because of Medicaid laws. The agency can't afford to lose government funding because a lot of these kids couldn't get help without it."

"Of course I will, if she doesn't mind my appearance," Lorraine relaxed. She sensed that somehow she already had the upper hand in this situation. It was the first time she had felt like she was in charge of some aspect of her life in quite a while. It felt good.

The secretary opened a door to the side of her counter and Lorraine entered the office area of the center. A youngish-looking man came out of an office and handed the secretary some papers to copy, while smiling at Lorraine. It was obvious he thought Lorraine was the PhD. here to interview. He quietly introduced himself as Dr. Goodfellow, the psychiatrist. He told Lorraine he hoped she liked what she saw here. Then he returned to his office.

The secretary showed Lorraine into a large, much disorganized office. Stacks of file folders sat around everywhere, on chairs, on the desk, and even on the floor. She accurately guessed that the workers here were overworked. Organization was not one of her great skills, but she managed to get files in their drawers (or at least a drawer. Often she could not retrieve what she filed without considerable work).

The secretary cleared a straight oak chair for Lorraine and gave her an encouraging smile. She smiled back and thanked the secretary as she left the room. Sitting gingerly in the chair, for the hard wood hurt her painful joints, Lorraine thumbed through her resume. She had not looked at it very carefully before coming today. She had not seriously believed she would find a job to apply for today, let alone this one. With all her health concerns, she figured her hopes for employment were just hopeful wishes.

After several minutes, the door opened and a short dark woman entered smiling. She looked to be about her age and was obviously very nervous. "Good afternoon!" Boomed from her tiny body, surprising Lorraine.

"Hello, I am Dr. Hawkins," Lorraine smiled in response and handed the supervisor her resume. The secretary had said this was Mrs. Wright. She looked very much as if she was the owner of this disorganized office. Her hair flew in six directions at once. Her blouse, perhaps neat in the morning, was wrinkled and had a lunch stain prominently placed. She smiled to herself. At least this would be easy interview practice, if she was not offered the position.

Mrs. Wright took Lorraine's resume and spent the next several minutes reading it carefully. "Been living in the ivory tower of therapy lately, huh?" She joked.

Lorraine had remembered saying the exact same thing to a friend of hers who left clinical work for university teaching some years ago. That was before she knew how much university teaching demanded. That and how many students expected her to be therapist as well as teacher, because of her training. She smiled at the supervisor's joke just the same, and told her she had completed clinical work before her teaching career. During the last nine years, she had been teaching in the field while keeping a small practice on the side.

Mrs. Wright finished reading and threw the resume on her desk. "When can you start?"

Caught off guard once more, Lorraine blinked. This was one day full of surprises! "I will have to find housing here in Charlotte for myself and three daughters. I could probably get us moved within a week.

"Good. Then you can start a week from Monday, OK?"

"Don't you want to know anything more about me?" Lorraine blurted out.

"I am usually a good judge of character," Mrs. Wright smiled, "My first impression of you is you are compassionate and warm despite your many years of training. That is unusual, and much needed when working with the kind of kids I am hiring you to take on as clients. You say you have kids of your own. I thought so in looking at you. Something in your demeanor told me that you had a strong mothering instinct. That will also be an asset here, as most of these kids come from very troubled homes and could use a good parent role model. You enjoy parenting, don't you?"

Surprised once more, Lorraine nodded. "My kids are the most important thing in my life."

Mrs. Wright smiled, "Good. You are likely to gain forty-five new children in this job. The difficult thing will be leaving them at work when you go home. I will help you if you run into trouble with mentally taking clients home. My only question is how in the world did you end up in a God-forsaken place like Chester's Crossing, South Carolina?"

Lorraine felt an immediate camaraderie for this bustling, let's-get-on-with-life- type person. If her story cost her the job, she knew she needed to be honest with Mrs. Wright. Lorraine soon told her of her illness and her continuing pain struggle. She ended with her fear of what her husband had dragged them into when she was defenseless. Mrs. Wright listened without comment or judgment.

"Maybe some higher power knew we needed you," She smiled, "And maybe, you needed us, too." She held out her hand and shook Lorraine's hand, welcoming her to her staff. Then she took her around to any of the offices whose doors were not closed (closed doors signaled a client session in progress), and introduced her to several of the many therapists. Finally, Mrs. Wright explained that no one had training beyond a master's degree, but all were dedicated clinicians. They would be glad to have Lorraine in their midst. She was sent back to the secretary to do paperwork and to set up a schedule for her first day at work.

Once upon a time, this position would not have been Lorraine's first choice, but she sensed it was God's newest choice for her. She must still convince Justin that they needed to move to Charlotte, or she and the girls would move alone. Daniel's hold was great over Justin. She greatly doubted her ability to extricate him from his brother's mental and emotional grasp, and this frightened her greatly. Being finally free, however, began to sound like a relief.

Gathering her children, she began the two-hour drive to the compound. Often the speed limit slowed to twenty or twenty-five because of road conditions, explaining the time it took to go to Charlotte. Exhausted, yet elated, Lorraine pulled into the compound's yard with last instructions to the children that they were to tell no one, for any reason, where we went today. Secretly they were excited about leaving Chester's Crossing and their uncle. Recent lurid looks and unwanted touches from Daniel when Mom was not in sight raised Autumn and Ariana's guard. They wanted out of this terrible place!

As evening sunset came into the late August sky, Lorraine asked Justin if he would walk with her and watch the sunset behind the beautiful Smoky Mountains. He seemed pleased with her desire to try something physical, and they set off down the gravel road. Topping a hill, Lorraine turned to face Justin. Without preamble she stated, "I found a job I like today. The girls and I are moving to Charlotte tonight. Will you come with us?"

A look of disbelief came over Justin's face. This look was followed by an angry attack. "You won't accept the care I can give, will you? It isn't good enough that Daniel will take care of you and the girls, is it?"

Lorraine sighed. His reaction was expected, but it still hurt. "This is not a healthy place for the children. It is also too far from medical care for me. The doctors want me to move to town so they can supervise my care better. I am going, Justin. I don't want you to blab to Daniel about my leaving until I am gone. He may try to stop us."

Justin stomped angrily away. His plans to take it easy for a long time had been foiled. He fumed. Lorraine would never be satisfied just to let him enjoy life! He sensed correctly that she would indeed leave the cult without him. He was not ready, however, to give up what he saw as a potential gold mine for himself in his future.

The Minnesota bank had allowed him to liquidate Lorraine's accounts while she was ill without even calling her. He knew she had no idea he had dispensed of a rather nice savings and retirement account to force her dependency on him. This way he knew she could not pack up and go back west if she got much better. No, he promised himself, his wife would not get away from him. Her potential to keep him financially sound in the long run was worth the games he played now. He slipped and bragged to Lorraine about these thoughts out loud that night, not realizing he had revealed what she had already guessed. He had given her life savings to Daniel and that was why Daniel was willing to take them in as dependents. Justin angrily kicked at a stone in the road as he turned into the drive at the cult's grounds. He would follow her into town, he agreed, but he would not go any farther, because it took money to travel. He smirked to himself and entered the compound's large housing project.

Once more Lorraine felt trapped. She followed behind slowly, making plans to escape that night once everyone was in bed. She could pack their few belongings in a matter of minutes. Most of their things remained in Minnesota in storage. Justin was the main problem. If he let on that they were going to flee, Daniel might indeed do something to stop them. She did not doubt that he would try anything. He recently gloated to the group about finally capturing Lorraine and her children for his group. He would not give the children up easily. She walked slowly back to the compound while plotting their escape.

That evening Justin unexpectedly asked the girls if they wanted to go to the local gas station that also housed a small restaurant. The restaurant imported some wonderful ice cream from Charlotte. It had been one source of joy for the children since arriving in Chester's Crossing.

Justin told Daniel they were going to get ice cream. Daniel

readily approved. One sore spot for Lorraine in this living situation was that Daniel had to approve every move of every person in the compound. He also required all adults to work and hand their wages over to him as spiritual leader. All but Justin, she thought wryly. Each member received twelve dollars a month in return to spend on personal needs. Years of observing the group from a distance convinced Lorraine that Daniel squandered much of the money. Members, though, seemed to utterly trust this man. Now he had every dime she had saved for years.

Oh, how cunning he was to convince these people that he was "God's voice." He firmly believed He was the one in direct contact with God for everyone in the group. They need only listen to him to know the right thing to do. They need never pray for themselves.

Lorraine shuttered as these thoughts ran through her head. Brainwashed, the members looked slightly dazed as they carried out their duties in the compound. Even their work contacts seemed to have little influence over the blind trust in their leader. Lorraine knew Daniel was a charismatic schizophrenic personality. Sometimes people with this disorder are able to exert mind control over others. Jim Jones, of the famous cult that had all committed suicide in the 1970's, came to mind at this thought. Yes, she thought, these people would probably follow Daniel to the grave, too, if they were cornered. How terrifying and sad.

Coming out of the restaurant, Lorraine noticed a dark car next to the building. She had seen this car a number of times in recent days. An uneasy feeling came over Lorraine. She wondered if Daniel was having them followed but kept silent. She was, therefore, surprised when Justin looked at her and asked if she thought someone was following them?

Justin pulled out of the gravel parking lot rather quickly. The dark car pulled up behind them and continued to follow them to the compound gate. When they pulled into the compound, the other car continued on down the road.

Frightened, Justin tore into the building with the children and Lorraine right behind him. Finding Daniel, he asked if anyone else from the group had been tailed lately.

"Oh, that," Daniel tried to act unconcerned, "The police are forever trailing my members. Seem to think we are up to something illegal and trying to catch us off guard. We're different and that makes people not like us. Don't worry about it," he laughed. "You get used to it after being in the group for a while."

Visually shaken, Justin and Lorraine took the girls back to their rooms. Justin told the girls to sit on the bed and paced the floor. "I didn't know about this. Honestly," he whispered so that anyone listening at the door would not hear. "OK, OK, We will try your plan. I will go with you and I promise to find work, too. I also promise to get more anger control therapy, so I don't go into such rages at home anymore. My plan did not work. We can't depend on Daniel's group to care for us."

Secretly Justin plotted as he talked. He would see what Lorraine could come up with for income. See if he could find some work he liked. If it didn't work out, he could return to Daniel's with the children and without his wife. Lorraine was just too much trouble anymore. She could drop dead for all he cared, but he was going to eventually give Daniel their children just as he promised him. (This plot later came out as overt action on Justin's part).

Unsuspecting, Lorraine sighed with relief at Justin's overt show of concern and change of heart. Perhaps God had intervened again, or was she making a mistake by thinking Justin was sincere this time? She prayed quietly for peace and felt God's presence once more. Joy filled her heart. God had not forgotten them. She would follow Him as He led and take this small step into her unknown future.

It was two AM before Justin and Lorraine determined that everyone was sound asleep. Justin finally sneaked down to the car in his stocking feet with their suitcases so that others could not detect them. Lorraine woke Ariana and Autumn. They got dressed quickly, while Justin gathered Allison in his arms. After what seemed like an eternity to Lorraine, the family, shoes in hand, slipped quietly into the night.

Chapter 13:
He Renewed Her Strength When Her Strength Was Gone

Lorraine pulled her car into the narrow, gutted one-lane road and stopped. She had been working for mental health for eight months. Her client load rapidly increased, as her supervisor was reassured that she was returning to health. Altogether, she now had forty children under her care. Today her schedule required a home visit up the side of the mountain in front of her.

Already struggling with claustrophobia resulting from the dense tropical foliage in this part of the country, Lorraine panicked at being unable to see the sky since leaving the main road five miles back. Now she realized that she was going to have to challenge her other secret fear, too. She had always been terrified of sharp drop offs. Her hands, still the most painful part of her body, froze to the steering wheel as she stared at the path that was called a road in this part of the country. Fear always seemed to cause that kind of physical response in her nowadays. She gulped and tried to talk herself out of her anxiety.

Added to the fear of drop offs and claustrophobia was the plain fact that this little dirt road did not look passable for her small, front-wheel drive car. Lorraine also dreaded this new home visit. She really doubted she had any hope to offer this family and hated coming to a home without any good news. Lorraine wanted so badly to help "her kids."

Enough time for doubts and fears, she chided herself. Finally, the responsibility of the job reasserted itself in her mind. Lorraine shifted the car into low gear. Unable to pry her left hand from the steering wheel, she eased the car up the side of the mountain. After what seemed like forever, she saw the mobile home clinging to a widened spot of ledge that the family called home.

Feeling encouragement from successfully making it up the road, she pulled into a obvious parking spot at the end of the short driveway. From this high point on the mountain, the sky was visible, and she sighed in delight. Refreshed, Lorraine jumped out of the car. At that same moment, a large mixed breed dog lunged from under the small porch attached to the trailer with a menacing growl. "Oh, no, not a mean dog, too!" she cried in exasperation as she quickly jumped back into her car.

When no one came to the door, Lorraine honked the horn. Still, no one responded. She must have "hit a dry run." A child client's family sometimes chose to avoid the professional by not being at home at appointment time. Her fellow workers jokingly called these "dry runs."

Sighing, Lorraine pulled out her logbook to enter the no show just as a banged up sedan pulled up and inched around her. The client's mother waved frantically at her, and then came over to her car window. "I am so sorry I am late. My boss kept me late. I work in the hosiery factory down in the hollow. My son won't be home from school for a few minutes yet because of riding the bus. Won't you come in?"

Lorraine nodded and then explained her fear of the beast under the porch. The mother reassured her that he was just protecting the vacant home. With the owner present, he would be friendly. Sure enough, the dog simply came over and sniffed Lorraine as she disembarked from her car. Trying to display calm for the dog, she followed the mother into the house.

Lorraine had discovered over the previous few months that many of her clients lived in isolated mobile homes tucked into crannies of mountain roads. The views, when trees did not block everything, were beautiful. Today the Great Smokies loomed blue in the distance. Too often, all she saw were trees and underbrush that made the whole world look green. It was lovely, too, but she had lived too long in places where seeing wide-open skies was taken for granted.

Lorraine badly missed the wide open skies. She actually

ached sometimes to see the wide blue expanse over the prairies. Never admitting she actually felt physical pain associated with such a loss, it sometimes consumed her. She especially felt this loss at sunset time. Like many recent days, today she longed for places wide open, and, yes, the yet taller peaks of the Rocky Mountains. She had lost her Rocky Mountains years ago when Justin moved the family back to the Midwest from Colorado, where she had lived since her teen years, to be closer to his parents. Lorraine protested loudly that this meant leaving the one place on earth she considered "her hometown," but he did not listen.

Lorraine now remembered moving to Colorado as an adolescent. Wanting to remember more than PTSD flashes, she began asking relatives a lot of questions. One aunt sent her reams of pictures of people and places she could not recall. Gradually, she began to remember the fast moves across state lines to avoid the police. Her father, wanted by the law in several states, had finally deserted when she was twelve years old. She was yet to remember why he had gone away.

After her father left, a minister and his wife supervised her adolescence and acted as guardians. These were the people Lorraine called her family. They helped her to get into the college in Colorado as a means to help her disappear more completely after the police helped them to realize that Lorraine was still not safe from threats from her father. Her mother and sister had driven her to college. There, under a new name, she felt happy for the first time she could remember. Feeling safe from the constant death threats helped her to learn to relax and enjoy life. It also afforded her another chance to erect blocks to hide her past from herself.

Lorraine married, completed college and began her career in Colorado. Those first married years she felt safe. In the trauma of her current life, therefore, it was not surprising that she increasingly turned back to the days symbolized by Colorado sky. She glanced out the mobile home window to reassure her the sky was here in North Carolina, too.

Lorraine came back to the present and the client's mother. They began discussing many difficult questions about the child before he came home from school. She ended her visit after spending an hour with her client. She was exhausted. Her supervisor once told her most workers lasted six months at the most on her staff. The stress from dealing with impossible family situations, and equally impossible red tape to try to get them help, wore even strong professionals out quickly.

Lorraine understood the high burn out rate. She had had more success than most workers in her position. For example, a four-year-old child, one of her first clients, had never talked; but, he began talking a blue streak one day after several months of frustrating work with her. To her delight, he progressed rapidly after that. The state, which had custody of him in foster care, approved him as a candidate for adoption because of his progress. Lorraine felt he was one reason God opened doors for her to work in the South. Many other children were also taking great strides in getting better. Still, she was beginning to think she really ought to "go home." The doctor in Minnesota had told her the University of Colorado in Denver was where she needed to be if she was to get the long term care she needed. Yet here she was 2,000 miles away and broke.

Yet on the mountainside, overlooking the Smokies, that conviction of needing to return to the Rockies grew in strength. Lorraine knew she must flee soon to protect herself and her children, so why not go home? Justin kept his promise about getting work, but not about getting anger control therapy. In the last few weeks, she found him terrorizing the children when she got home from work. This had to end soon for their sake, but she discovered her bank accounts were continuing to magically empty when trying to plan an escape. She knew they could not flee just yet. She had to figure out how to protect her funds better.

Justin's brother, Daniel, also continued to show up several

times a week despite the two hour drive from their cult home. Unable to accept Daniel's unstable mental condition, Justin readily supplied him with their new address and phone number. Lorraine came home from work day after day to discover Justin "visiting" with Daniel in their apartment. She was beginning to believe any hope for Justin was lost. Autumn, home from high school before her, more and more frequently kept the younger girls away from Daniel until Lorraine could get home.

More likely as not, if Daniel did not leave the apartment when Lorraine arrived, she took the children out for supper, to the library, or to window shop. The number of times they had to do this was increasing, though, and she, already exhausted from work and home responsibilities, felt herself once more physically slipping. She could not compete with Daniel and he knew that.

Somehow, moving here was not far enough away. Lorraine also knew this, and yet she hesitated. After several moves in one year, the children needed some stability. She kept praying that God would give her a sign that she was supposed to leave, and then dreaded the possibility He might answer that prayer.

It was the same day as the visit on the mountain that God shouted the answer out to her. Lorraine arrived home feeling like she could not walk one more step. Then she discovered Daniel firmly planted in their living room. Resentment rose in her throat. Once in the apartment, she thought the girls were in their rooms because of music coming from that direction. Minutes later, though, she heard a scream from thirteen year old Ariana, who was actually in the bathroom. Alarmed, Lorraine ran to the bathroom and pounded on the door.

"Ariana, Ariana, let me in!" Lorraine cried. Ariana opened the door and pointed to the toilet, which was covered with chunks of tissue and bright red blood.

"Oh, no, what is it?" she responded and pulled Ariana to

herself.

"I just threw all that up," Ariana sobbed.

Shaken, Lorraine called to the other girls and rushed them out to the car. She put Ariana in the front seat. The doctor's was only a few blocks away, but she wanted to keep an eye on her. The other girls piled into the back seat. Today was Thursday, the doctor's evening pediatric clinic day. He could surely help. It seemed to take forever to reach their doctor's clinic. Once there, the doctor ordered them to the hospital for tests. As suspected, Ariana had a bleeding ulcer and it was critical to treat her immediately.

"What kind of stress is this child under?" the doctor demanded when he arrived an hour later to go over the tests with Lorraine. They soon told him everything.

Then Ariana started talking. "I want to go home," she sobbed, "Please, just let us go back out west. The kids at school throw things at me and call me names all day long here. My accent is funny. My clothes are weird. They make fun of me because I can't do athletics with my warped joints. They don't want me to belong. Today in choir, the teacher asked me to sing a solo. I thought it might help the other kids like me better. Instead, the whole class laughed at me. Momma, out west I was the star of the choir. Why do they make fun of me here?"

"People are afraid of new things, sweetheart. I am afraid we are 'something new' to some of the kids at school."

"Then in math class the teacher held up my paper today and laughed at it. Mom, I get straight A's in math. Why should she make fun of me to her class? She made us draw a folder picture to hand in today. You know I can't hold a pencil enough to draw. She said I was just making that up to skip work. Mom, didn't you put that in my school records? Don't the doctors' notes explain that? Teachers could not grade me on my homework if they didn't let me do the work on the computer before, because

114

my hands don't work right. Why did she have to make so much fun of me?"

Stunned, Lorraine realized the children were facing real prejudice. Ariana struggled to learn to walk because of malformed joints. By the age of three Lorraine knew Ariana would be unable to write like most kids and taught her to use a computer. The teachers were required to accept her assignments done on computers. They could not require handwork from her. How dare that teacher pick on her! How dare she! Livid, Lorraine held her daughter and cried with her.

The doctor left for a moment and came back in with paperwork. He told Lorraine he would like to call the principal and discuss this obvious breach of doctor's orders. Something had to be done to protect this delicate child. She agreed and signed consents. Then the doctor gave her a note for the school. Exacerbated by stress, Ariana was obviously getting worse from whatever was afflicting her. *It was time to go home.*

Long ago Lorraine taught her children to be open and accepting of others no matter what. Having Ariana in the family helped the other girls more readily accept children with special challenges. Some states were further along in enforcing equality in schools than others. Here even the buildings did not meet the federal disability codes. If only for Ariana, they needed to go back to where she knew they would find more understanding. Lorraine had found acceptance at work, but she could not allow the children to pay for her success.

Angrily, Lorraine slammed her fist into the wall of the emergency cubicle the staff placed Ariana in after her tests. No teacher should laugh at a child—no matter what. Kids could be cruel. They were kids. Teachers, however, were a big example for kids and needed to be kind. She knew what she must do. With medication and instructions to call an ambulance if more blood showed up, Lorraine started back to their apartment. Driving slowly, she edged her way in and out of heavy, rush hour traffic. Perhaps if she took her time, they could avoid Daniel.

Not surprisingly, an empty apartment greeted them. Most probably, Justin had gone with Daniel. So much for fatherly concern, Lorraine growled under her breath as she helped Ariana into bed. A week of bed rest, the doctor said, might help.

Autumn would graduate from high school soon. Upon starting the eleventh grade this year, she jokingly challenged both eleventh and twelfth grades with overwhelming success. Scoring the top SAT in the state, she was offered scholarships to colleges all over the nation, including Ivy League schools. Her choice, however, was yet another sign that Lorraine realized she needed to listen to—she chose a school in Colorado. Shortage of funds from their unending crises had left Autumn dependent on scholarship funds. If the Colorado school could not offer her enough aide to pay her bills this fall as an out of state resident, a private school in Kansas did offer her a complete free "ride." She could go there. That would only be eight hours from "home," the Colorado town where she had been born.

Why could Lorraine not have read the writing on the wall? she asked herself. Why? She knew it was in large part because she now knew Justin had spent all their savings to ensure that Lorraine and the girls could not escape. This had included giving large amounts to Daniel's group. It almost worked, she thought bitterly. Time and again, Lorraine almost gave up in frustration when calculating what it would cost to retrace their cross country move. Still, she began taking steps to ensure their getaway.

Back at work, she arranged for part of her paycheck to be deposited in a bank close to work. She lied to Justin about the amount of income she made, telling him everyone had had to take a pay cut. She also made sure she never brought her check stubs home. The nonprofit she worked for was privately owned, so, she figured she could get away with this lie until tax time. When she worked for the government, her salary was published in the paper, so Justin always knew what she made. No more, thank God.

Over the next few months, Lorraine withdrew her secret funds and hoarded the money in a large spice can at the top of her spice rack, being careful to be sure enough spice seed remained so that it made noise if shaken. Since Justin refused to help with the cooking, though, this was the least likely place he would ever look for money. Coriander seed must be something she used in something, she could just imagine him thinking. Banks were the last place she wanted her money after they had given Justin access to her accounts even though the new account was secret.

Several weeks after putting Ariana to bed to rest, Lorraine pulled the large bills out of the can after Justin had left with Daniel. She counted $3,600. It was not enough, but it was better than nothing. After Autumn graduated, she figured she would have $4,000. They would have to make the move on that. Perhaps her boss could help her secure a similar job in Colorado before she got there. This dawning thought spurred Lorraine to call Mrs. Wright.

Her supervisor almost laughed when she heard her on the line. She told her she knew this was coming the day she met her. She knew she would be unable to keep Lorraine from fleeing back out west.

"There was too much sunshine in your eyes," Mrs. Wright told her without explaining. "I think I can get you a transfer. This nonprofit owns agencies all over the country. You just tell me where you plan to go, OK? You have been doing an excellent job for us, so I think I can be of help. No, I don't want to lose you. Some of those kids were hopeless until you came. You need to take care of yourself and your girls, though. Daniel is not going to stop bothering you until you get a lot of distance between you and him."

Once more, the girls and Lorraine made silent plans to run. This time the distance would be great—over 2,000 miles—so they must calculate carefully. Yet, in a way, deciding to go home brought peace. She could sense the same from her children. The younger children barely remembered Colorado, but she now brought it back to life in the many stories she told.

Lorraine had forty-nine children now at work she cared about deeply. Yes, she struggled to leave them at work. Her most important children however, needed her more. They needed to "go home," too.

It was getting more and more important that they be taken away from Daniel's presence and the constant stress it stirred up in them every time he visited. They needed a change in environment, too. Justin would probably stay in South Carolina with Daniel. This would be best for them anyway, she concluded. Right or wrong, Justin needed to either get professional help or get out of their family. Lorraine could now remember the long lost time when things were good between them. She secretly hoped that this might be the move that forced him to decide to get the help he needed.

Everyone has a place in their hearts that calls to them. It might be the place they lived as children. As in her case, it might be the place they felt the safest. With the increasing pressure from Justin and Daniel to go back to the cult, her stress mounted. Seeing the stress in her children's faces also increased hers. Her worry about Ariana's health, so obviously deteriorating, also increased her stress. These all contributed toward her feeling that her heart was calling them "home," home to Colorado.

The night Ariana threw up blood, Lorraine again dreamed of the great metal door and the abyss. Thank God, these PTSD episodes remained in the night. The business of work seemed to keep them at bay during the day. The reoccurrence, however, further strengthened her resolve to go home. Somewhere out west, perhaps the children would be safe. Deep down, somewhere close to her heart, she also knew that in going home, she might finally find peace over her past.

Chapter 14:
He Gave Her Hope When All Hope Was Gone

The school semester ended. Sadly, Autumn's graduation
came and went without much excitement for her. Having spent
only a year in Charlotte, she had few friends to invite to a
graduation party. Lorraine made an effort at celebration, though,
and had a small graduation party at Autumn's favorite restaurant.

The only people who showed up were Justin's relatives.
Daniel came, invited by Justin, and his wife. They showed up with
a flourish of bizarre behavior that left Autumn embarrassed.
Justin's other brother, John, and his wife, Barbara, had recently
moved to North Carolina after retiring from the Navy. They came
to the party. Lorraine enjoyed this new company, as John
appeared to be sane in comparison to Justin's other brothers. His
wife was from North Carolina and wanted to spend their retirement
close to home. They settled 100 miles southeast of Lorraine's
family a month before graduation. John joked at the party that
Barbara *had* to come home, and he *had* to stay close to the
ocean, because it was in his blood. How well Lorraine understood
those longings for the familiar.

Urgency fell upon Lorraine as Autumn's graduation
passed and summer went into full swing. The girls enjoyed a
church youth trip to Myrtle Beach as a highlight for June.

At work Lorraine found more families failed to show up for
appointments in the weeks of hot weather that followed.
Sometimes she would not see a client for six weeks. She realized
much of the work she accomplished in the spring was destroyed in
their absence. These apparent failings filled her with frustration.

Lorraine kept telling herself that the only hold for them in
North Carolina was behind them because of Autumn's graduation.
She was thrilled that Autumn performed well in school despite the
move. Graduating with highest honors, she looked to the future
anxiously.

Yet, Lorraine hesitated. Summer seemed to bring some reprieve in the stress level, and Ariana's health improved a bit. The job transfer and savings seemed to take its time in developing. Discouraged, she prayed that God would still make a way for them to return west. August came to a close and found them still in the South. She registered Ariana and Allison for school, while Autumn announced she wanted to take a semester off and work. She claimed she was burned out on schoolwork but was really hoping to help her Mom move before going to the Colorado college. They would hold her scholarship for one semester.

The new school year began for Ariana and Allison. Only three short weeks into the year, though, violent hurricane warnings filled the TV screen. The hurricane was so strong that it was supposed to jump onto land and wreak havoc. The closer it came, the more frightened Lorraine became.

Driving home from work the day the hurricane hit the North and South Carolina coast, Lorraine fought fierce winds that kept pushing her off the road. The air smelled funny. Thunderstorms broke over her with a violence that left her breathless. Lorraine pulled off the road under a gas station canopy just as large hail began to hit her windshield. Turning the car off, she sat in petrified silence. Why was she so frightened?

As the car rocked, Lorraine turned inward once again as the present slipped away more and more with each lightening flash. She found herself running through the open door to the abyss. Rainee cried out loud, as she was hit by hurricane-force winds on the other side of the mental medal door. This was why Lorraine was so afraid, she thought. She was back in the past hurricane when Elaine had rescued them from hunger with chocolate cake.

Lorraine shook herself back to reality as a semi-truck that had pulled in beside her honked. "Are you OK?" the driver hollered when she opened the window. She yelled back that she was fine, just a little scared. As the eye of the storm came over their vehicles, she drove out quickly, trying to get home as fast as possible before the winds started again.

Arriving home, Lorraine ran up the stairs to her apartment. The girls had arrived first because Autumn picked up Allison from day care early now that she had her license. Scared of the storm, they huddled in the hallway where there were no windows.

Another memory surfaced as Lorraine joined her children in their apartment hallway. When Allison was a baby they had survived an F5 tornado when Lorraine was attending graduate school. She was able to pull all her children into an inside-wall closet with herself just before the roof was ripped off above them. Looking at their faces when she arrived in this storm, Lorraine could feel pain for their pain. Yes, indeed, a hurricane *and* a tornado in one lifetime made for one big scared attitude!

Gathering her children about her once more, Lorraine began to tell stories of when they lived in Colorado. Then she suggested they all sing some of their favorite songs. The wind continued to howl. Hail pounded the windows off and on, yet she continued to sing with her children. She could even make jokes when the lights went out. This building was shaking so much that it would be a miracle if it stayed in one piece. They prayed for their safety and Justin's, who never came home from work.

Ariana crawled into her bedroom and brought a portable radio out into the hall. Listening to the news reports, Lorraine realized that full force hurricane winds raged outside. She tried not to look fearful for the children's sake, but she wondered if she would live through the night. She knew if God chose to get them through this night, it would be one of their last in North Carolina. Enough pain was enough. Money or no money, job or no job, they were going home.

The children slept on the floor of the hall. Everyone cried intermittently. Finally, the storm quieted. In the wee hours of the morning, Lorraine heard Justin come into the apartment. He excitedly described downed trees and smashed buildings all over town. He walked the last mile because of downed power lines on the street, so the bus could not get through. Lorraine shuttered at his stories while helping the children into their beds. No one would go to work or school this morning.

In the late morning, Lorraine opened the apartment door and looked out onto the chaotic world the hurricane had created. In horror, she realized that a tree lay across her car in the parking lot. It was small but could have done a lot of damage. When the girls got up, she convinced them to try to help her to remove the tree. With Justin's help, it was soon on the ground. Still intact and only badly scratched, the car was a welcome sight to her. After all, it was her way out of North Carolina.

Underground phone lines enabled her to call into work. Her boss told Lorraine she spent the night at the office. Nobody was to come into work. All appointments were cancelled. "Were Lorraine and her children all right," Mrs. Wright asked? At this question, Lorraine began to sob, "I'm going to need that position in Colorado right away, Mrs. Wright. I'm just going to try to call them to let them know I am coming, and see if the position has opened up at last. I can't stay here. We can't stay here. It is time for us to go."

Mrs. Wright did not seem surprised. Instead, she soothed with calming words and told Lorraine she wanted to thank her for letting them work with her this last year. She knew what hardships Lorraine's family wrestled with, but Lorraine had blessed so many by being in Charlotte.

"Someday, you will look back on this time with kinder eyes," Mrs. Wright reassured her. "What you accomplished for our kids has permanently and positively influenced their lives. I want to thank you for us, the staff, and in behalf of all "your" children. God bless, you, dear. Go. Go home. You need to be as far from here and Daniel as possible—and you need to be at home. God bless." Mrs. Wright hung up the phone with a sigh. Losing a gifted therapist left her exhausted and frustrated. It was time for Lorraine's family to return home but how she would miss her colleague and friend.

Lorraine packed the still meager belongings after calling the center in Colorado. That same day she received a surprise phone call from her dear aunt. She knew God wanted Lorraine and the girls out of that place. "I can help," she told her with great glee, "There is a money telegram waiting for you at Western Union. Just don't tell Justin, OK?" Lorraine went to the location she quoted and discovered a telegram for $6,000. Utterly astounded, she traded it at the bank for traveler's checks. They were going home....home, to Colorado. She called her Aunt to cry out her thanks.

Lorraine told Justin she was not wasting another day but heading west. He agreed that the storm scared him to death. He would help with the drive to Colorado, he told her in a surprising gesture of caring. However, he belonged here. He was coming back to Daniel. His boss would let him have a few days off to take Lorraine and the girls out west.

The following day Lorraine's family wound its way around downed trees and out onto the freeway that connected them to Interstate 40. This highway would take them to Oklahoma. There she planned to stop and rest and visit old friends from graduate school. There was no hurry, the job would not start for three weeks, Mrs. Wright had told her. Heading through Smoky Mountain National Park, therefore, they took their time to enjoy its great beauty. Then they pointed the car toward Oklahoma and friends.

Two driving days later, sunset broke just as Lorraine's family cleared the foothills of eastern Oklahoma. In awe, they drove out of the Ozark mountains and onto the wide-open prairie. Pulling into a rest stop with their car, the girls and Lorraine got out to walk around. Walking the rest stop trail, Lorraine twirled around and around, thunderstruck by the sunset in all four corners of the sky. It was more beautiful than she remembered. It was, however, what had fed her soul for so many years and fed her now. She lifted her heart in a song of praise as the colors slowly crept from the wide-open prairie sky. Sky, her sky, she smiled to herself. God was taking them home.

Three weeks later, Lorraine began her new job as a rural mental health worker in eastern Colorado. Autumn contacted the private school in Kansas and learned she was still more than welcome on her full scholarship there. Colorado would require the family to live in the state for a year before granting residency and in-state tuition. She seemed very anxious to move on with her life. She could begin school in a few weeks if she went to the Kansas school, a short train ride from her family's new home.

Ariana and Allison contentedly explored the small town of Alameda that they had settled in after arriving in Colorado. School would start soon enough. They found a small house where they might be able to get another dog, which made them happy. Dad said no more dogs ever, but he quickly returned to North Carolina, so they would hope.

Then, a month after settling in, Justin showed up. He quit his job in North Carolina and decided to come live with his family. After all, Lorraine's job paid enough for both of them. He found a low paying job that he felt was good enough. She consoled herself by remembering at least he was away from Daniel. He had once again promised to get help with his anger, too, which renewed her hope.

The peace lasted for two more weeks. Then Daniel, driving more than 2,000 miles, showed up at their new home. Lorraine was at work when he and his wife arrived. Later Justin confessed to telling him where they lived again!

Autumn fretted nonstop when Lorraine arrived from work until Daniel left for his motel with Justin in tow. Safe once more, the girls told their mom what Daniel had told them. He claimed God ordered him to come and get the girls away from their evil mother. The group was going back to Alaska to live. The police were investigating their group in South Carolina. God told Daniel, he claimed, that her kids were to go with him to Alaska. No, not Lorraine. She was too rebellious. God told him just to bring Justin and the two younger girls. Autumn, too, was too rebellious and could go on to college.

Daniel arrived at their home the next morning before Lorraine left for work. Cocky and self-assured, he told the girls to pack. Lorraine picked up the phone and called work. She had an emergency and would not be able to come in, perhaps for the day. Setting the phone back on the table, Lorraine turned on Daniel with a vengeance. "You are to get out of my home!" she cried. "And don't come back! These are my children, not yours. Do you hear me? God has never told me to let you have them and He never will. They have been special gifts from Him to me; a woman whom doctors said could not physically have children. *You will never get my children, even if I am dead! Now get out before I call the police! They will be glad to know you are back in Colorado, because I know you are already wanted for kidnapping here!"*

Justin walked Daniel to his car, telling him he and the girls would come to Alaska as soon as he could manage to get them away from Lorraine. Daniel realized Lorraine was serious about her threat and took his leave. Fully frustrated, Justin stormed out of the house and stayed away for two days.

In the meantime, the younger girls started their new school. Lorraine felt safer in having the children at school where she informed the office that only Autumn could take them out of school besides herself. She also informed the school and the local sheriff that someone had threatened to attempt to kidnap them, and she needed their help in keeping them safe. They readily agreed. They even notified the state police that there could be possible trouble, so she would feel safer going to work. Once Autumn went to college, Allison and Ariana would stay in the after school day program until she picked them up after work.

Justin's job kept him away from home for long hours. The work was in the next town, so Autumn felt relatively safe during the day, too. Too long, she told her mother years later, she kept her secrets because she feared if her mother knew the truth, it would kill her. She also knew, though, that she needed to get away as soon as possible. She was her father's target, she rationalized. Everyone would be safer with her gone. She did not understand or know that Ariana, too, had her secrets.

Autumn knew the truth behind her decision to challenge her last two years of high school. She knew she needed a way of escape and college would be one. Her goal was to get away, far, far away. She felt so glad when her Dad said he was staying in South Carolina. Now her problem was back. School in Kansas would be a good choice.

Chapter 15:
He Tested Her When She Thought She Could Only Fail

Lorraine pulled the car off the desert road and paused at the top of the giant hill. She sought out the distant Sangre de Cristo mountain range. The sun was setting behind the purple peaks in a glorious riot of oranges, reds, yellows, and even a streak or two of green. She smiled with contentment, content in her decision to come home to Colorado.

She had spent some difficult, but rewarding, moments with her clients this afternoon. At long last, she turned the car toward home. The setback about this job was the long hours on the road, as it required Lorraine to visit the clients in their homes to do initial diagnosis. Sometimes her clients lived a hundred miles apart in this wild, semi-desert terrain. Thank God, her partner traveled with her when she would feel unsafe.

Lorraine reminded herself daily of the advantages to the travel distance as the late afternoons crawled by. Today was no exception as she took a long, deep breath of the clean air. She also appreciated the time to enjoy the beauty of her surroundings and time to think about her blessings--being alive after her long struggle with kidney disease and its treatment. Nightmares about not being really well still haunted her dreams, but she would not listen.

Her children, now seventeen, fourteen, and almost nine, deserved a happy home. Their lives were already so full of serious pain. Lorraine had come to believe she would never be able to get away from Justin, as he threatened to kill her if she ever seriously tried again. He said he was joking, but she doubted that. He told her he could go to Daniel's with the children...but if she insisted on keeping the children, he would keep Lorraine from leaving. Lorraine determined that she must try to protect the children and live with the fact she may have to continue to contend with the stress Justin brought her.

Christine, her partner who was with Lorraine that day, interrupted her thoughts with a reminder they must drive a long ways yet to get home. Lorraine sighed with contentment and restarted her engine. Edging back onto the road, she turned westward into the sunset. The empty road meant they could travel quickly, provided an antelope or coyote did not choose to cross their path at the wrong time.

Lorraine applied the gas and her new company car purred on at the speed limit. She was so glad her route did not require her to travel busy I-25. She hated the time spent on that highway. Too often she spent hours totally stopped in traffic jams on that road. This state highway was rarely used and in good condition.

Lorraine looked to the northwest and caught a glimpse of Pikes Peak on the horizon. Turning her eyes westward once more, she suddenly realized she was seeing nothing. In one moment her world completely vanished. In full panic, Lorraine cried out to her partner that she could not see. Christine grabbed the steering wheel while Lorraine pumped the brakes. Gradually they came to a stop halfway off the road. Christine barked for her to move into the passenger seat. Christine then came around the car and got into the driver's seat.

"Do you know what is wrong?" Christine asked.

"No, no," Lorraine sobbed. "It was just like a curtain came together in front of me and I can no longer see!"

"OK," Christine, a trained social worker, tried to stay calm. "We are only twenty minutes from Merrington. I am taking you to an emergency clinic."

Lorraine sat up as straight as if she had been shot at, for her vision reappeared as quickly as it had disappeared. "I can see again," she almost shouted, "Let's just go home."

"I don't think so," Christine disagreed, "As senior therapy partner, I have to be sure we are safe, and I am taking you to a doctor!"

They rode on silently as twilight came into the sky. Christine glanced over at Lorraine every few minutes to see if she was all right. Christine knew Lorraine's medical history even though she never shared this with Christine. It was illegal to check on medical records for employment purposes, but she knew that her boss got curious and checked anyway.

The boss could not understand why Lorraine walked away from first, a lucrative faculty position, and then, second, a thriving clinical practice. She told the employment committee what she discovered, only to be reminded by Christine that it was illegal to use that information to deny employment to Dr. Hawkins. They, therefore, hired Lorraine on her work record. When she arrived, she honestly shared her health information with her boss, but Christine did not know this. Christine wondered if this blind spell was related to past illness.

A cry from Lorraine caused her to pull the car over to the side of the road once more. "What is it?" Christine asked in a voice calmer than she felt.

"I can't move my right hand. I tried to brush my hair off my face and in my mind I did. When I looked down, though, my hand was still in my lap. I can't move it!" Lorraine sobbed.

Used to working with the elderly disabled, Christine knew what her partner was probably experiencing. It was vital to get her to help right away to minimize the stroke damage. A stroke in the early 40's is very atypical, but that is what the symptoms suggested. She tried to reassure Lorraine and then drove as fast as she could to the Merrington hospital.

In Merrington, the emergency room doctor ordered an EEG and many tests. Christine got her home phone number from Lorraine and called her husband. As calmly and simply as possible, she told Justin doctors suspected that his wife had suffered a stroke. She also told him what hospital they were at in

Merrington. Justin told her he and the girls would be there within the hour.

Christine hung up the phone and sighed. She ate dinner with Lorraine's family recently, as a "let's get to know each other" exercise. She instantly disliked Justin. He reminded her too much of her own abusive ex-husband. It took her ten horrible years to leave him because of death threats. It was none of her business, but she wondered why Lorraine, with her medical history, was expected to be the breadwinner when Justin had a good Master's Degree gone to waste. She suspected that Lorraine covered a lot for him, and this made her feel sick at her stomach.

Christine returned to the emergency department when Lorraine was brought back from her EEG tests. An IV was running and doctors seemed everywhere. She listened without surprise as the doctors informed them that they suspected a vascular stroke. This meant a blood vessel in the brain broke, poisoning brain tissue. Breakage in very tiny capillaries could cause these symptoms. The brain tissue that looked affected was in the vision part of her brain, and in a couple of other spots, explaining her numb hand. The doctor then began to ask Lorraine questions and concluded she suffered temporary memory loss, too.

"Am I going to be OK?" Lorraine asked defensively.

"I am 99% sure you have had a stroke. It has not affected your speech and the spots on the brain are small, so we believe it is a vascular stroke. We will keep you in the hospital to be sure you are OK. If one capillary broke, another could easily. We will want to get you started on some stroke medicine and physical therapy before you can go home. Do you have any medical history that might give us a hint about why this is happening?"

Lorraine filled the doctor in on her kidney failure and treatment. He nodded as she talked and then concluded, "This is probably a result of the steroid treatment. Steroids weaken blood vessels if used long-term." With this, he gave her a brief smile, shook her hand and left the cubicle. A nurse then came in to ready her for moving to the medical floor. Christine also slipped into the cubicle and took her hand. Although they only worked together less than two months, both felt they were friends.

"My job," Lorraine suddenly blurted out, "The boss will never let me keep my job after getting sick seven weeks after hiring!"

Christine shook her head. "She can't fire you. She would be breaking the new ADA Law. Don't worry. I will try to make sure you have a job to come back to."

Two young men moved Lorraine to the medical floor. Justin arrived with the three children in tow. Autumn was due to leave for college soon. The unexpected visit to her mother in yet another hospital left her feeling threatened. Would she have to give up her college plans, too? Would she never be free to have a life of her own? Why did she always have to make her plans contingent on her family? She was ready to break free!

Seeing her mom white and scared in that hospital bed, though, made her second-guess herself. "It's just a small stroke resulting from the steroid use," Lorraine reassured the children. "The doctor thinks they caught me in time to eliminate a lot of damage. I can go home as soon as they get medicine and PT set up."

As Lorraine expected, Justin's first question was about how she was going to keep her job when she kept checking into hospitals. Lorraine simply turned her back to his angry questions, trying to block the hatred she felt in his voice. When did he start hating her? Had he always hated her, and she had just been too busy to notice?

Fear grabbed at her causing panic to rise in her throat. Why did he not leave? It was obvious that he did not want her for a wife. Why did he not just leave? Lorraine curled into a ball as the tears began to course down her face. She felt his hands grabbing at her, forcing her to face him. Arms badly bruised, she finally relented, only to stare at him silently, for his face had become a blank slate, and his voice as if it came from miles away.

Rainee appeared behind the faceless man. Rain began to fall, melting the faceless man. Rainee laughed out loud. Dancing in the rain, defying her fear of lightning, Rainee, chased her two older sisters, Eileen and Jenna. Whomp, they splashed through the mud puddles laughing. Lorraine relaxed. Today, she might gain a good memory, she thought.

Rainee leaned over a place where the water burbled over stones as it swept down the gutter of the street. She grabbed a tiny branch and placed it in the flow. Together, they chased the makeshift boat, still laughing. Eileen shouted, "Remember the ocean, Rainee? We chased the waves out to sea. Remember?"

For a moment, Rainee paused in her play. Then Lorraine saw herself become a younger child, and the rain disappeared. In its place was bright blue sunshine. They were on the white sandy beach in Florida. Rainee was once more chasing Jenna. The sound of the waves somehow comforted Lorraine. This, she momentarily thought, must have been a better time of her life that she had forgotten.

Only the moment did not last. As Rainee ran away from her sister, Jenna let out a terrified scream. Rainee turned to see Jenna grabbing at her leg, continuing to scream. The faceless man appeared. Picking Jenna up, he knocked a stinging jellyfish from her leg with a bottle of suntan lotion. He then began screaming at Rainee. "Look what you have done! If you would have stayed where you were told, Jenna would not be hurt!"

Stunned, Rainee froze in the water. The high-pitched screams continued from Jenna. It was her fault Jenna was hurt. She was bad. If Jenna died, it was her fault. She ran forward and grabbed the arm of the faceless man, adding her screams to Jenna's, "I'm sorry, I'm sorry," she cried. The man shook her hands from his arm and carried Jenna to the car. "Stupid girl!" he called behind him.

Rainee, cowered behind Eileen until the faceless woman took her hand and led her to the car. The woman was screaming now, too. The lifeguard had informed the woman the jellyfish was poisonous. Jenna needed to get to the hospital right away.

Rainee believed it was her fault. She was stupid. Jenna would die. It was her fault. The grownups said so. It must be true.

At the hospital, Jenna was treated and released. Quick attention reduced the danger of the stings. Jenna was coddled and praised on the way home. Rainee, though, crouched in the back seat beside her sisters, Marta and Crystal. Eileen kept totally silent except for the dirty looks she threw at Rainee. Her fault, her fault, forever was buried in her head.

Lorraine gasped for breath as she flashed to another time. This time she was twelve. She showed signs of beginning to develop into a teenager. Tall and gangly, her blond hair was pulled back from her bony face with a headband. She could hear Eileen screaming.

Eileen was in the condemned three room house in Indiana where they moved when she was seven. With no running water and only bare electric bulbs for electricity, they hardly survived. Her tattered dress hung two sizes too big from her bony frame as Rainee reached up to pull herself even with the cracked window. The screaming worsened. What should she do? She was so scared. What could she do to help Eileen? What?

The faceless woman slid up behind Rainee. She pulled herself down from the window, "That's your fault, Rainee," a female voice growled, "If you weren't such a brat, Eileen wouldn't get hit so much!"

Rainee tore herself from her female torturer's hands and ran. She ran until she put the old pasture with its broken down fences and a hay field between herself and the house. Sobbing, she crumpled up in the full-grown alfalfa. Her fault! All this pain was her fault. Why could she not get it right, so all the pain would stop? Rainee turned on her back and gazed into the cloudless sky. She felt God's presence as if God wrapped her in His arms. She knew love surrounded her in these few precious moments alone. Grandma's God was real. He was here, and somehow he would make a way for her to survive.

Chapter 16: He Stayed Beside Her and Comforted Her

The plain hospital room replaced the blue sky and green fields as Lorraine felt the same peace once again flood her soul. God showed Himself to her when she was twelve. He would not forsake her today, either.

A young adolescent voice called to Lorraine. "Momma, Momma! Please come back. I need you, Momma." Lorraine smiled into the tear-streaked face of her middle daughter, Ariana.

"It's OK, sweetheart. I'm here. I'm here."

"I love you so much, Momma," Ariana cried as she wrapped her arms around her neck, "You have to get better again. We need you."

Lorraine held Ariana tightly in her arms, "I will do my best, sweetheart," she reassured her child. "Where are Autumn and Allison?"

"Dad took them to the gift shop to try to find something for Allison to do. She is awfully bored."

Lorraine nodded and closed her tired eyes, relishing the hugs of her more private child. Ariana was not demonstrative on the average day anymore. Fourteen year olds aren't demonstrative, in general. She would cherish this moment for years to come and hold it close to her heart when she would feel like quitting the game of life. She was a good mother, loved by her children. She loved them so much! She would do anything to be sure they were cared for and knew they were loved. Anything.

Fight she must. She must get well quick and go home so the children were not in Justin's care. Then she must figure a way to somehow get away from him despite her recurring health problems. If she died, who would care for her children? she asked herself. She could not let them end up under Daniel's care.

Lorraine was gaining a bettering understanding of why she had not ordered Justin out of our home in the last few years. There was no relative to take custody of the children. Justin kept promising to get help, feeding her hope it would be safe to leave her children with him if she died. He also would intermittently make death threats. Now, however, she began to believe that if she died, Justin would take the children back to Daniel's or, at the least, take his problems out on them. He was once again threatening to take them to Daniel, who had recently escaped to Alaska. She must not die. She must live. Lorraine gently stroked Ariana's long dark hair as she wondered when God would show her the next step to take in this terrible journey her life had become.

Chapter 17: Rainee's Terror Remembered

Rainee ran and ran as fast as her awkward thirteen-year-old legs could go. Behind her could hear a man shouting, cursing, and the roar of a .308 hunting rifle. In horror, she heard the plunk of a rifle bullet plowing into a cedar tree not three feet from her. She glanced around feverishly and then plunged to the right. Crashing through the brush, she found herself in a meadow. Quickly she turned left to re-enter the woods.

The shouting faded slightly as Rainee continued to run. Suddenly, she caught sight of an evergreen tree whose branches reached completely to the forest floor. She dove under the lowest branches. Clawing up the trunk until she was several branches off the ground and completely hidden, she rested.

Totally covered by the ancient tree, Rainee prayed for help as she silenced her breathing. The sound of heavy hunting boots came within inches of her hideout. She smelled the rifle's gunpowder. Cursing, the booted man continued down the path away from her hideout.

When Rainee could no longer hear the man, she slid from under the tree and ran toward the house. She saw her sisters playing softball in the field beside the house. She had been playing with them before leaving under orders from the faceless man for her to go hunting with him. He told her he wanted her to learn to hunt deer. She ran in a beeline for the field in which her sisters played softball. In the past the faceless man cowered when more than one of the children were present. Today, she counted on his cowardice to save her life.

Finally, Rainee heard the heavy hunting boots clumping far away on the path she had followed. A man's voice shouted, "I can't find my prey! Where did she go?" Terrified, Rainee hurried her steps, praying he would not get close enough to shoot again. Just as she reached the road in front of the field and her sisters, Rainee heard him break out of the woods a long ways down the road. He started shouting and laughing as the other girls ran into the road to greet Rainee.

"I missed my prey today," he hollered in a roaring laugh, "She was too crafty for me. Maybe tomorrow, eh?" He shouted again and laughed. "I won't miss my deer forever, eh?" With this shout, he wandered back into the woods. Her two older sisters, Jenna and Eileen, grabbed Rainee and kept her running toward the house. Both were crying.

In horror, Lorraine realized Jenna and Eileen knew something she had not quite figured out. In her gut she knew it was an ugly monster she did not really want to meet. They also knew, Lorraine was sure, the faces behind the featureless masks that haunted her nightmares. She was sure they were her mother and father, but she could not remember how they looked. Why could she not remember?

Reaching the relative safety of the old screen door at the back of the house, Eileen shoved Rainee into the kitchen. "He's hunting again," She gasped to the faceless woman. Unbelievably, the woman laughed. "Good, we need meat. You girls better go find him and help him. Eileen, here, take your rifle." She put a 30/30 rifle in Eileen's hands. "Go on, Go!" The woman cried as she handed her shells and pushed them out the door. "I want him to catch something today!"

Frightened, dazed, the three young teens cautiously crept down the road, looking this way and that. Suddenly Eileen slammed a shell into her rifle. "You girls stay here," She growled just loud enough for the others to hear, "He won't play this game again." With this, Eileen slid off the road and into the underbrush. Rainee shuttered. What did she mean?

Chapter 18: He Kept Her Safe When No One Could

Lorraine felt Rainee's shutter and came back to the present. Gasping for air, she treaded the air around her with her arms. She felt unable to remember where she was. "Help, oh, God, please help," she heard a voice strangely her own cry out.

A gentle hand applied warm pressure to her shoulder. "Dr. Hawkins," a soft voice called, "You are safe. You are here with us. Remember?"

Lorraine lifted her head and met the kind eyes of her new kidney doctor, Dr. Engler, from the Merrington hospital. "I need you to stay with us. I know you suffer from PTSD and I will get you help for that. Right now, though, I am here to help you with your kidney problem. Can you listen to me now?"

Then Lorraine remembered. She had been in the hospital for three days for the small stroke and then gone back to work. Autumn had just left for college when Lorraine knew her kidneys were shutting down again. She did not want to remember. Terrified, she met the doctor's gaze.

Lorraine nodded, "My job," she muttered, "My partner told me I was fired Monday because I got sick again. This is despite the ADA law. They say they are exempt from that coverage. What am I to do? The doctors in North Carolina guaranteed I was over my illness, so I could work. I need my job. I can't let my children go hungry and homeless. I can't! I used to be hungry as a child. I never had a pair of shoes to wear until I started school and they made my parents buy me some. I used to live in a gutted out school bus my dad found in a dump. Dr. Engler, please, tell me my children won't go through the pain I did. Please." Lorraine looked into her worried doctor's face. He would care, wouldn't he?

"Worrying is going to make you worse, dear. I will help you with figuring out what to do about income and your job. ADA laws prohibit an employer from firing an employee because of illness, no matter what their history was before. You might be able to go back to work if we can get this thing turned around fast. Right now, I need you to concentrate on what I say, because your life depends on it, OK? Your children need their mother more than they need income right now. Listen, listen to me."

Lorraine began deep breathing. She had to get control of her fear if she was to get better. She won over this thing once. She could do it again.

Dr. Engler looked over at Justin, who had decided to join his family at the hospital. The doctor pulled Justin into the conversation with his eyes. "Your wife does not have just a kidney disease. That would be bad enough. The kidney problem is just a symptom of something much broader and more difficult to treat. I am running more tests to confirm my diagnosis, but I am sure I know what is wrong with her. Strokes are another common symptom of the illness."

"There is nothing wrong with her. She just doesn't want to work!" Justin jeered. "The doctor in Charlotte told me she was completely well. You tell me why she is so crazy!"

The doctor's face went pale as he stared at Justin. Dear God, the man wanted his wife dead, crossed the doctor's mind as he searched for a response to the jeering.

The doctor sat down in a chair next to Lorraine and took her hand, choosing to turn his attention to his patient. "I don't know how you found me. The only answer I can come up with is God. I am one of three people doing research on your disease in this whole country. One of the doctors is at Johns Hopkins back east. The other is at the University of Colorado research hospital in Denver. Our research is not finished. We do know what causes your disease, thanks to new research. The treatments, though, are very experimental. No one knows the end results yet. I want you to trust me. I am going to do my best to get you on the road to recovery. I want you to promise me, though, that once treatments are started, you will move to Denver. The hospital here is not equipped to take care of you. I need my colleague at the University Hospital to take over your care. We have to get this thing turned around, OK?"

Numbly, Lorraine nodded. Denver. She hated big cities. She intentionally raised her children in small university towns and the country. Denver would be like another world. Could they handle that kind of change?

Dr. Engler squeezed her hand to get Lorraine to refocus her attention on him. "I am serious. Without this experimental treatment, you have only about two weeks to live. We have to get the illness into remission so your organs have a chance to at least partially heal."

"What do I have?" Lorraine whispered as she stared into the concerned face of the doctor. For the first time a doctor understood what she already knew. She was dying and there was no one to help—until now. He said he knew her disease. Lorraine wanted to know what she was facing now! She realized she was no longer a professional fighting for her job. She knew she had lost her fight for her marriage long ago. She could sense that. She had one last cause to win this battle over disease for—her children, they needed her.

"I think God did send me to you, Doctor." Her voice trembled as she spoke. "I somehow sense my work on earth is not done. My children need me," Lorraine looked deep into the doctor's eyes as a realization came to her—"and the world needs to hear my story."

Dr. Engler smiled and nodded. When she had met Dr. Engler yesterday, she thought this doctor too young to be a specialist. She quickly realized, however, that he was capable of helping her.

Dr. Engler quietly told her he cleared his afternoon calendar to spend with Lorraine and her family. He needed to fully explain her disease, its sources, and its treatment to the whole family. They would be needed to be sure she made it through the treatment. The experimental chemo he was about to propose could kill Lorraine if great care was not taken to ensure her safety. He also wanted to get a good look at as many of the children as possible. This dominant disease was an inherited female disorder. It was highly likely that at least half of Lorraine's children had inherited the gene. Physical features would give away which ones were most likely to also need medical care.

When the children were ushered into the room, Dr. Engler explained that Lorraine had a rare inherited autoimmune disease that only a handful of families experienced. The early studies were showing a yet to be named syndrome, although her variety might be unique to her ancestral line. The research team recently discovered that these diseases seemed to develop only in extended families. Dr. Engler suspected Lorraine's illness was somehow related to people with British royal blood in their veins. Most of the cases in the study all seemed to have this connection.

"Does your family of origin make any claim to being somehow related to the crown of England?"

Startled, Lorraine looked at the doctor in surprise, "What a curious question!" Then she heard Rainee cry out in shock, too. Momentarily back in childhood, she could hear her mother as if she was in the room, talking about her pride in being of British royal ancestry. Coming back to the present, she told the doctor that she remembered her mother's pride in her heritage and her pride in also marrying someone else with British royal connections. Her one older living relative, her mother's older sister, completed a family tree search and found her mother and father were 23rd cousins. The aunt, the one relative who continued to keep in touch with Lorraine, only recently told her about this finding. "I thought it was a bunch of poppycock snobbery," Lorraine sighed as she told Dr. Engler this information.

"My father was a mix of Irish and British, but mostly British.

My mother was pure British except one of my grandparents was Native American. The family covered that up to anyone asking questions. I knew of my Native American roots from my aunt, because when she called about my heritage, I got snoopy. I asked if there was any explanation for two of my girls looking Native American if the family was British!"

Dr. Engler chuckled. He knew Lorraine was a professional researcher. He could not imagine Lorraine not being snoopy! Researchers, by nature, just are or they would not do research.

Slowly, the doctor explained that the disease was in her blood, making every tissue blood touches at risk of dying. Brain tissue is protected from blood except in cases where blood vessels break, as hers had with her stroke. Then, they, too die when the blood touches them. This happened sometimes when blood clots travelled to the brain, but he did not know why Lorraine's vessels had broken. That information had not yet been discovered. "Do you know what lupus is?' he asked.

Lorraine nodded. She knew only one relative with lupus and it had been a very difficult disease to watch progress.

"Do you know any relatives with rheumatoid arthritis?" he queried further.

"My father!" she choked out, as she remembered even more of her family history.

"OK. Did he or his siblings have any other diagnoses you have wondered about?" the doctor queried

"Yes, my dad had rheumatic fever which damaged his heart. His sister was diagnosed with a thyroid disease and had a thyroid tumor she had to have removed. My paternal grandfather appeared totally insane. He was never charged with a crime, but I am relatively sure he killed six of his wives and most of his nine children. He was married eight times and only one wife outlived him." She shuttered. She did not want to remember these things, but the pieces seemed to come forward anyway. The mental medal door stood ajar now, and she could no longer block anything from her past..

"Do you remember anything unusual about your mother's side of the family, medically speaking?" the doctor pushed on with his questions.

Lorraine concentrated all of her energy on turning back her mental clock. Sad thoughts engulfed her. She remembered her mother's mother, Grandma Benson, the only relative who seemed to care for her. Finally she spoke, "All the women on mother's side of the family seemed to die young. Some died by age thirty-six. As early as the late 1700's my mother's relatives died young with weird diagnoses. My great-great grandmother collapsed after her last child was born and was in a wheelchair for several years. When she died, she had a growth the length of her neck. Their deaths, however, were all blamed on heart failure. But it was only the women who died young. If heart disease was that bad in the family, should not the men have suffered more?"

Dr. Engler began explaining the scientific facts surrounding her disease, telling Lorraine that although no name had been chosen for the specific variety of her illness, most illnesses were named after the doctor who discovered them, or the family of the patients who suffered the disease. He also told her he was not surprised that the women in her family all died young. "Your illness tends to affect women 80% more of the time than men, although some males are showing symptoms. Also, your disease, unfortunately, has symptoms involved in several autoimmune diseases—like lupus, endocrine disease, rheumatoid arthritis, pernicious anemia, fibromyalgia, MS,—because the blood affects all those tissues. That is why I am telling you no tissue in your body is safe from your blood."

"The antibodies in your blood appear to have been programmed to kill any part of you. These cells normally kill bad bacteria and viruses. Yours, however, were misprogrammed and attack your own cells. Because they are permanently warped, they must be destroyed."

He continued, "My research team has discovered a chemotherapy used for breast cancer that slows lupus down. We believe it would do the same for your form of the disease. I must warn you it has not yet been tried on your illness, because we have not found a patient in the final stage of the disease that is still alive. Only then could we risk such a dangerous experiment. You are in that stage. Would you trust me and risk such an invasive treatment to save your life?"

"What is this treatment called?" Lorraine murmured in terror.

"It is called massive doses of Cytoxin. It is given as an IV. You will also have to go back on massive steroid dosages for a very long time. Every month we will check your blood to see if the antibodies are dying. As you get weaker, hospital stays will be a must scenario. When we have killed all the antibodies in your blood, we will do a bone marrow transplant to replace your blood with healthy tissue. Do you understand?"

"I don't think I can do this," Lorraine whimpered.

"You have to, because otherwise *you only have about two weeks to live*," Dr. Engler told Lorraine firmly, "Your children need you. And the world needs your story. I know this is tough, but it is the only decision you can make. I am not willing to let you die. I have already notified the cancer unit at the hospital that you are to receive your first chemo tomorrow morning. I will see you in a few days to be sure your body is responding appropriately to the chemo. I suggest you find a motel in town, as the commute to Alameda is too far for someone as fragile as you are."

He finally turned to Justin to gauge his reaction. Justin's look of disbelief seemed greater than ever. "She can't be this sick!" he spat out, "Her whole family is crazy. That is all that is wrong with her! I am going to take her home! I need her to support us!"

"No, you aren't," the doctor responded. "She has all the rights over her life, not you. If she chooses to go into treatment and save her own life, you cannot stop her from getting treatment. It is against the law. Do you understand me?"

Justin slammed out of the room, shouting insults at the doctor. Doctor Engler shook his head and turned his attention back to Lorraine, who was muttering, "Why can't he just get a decent job himself? Why must I bear the entire financial burden?"

Doctor Engler sighed. "Something is very wrong with your husband. I am going to notify Dr. Proctor, my colleague in Denver, so that he will keep an eye on him and try to get him help. I am setting up counseling for you and the girls here and it will be continued in Denver, OK?"

"Can we wait a few days to start treatment? I am so scared," Lorraine whimpered.

""No, every day is critical now. Tomorrow we will start the IV treatments." He patted her hand, "You will be OK. I will be right here to help you, and Dr. Proctor is the best doctor in the nation for you. Just trust me, OK?"

Tears in her eyes, Lorraine nodded. Did he have any idea what he was asking? How long had it been since she had trusted anyone except God? She could not remember. Long ago, she trusted her parents. They had violated that trust greatly. Then she trusted Justin—only she finally knew she could not trust him either.

The doctor frankly discussed her illness and treatment with the two younger daughters since Autumn was not available. Someone had to help Lorraine. The doctor then turned to Ariana, grieved that he must ask a fourteen year old to do one of the toughest jobs he could give a family member. Justin could not be trusted. He was pleasantly surprised when Ariana told him "my father cannot be trusted with my mother's life. I can handle it. I *will* help my mother. Allison can do her small part, too," she told him very seriously.

Doctor Engler next told the children he needed each of them to go through tests, too. The researchers now knew a dominant recessive gene caused this illness. In other words, the gene could express itself with only one gene. It was likely that two out of the three girls carried the gene. That meant they would express some form of autoimmune disease in the not too distant future, if they were not already symptomatic. He could reassure them they would not need to get as sick as their Mom was if they started some preventative care right away.

Ariana, the science buff of the children and tiny for her age, listened attentively. Finally, she interrupted with an exclamation of discovery. "I have been sick since I was born. Could this be what is underneath all my problems, too?

Dr. Engler started asking her specific questions and soon nodded his agreement. It was highly likely that Ariana was a full-blown case of the autoimmune disease, and it triggered before birth. He immediately called Children's Hospital in Denver to alert doctors there of his suspicions and to set up in-depth tests for her.

After observing the youngest, he concluded she probably had some form of the disease also. Her swollen eyes and red-slapped face indicated she was becoming symptomatic, too. He could not assess Autumn in her absence but he wondered if she, too, was ill.

Dr. Engler turned back to Lorraine. "I wanted to be sure and tell you the kidney connection before you leave today. Your biopsies actually showed that your right kidney is 95% dead. Sometime in your past, your kidney suffered a great deal of trauma. The symptoms of this disease do not cause that kind of injury to only one kidney. If one is diseased, they are both diseased. I would guess you had a severe kidney injury when you were about twelve years old. Did Dr. Semdka discuss this injury with you?"

"Yes. It happened when I was about twelve, but I didn't die," Lorraine whispered.

"No, you didn't, and I cannot humanly explain that. In all fairness, I will have to tell you that you should have died. I do believe God has a reason for keeping you alive, just as He did back then. And we need to do what we can to be sure that you stay alive, OK?"

"Just a few more questions. I know you are exhausted. First of all, do you remember your pattern of growth as an adolescent?"

At first, his question drew a blank in Lorraine's mind. Then she was in her past again. She was standing in front of the faceless woman, asking if she could go to a doctor. She had not had a period in six months, and that just did not seem normal for a fourteen year old. The woman laughed at her and told her it was probably just because she had talked herself into believing she was sick. Rainee was certainly strange. That did not mean she was sick—a little stupid maybe, but not sick.

The doctor's continued touch on her shoulder brought Lorraine swiftly back to the present. She told him what she remembered.

"How big was Rainee when you saw her at age fourteen?" Dr. Engler asked.

"I was tall, but I looked like a boy—flat chested and small hips. My sisters teased me that I was not a girl, because I looked 12-12-12." (her measurements)

Dr Engler nodded as Lorraine talked. "Your disease was affecting your development by then. As an adult did you notice unusual female symptoms?"

Lorraine told him about being diagnosed as sterile before Autumn's birth. It had taken seven years to get pregnant with her. Then she surprised the doctors and had Ariana without having normal periods. After Ariana, her periods disappeared completely. The doctors diagnosed it as early menopause. Said that was it for childbearing, so she might as well get on with her life.

Six years later Allison came along. Doctors diagnosed that pregnancy as an ulcer. She was twenty weeks pregnant and the baby was moving when she informed the doctor she did not think it was an ulcer at all. Lorraine spent the rest of that pregnancy in bed. After that, they kept her on female hormones to force periods for a while. Then periods became normal for many years. No one ever questioned why her female organs did not function normally. They just told her to be grateful she had three miracles for children. Lorraine had been extremely grateful. Her whole life she had wanted to be a mother.

Dr, Engler explained that the disease had probably gone into temporary remission on its own long enough for Lorraine to become pregnant those three times. Her difficulties during her pregnancies were probably because the disease tended to come out of remission before the babies were born, and it acted as if the babies were "an enemy to attack." Lack of periods indicated massive clotting in the uterus for long periods of time, not early menopause. The hormone treatment probably cleared these, allowing regular periods later on in life.

"Can this disease cause depression?" Ariana interjected.

"Very much so. In fact, we are finding that if the disease hasn't killed its victims, patients eventually kill themselves because it is an extremely painful disease in its final stages. Sometimes the depression is our only hint that something is wrong physically."

Justin slid back into the room and snickered just at that moment. "I told you she was crazy. Just like her whole family."

The doctor looked at the man impatiently. "She is not crazy. Depression is a normal part of autoimmune disorders. Once the medical condition improves, the depression gets better. This, sir, is a physical illness we are dealing with, and not a mental one."

Justin snorted and left the room again. Discouraged, the doctor watched Justin go. He would have to warn Proctor about that guy. His attitude could kill his patient, who was already poised on the brink of death. He watched as the girls huddled protectively around their mother. They knew something was wrong, too, he thought. Thank God, they saw it and would protect their mother.

He knew he needed to get Lorraine into some positive thinking if the chemo was to work. A friend of his, a psychiatrist, recently published research about the positive effects of pet ownership on illness. He wondered if Lorraine owned a pet?

Dr. Engler asked the girls out loud, "Do you have a dog?"

Ariana shook her head violently. "Dad said we could never have another one after we left our dog in Minnesota. Said dogs in a house made a nasty house. I love animals. I have wanted another dog as long as I can remember."

Allison's face lit up. "Does this mean we get a dog, Momma?"

"Let's hear the doctor out," Lorraine cautioned.

Dr. Engler smiled at the girls. In his estimation, Justin was leaving this family anyway, so why not let them have something to comfort them? "Tell you what, when you leave chemo tomorrow, I want you to go over on Commerce Street. The dog shelter is there. I happen to know they got a new litter of puppies recently. I want you to get the smallest, most dependent pup you can see. I want you to do this, because your Mom needs something whose very life will depend on her care. You guys can help take care of the puppy, but she is to be your Mom's main charge, OK?"

Allison began to jump up and down as the doctor asked the nurse to show them the way to the door. He had a feeling this prescription was going to be easy to fill.

True to their promises, the girls went with Lorraine to her first chemo session and then they wandered over to the animal shelter. Once there, however, Lorraine felt extremely tired after her chemo ordeal. She sat down in the waiting room. The girls followed a worker back to the kennels. Soon Allison came charging back. They had twenty puppies! Mom must come and look!

Privately, Lorraine wondered how she could care for a puppy if she was already this tired after her first chemo.

Lorraine followed Allison rather slowly. Back in the kennels, the worker surrounded the girls with a litter of puppies. They giggled, enjoying the feel of a new puppy. Lorraine looked around. There was one puppy that looked too weak to participate. She pointed at that puppy.

"The little black one with the curly fur. What breed is it?" Lorraine asked.

"She is half Sheltie (miniature collie) and Welch Corkier Terrier. Both are small working dogs, so she would be easy to train."

"So it is female?" Lorraine asked.

The worker picked up the puppy and checked her over. "Yes, she is female. She is awful weak, though. She is only three or four weeks old. She has just opened her eyes. Someone decided to get rid of the pups before they were ready. She requires bottle feeding, being kept warm. We weren't going to adopt these out because they probably won't live."

Lorraine thought back to what Dr. Engler said. She needed something dependent. Well, here was a very dependent little puppy, indeed! She held her hands out, and the worker placed the puppy in them. Bringing the pup to her chest, it nuzzled her and then rooted until she found a warm place under Lorraine's arm.

"I think we have been adopted," Ariana laughed. So began Lorraine's pet therapy program to compliment her experimental chemo. And so also began a close relationship that would often bring the children comfort. The children named the dog Joy. Lorraine would come to believe they had picked the right name. Joy would spend her entire life with Lorraine and be trained as her assistant. She would continue to bring joy for the next seventeen years as she served her owners faithfully.

Chapter 19: He Made Her Feel What She Would Not

Lorraine's family had been in Denver for a month. During the previous three months, Justin had driven Lorraine to Merrington for her chemo and checkups a couple of times. He said he was trying to prove he was doing his part. Other times he asked people from the church they were attending to take her or put her on the bus for the hundred mile round trip challenge. Six months into Lorraine's chemo, Justin announced he had accepted a good, professional job offer in Denver that started at $50,000 annual salary. He planned to move them to Denver the next week.

Lorraine, weak from her illness and chemo, and under unbearable pain from the return of her joint immobility, watched as Ariana and Allison packed the few things they had brought back to Colorado.

Dr. Engler had become agitated because the family had failed to go to Denver. Lorraine informed him, therefore, that Justin had finally found a Denver job and they were going there. He looked obviously relieved. He told Lorraine he was getting Dr. Proctor on the phone while she was in the office.

Assured that Dr. Proctor would see Lorraine within days after arriving in Denver, Dr. Engler wished her well. The test results showed that her autoimmune disease was still active, but the antibody count was going down noticeably. He figured Lorraine needed another three months of treatment before she could have a break from the chemo. In excruciating pain, Lorraine felt like she had to fight just to stay alive.

A deep misgiving about Justin's apparent change of heart also spurred Lorraine on to stay alive. Something was not right. He seemed to magically change from his old hostile attitude, but too many years of torture left her in doubt. What did the change mean? Was he genuine?

Autumn continued to go to college in Kansas. Lorraine

told her she must get away after Justin threw her against the living room wall with Lorraine present. She left with her mother's blessing, even though she had just turned seventeen. She never again trusted her father. And Lorraine decided not to tell her of her chemo until she felt there was no other choice. She was better off away at college.

Autumn, shy, pretty and small boned, did not need a big man to beat up on her. Already quiet by nature, her increased quietness now alarmed Lorraine. Autumn seemed to talk openly to her mother about everything, including sex and boys. The bruises from her father from the past were never on parts of her body that were not obvious, so Autumn never showed them to her very ill mother. She simply claimed she preferred sweaters and jeans. She practiced hard to keep her secrets, because she feared what the knowledge would do to her mother's already weakened state. She completed her task well, because Lorraine never guessed how great the physical abuse in their home had become until years later when she was stronger and Autumn revealed "the rest of her story," to her mother in tears.

Autumn called one day from college with a pleasant surprise she thought might cheer her mother. "I met the dorm mother today," Autumn told her, "You wouldn't believe who she is." She chuckled out loud.

"Do I know her?" Lorraine asked, puzzled.

"Very well," Autumn laughed again, "I think God answered your prayers to have someone watch over me here, because I am too young to be away from home."

"Well, don't leave me in suspense!" Lorraine cried expectantly.

"It is Beth Cameron, our babysitter from Minnesota. Her husband is the treasurer of the college. She said they moved here to take over these responsibilities last year. Can you believe it?"

Lorraine, terrified of sending her oldest away so young (Autumn had graduated from high school at age sixteen), visibly relaxed. God answered her prayer. Beth was a Christian lady who babysat for the girls off and on when they were younger. She was a very good person. Autumn *had landed* in good hands.

"I am so glad," Lorraine told Autumn as she broke into tears, "I am so glad. I miss you so much. You are my first-born, my first joy, and my first song. I am so sorry I did not figure the physical abuse thing out sooner. Your father got counseling in Minnesota. The counselor said the one time I knew about was a one-time reactionary thing that we wouldn't see again. I believed her, Autumn. I should not have. Forgive me. Forgive me."

"Momma, Momma," Autumn's voice also held tears, "It wasn't your fault. You did what you could when you knew what was wrong. I just didn't want to cause you more pain. You have been through so much, I thought I could bear this much. I hate him, though. Dear God, help me, I hate that man," Autumn choked out.

"You have a right to be very angry with him, Autumn," her mother responded in a worried tone.

"I think you should get away from him," Autumn's voice became concerned. "I do not think you or the other girls are safe with him anymore. I am going to pray that God makes a way for you to get away, too."

Deep in her heart, Lorraine knew that Autumn had a legitimate concern. The thought of being abandoned once more, though, left her with a sense of panic. "I know it seems the best thing. Let's pray that God shows us the right way to go," Lorraine told Autumn as she hung up the phone.

Autumn was safe. She was in a safe home. God would help Lorraine and her other daughters to find a way, too.

Justin came home a few days later and announced that he

had a counselor in Denver he agreed to see for a while to "learn to get his anger under control." He had, further, found them a nice apartment close to where he said he was working. The problem was it was a forty-five minute drive to the doctors and hospital, making distance still a problem in getting Lorraine to help. When she commented on this, however, she was reprimanded for criticizing his help "Again!" He began calling Lorraine names and verbally attacked her until he left her in tears.

The move to Denver was finally completed. Ariana and Allison settled into the new apartment. Allison started school, but Ariana contacted the Education Department to let them know the school in southern Colorado had graduated her early. She was now fifteen. That was old enough since they had no classes to offer her. She began studying furiously for the tests the Education Department asked her to take to prove she had high school competence at so young an age before they would allow her to start college classes.

By the time the nine months of chemo were over, her doctor appointments had to be made late in the day so the girls could help Justin physically load Lorraine into the car because of her weakness. Nurses helped her into the office when she arrived. She began to wonder if the end was near no matter what the reason for her to stay alive, and this frightened her greatly. Who would take care of her girls?

Lorraine joked with the girls about spending more time in her past than in the present, as her PTSD episodes came almost daily now. Ariana secretly talked to the doctor about these and armed herself with knowledge and training. He told her what she could do to help her mother. The chemo was, indeed, removing any remaining mental blocks Lorraine had left. "I don't want you girls to know about my past. It seems too ugly to share," she told Ariana, "I may have to tell you about it one day, though."

Ariana refrained from asking her mom questions, but let her know she needed to know about her past. Lorraine volunteered a fact or two occasionally. This helped Ariana to begin to piece together her mother's childhood.

A short time later, Lorraine was propped in her recliner listening to TV. She seemed to be doing a little better when suddenly she asked Ariana to come and hold her hand. Tears began to stream down her face and Lorraine began to talk in terror in a child's voice. "He is going to kill me; he is going to kill me!" she blurted over and over.

Justin came over and forced Ariana away from Lorraine, "You go to your room. She is just being crazy and you don't need to help her," he angrily pulled Ariana away and would not let her near her mother again. Lorraine continued to rock back and forth and cry.

Gazing up and seeing Justin as if from a far away distance, her fear took over completely and she jumped out of her chair. Having not stood up by herself in several weeks, this action took Justin off guard. It was as if she could not remember her pain. Pushing Justin away, Lorraine ran out the door of the apartment and into the street. Running up and down the street, she continued to scream, "He is going to kill me!" Several neighbors came to their windows and watched Lorraine run, but Justin stayed in the apartment. He wanted nothing to do with this raving maniac.

Night came, and Lorraine remained in the street crying even though it was a cold January night. The neighbor from the apartment above them came home, and seeing Lorraine in the street, got out of his car. He worked for Vocational Rehabilitation Services and sensed that his neighbor was in jeopardy of losing her life. Lorraine would be killed unless someone helped her to get out of the road.

Lorraine pulled at her hair and her nightgown as she cried and ran up and down the street. The neighbor man called to her gently, as to a little child, "I am here. I want to help you. The bad man is gone now. He won't hurt you anymore. Can you please come and stand here on the sidewalk with me?" He continued to gently coax Lorraine until he could tell he had her trust. Then he slowly reached his hand out and stroked her shoulder. Lorraine edged up onto the sidewalk with him.

"Can you tell me who is trying to kill you?" the neighbor asked gently.

"Daddy," Lorraine sobbed, "Daddy."

"How is he trying to kill you?" The neighbor asked. He suspected Lorraine was in a PTSD episode and had been for hours. He knew they could last up to eight hours. Why, in God's name, did her family leave her out on the street without any help on a January night? He looked over to the door of their apartment and saw Justin standing, blocking the way for a daughter, obviously distressed, from coming outside. "Stupid idiot," he thought to himself as he continued to stroke Lorraine's shoulder.

"He has a gun," Lorraine gasped.

"What kind of a gun?" the neighbor asked.

"A .308 deer-hunting rifle. He is chasing me and trying to shoot me. I have to get away. I have to get away!" Lorraine cried but did not pull away from the neighbor, sensing she was safe with him.

"I chased him away, he won't hurt you anymore," the neighbor soothed, "The bad man is gone far, far away. He will never hurt you again."

Dawn crept into the sky and then full daylight. Still, Lorraine stood on the sidewalk shaking and screaming that her father was trying to kill her. It was well past eight in the morning, when Lorraine looked up suddenly. The episode was over. She was back in the present and realized how cold she was even with the neighbor's jacket flung over her shoulders. The two of them had been outside for a long time.

"I'm so sorry; did I make you late to work?" Lorraine looked into the eyes of this kind neighbor, not fully comprehending why he was staying so close beside her.

"That's OK, I can do flex time. I thought you could use some company for a while." He would never tell Lorraine he had spent the greater part of the night keeping her company. Ariana would later tell her this fact. He also did not tell her that Justin refused to come out and help either. He now guided a very tired Lorraine back to their apartment, realizing she was running a very high temperature when he put his arm around her shoulders. Ariana threw her arms around her mother when she came through the door.

"What happened, what happened?" Ariana cried in bewilderment.

The neighbor kindly told her that he suspected an extended PTSD episode combined with some delirium from a high temperature. He asked if she could see that her mother was taken to the hospital immediately. Justin, listening in the background, growled. He was going to work. He was not taking that woman back to the doctor! Ariana led her mom into the apartment and helped her into her chair. Covered with her favorite quilt, a gift from her aunt, Lorraine soon collapsed into sleep.

Ariana made sure Allison caught the school bus and then quietly went about preparing Lorraine's medicines. She had taken over her mom's medication duty months ago when Lorraine started getting confused about what to take. Normally, Lorraine had finished her morning meds before Allison went to school.

Now that Ariana was finished with high school, she felt she had more time to help her mom. In the last few weeks, she completed studies in English, chemistry, biology, advanced algebra, and Spanish. She was set up to take the competency testing the following week that the Education Department insisted upon before she apply to the local college. She also challenged the junior college's entrance requirements. She was set to take a special test to show she met college entrance requirements the following week, too. These exams did not frighten her. Being in college would free up daytime hours for her to help her mom. After Allison was home from school, she could take college classes.

She had this all worked out before contacting the education office. Today she was grateful they were cooperating because she was more sure than ever that her mom was not safe in Justin's care.

Justin supposedly went to work. Ariana played computer games while keeping an eye on her mom, who did not seem to be able to awaken. She checked her temperature and discovered it had gone up to 104 degrees. That worried her. Ariana called the doctor and was told him that her mom needed to be seen right away. She called Justin at his message number, but he refused to come home and take Lorraine to the doctor.

In anguish and desperation, Ariana called Autumn's dorm in Kansas. Explaining she had a life or death situation on her hands, she asked if the dorm mother could find Autumn and have her call home right away. Beth, the dorm mother, knew Lorraine must be very ill and took Ariana very seriously. She called the registrar's office and got Autumn's class schedule. Then she sent a student to the classroom where Autumn was in class. Within the hour, the phone rang at home.

Sobbing, Ariana told Autumn she thought their mother was dying and did not know what to do. No, their father would not come home and take mom to the hospital. Mom was not really conscious. Autumn told her that she thought she had better call an ambulance after she made sure Allison could get home.

Then she told Ariana that her boyfriend, Tom, had a car.

They were on their way to Denver. She had recently told Tom her mom was really ill. He even volunteered to bring Autumn home if she ever needed to go.

Somewhat relieved that she was no longer alone in her concern, Ariana called the elementary school and told them there was a family emergency. Could she pick up Allison in a few minutes? She would come in a cab to get her little sister. Then she called the cab company. Within an hour, Allison was home and helping Ariana get their mother ready for the hospital. Then she called the ambulance.

By the time the ambulance came, Lorraine had slipped into an even deeper state of unconsciousness. On the ride across Denver she aroused briefly enough to pull her daughters close to her and tell them not to be afraid. If Jesus wanted her to come home, then she would have to go. But Mom knew they would be OK. Lorraine whispered that she had a plan to be sure they did not end up with Daniel that she had kept secret over the last few months lest Justin find out and destroy the plan.

Lorraine had already taken out papers against Justin and Daniel on child abuse charges so that they would be less likely to gain custody of the two younger girls if she died. She told them softly that she had hand-written her will, giving custody to her lifelong friend, Rebecca, and then to Autumn when she turned eighteen. If she did not make it today, Ariana was to call Rebecca to come and get them. Did Ariana understand? Ariana nodded through her tears. She did not want to live if her momma did not live, she cried, but Allison would need someone. She promised her mom that she would take care of Allison.

Arriving at the emergency room, Lorraine was rushed to intensive care. At the hospital, IV's and monitors were quickly started. Blood tests showed that Lorraine had eight different bacterial infections all at once. The chemo had succeeded in killing all her antibodies, but it had also destroyed all her bone marrow, and hence, her immune system; so Lorraine had nothing to fight off disease. Starting massive antibiotics and careful monitoring, the doctor told the children he was "guardedly hopeful. Your Mom has fought off a lot before. I don't think she is ready to quit yet."

The following day Lorraine and the younger girls received a wonderful surprise when Autumn walked into Lorraine's ICU cubicle. "Hi, Momma," Autumn whispered. She was dressed in hospital gear, with a mask to keep Lorraine safe. The doctors decided Lorraine needed to see the girls and overrode hospital rules. Even Allison visited Lorraine despite being nine years old, hospital garb and all.

Strengthened by their presence, Lorraine's body began to respond to the antibiotics. Three days later, the doctors cheerfully told the children their mother was "out of the woods." Justin tried to visit but was told he could not see his wife. He complained to Ariana that the doctors had no business telling him how to take care of his wife! In fact, the doctors told Lorraine she must sign charges against him under the brand new medical assault law in Colorado. She finally had the legal protection she so desperately needed.

The doctors knew Lorraine almost died because Justin refused medical treatment for her. She would have died if her daughters had not gone over their father's head and gotten medical help. The doctors were in no mind to allow him into the hospital at all. They sent a psychiatrist up to see the girls and Lorraine. She talked to them about life without Justin at home.

Doctors finally agreed to postpone charges if Justin started meeting with a good psychiatrist on staff. He could not see his family unless the psychiatrist approved.

The doctors released Lorraine two weeks later. For some reason, her own stem cells began manufacturing its own blood cells without a bone marrow transplant. This highly unexpected phenomenon proved a great medical breakthrough as many cases reported the same results. (It was later determined that the chemo had killed all her bone marrow and her blood cells but her stem cells were intact. In essence Lorraine had had a stem cell bone marrow transplant, only it was her own stem cells doing the work). No one really knew how this experimental chemo helped, let alone this new development. It was a miracle, Lorraine told them calmly. God had been with her through yet another of her darkest nights and chosen to once again give her back her life, at least for a while. She was so grateful to be with her children once more.

Autumn got permission from her professors to stay home for a few weeks, so her boyfriend, Tom, returned to Kansas alone once Lorraine started to improve. Autumn took over the household to give Ariana an emotional break. Their mom required twenty-four hour care for a while, so everyone was exhausted. Secretly, though, Autumn thought she knew there was purpose for her Mother's crisis. *He—her father--was finally gone.*

One day, sitting beside her chair enjoying one of their favorite videos, Autumn became fearful as she watched Lorraine begin to cry. "I want Ariana," Lorraine whispered.

Ariana came running into the room and took her hand. "I saw him. That is why I was so strange that night. I saw his face. I have not remembered his face in over thirty years. But that night, I saw him, the faceless man has a face, and it is the face of my father. The infections must have cleared any final small blocks." Lorraine squeezed Ariana's hand as panic edged her voice when she responded to her mother's statements. Lorraine could not tell her more. It was too painful. She was not sure she wanted to cause the children that much pain.

Ariana, however, added this piece together with what her mom had told her from previous PTSD episodes she had experienced. She was sure someone had tried to kill her mom as a child. After today, she knew that someone was her grandfather. No wonder Mom acted so forcefully when she had found their father beating Autumn. In a sense, it gave Ariana some peace of mind to figure this out. She now knew her mom would fight to be sure they were safe no matter what.

She knew that her father knew more than he explained, as he seemed to always have ammunition against her mom and them, blaming Lorraine because she must just be "white trash." These verbal attacks and emotional whippings used to be so sporadic one forgot them before the next one occurred. Over the last couple of years, though, they had become almost daily events.

Then the physical abuse began in random moments for what seemed like unreasonable causes. Autumn seemed to take the brunt of this; so, Ariana was glad she had found safety in going away. She was, however, really glad to have her home now with Dad gone, as Ariana needed help with Mom. When the massive infections were controlled, doctors discovered Lorraine's body was so weak that she had to be hospitalized more days than she was home. Autumn talked to her professors about incomplete grades so she could stay long enough to be sure her mother was stable. Life was forever changed. It was more painful than any of them had imagined it might be. They were together though, and they would work hard to face each day with hope.

Chapter 20:
He Gave Her a Song When Her Soul Could not Sing

Physical progress for Lorraine was minimal over the next few months, but she at least stabilized. By the end of six months, she had set a hospital record of eighteen hospitalizations.

In those months Ariana, now fifteen, was issued a driver's permit so she could drive her mother to her appointments. Since Lorraine still held her license, she could be the licensed driver in the car, even if she could not drive herself. A large computer corporation had a plant across the street from their apartment complex. Late at night when the plant's parking lot was mostly empty, Lorraine helped Ariana inch over to the lot. Then they practiced starting, stopping, turning and parking until Ariana began to feel in control of the car.

The first few road trips were scary, as they required Ariana to learn the fast way about big city traffic. On her first "street" day, she drove Lorraine to the store. She pulled slowly out of the large parking lot of the department store. Another driver, not as careful, ran the red light going quite fast. Lorraine screamed as she saw the shadow of the other car aimed right at her door. (Lorraine was once again suffering from blindness at this time). Ariana, an avid computer and video game player, spun the car as she would have in one of her games.

Lorraine sat in amazement as they spun back into the parking lot and out of harm's way. Lorraine was never afraid to ride with her new, young driver after that. Ariana's driving came as a natural gift, and she desired to keep herself, her sister, and her mother safe.

During Ariana's third day on the road, they were caught in downtown Denver rush hour traffic. Never daunted, Ariana gripped the wheel and picked her way through the crowd. Rather than terrify her of driving forever, these experiences seemed to teach Ariana that she could be in control in very stressful situations. Lorraine sat back in amazement as Ariana negotiated the rush hour traffic as if she was an experienced driver. Later Ariana would admit she was terrified, just as she was in that first parking lot drive. She knew, however, that God expected her to use her head and stay safe.

Lorraine was now deathly ill and alone in a big city with two children when she discovered that all her money was once again gone. Justin admitted that the money was gone. He had also cancelled her health insurance to prove she was not sick by preventing any more hospital stays. Lorraine became terrified for her life because she knew how fragile her health was now. What was she to do?

Dr. Berring attempted to help her. She set up a meeting with the hospital social worker, Mrs. Johnson, who told her how to apply for Medicaid, Aid to the Needy Disabled, the children's relief fund, and food stamps. She did not bother to tell Lorraine she knew the red tape these applications required would take weeks or that her previous year's income would disqualify her for the aid. Part of Lorraine's clinical work with mental health was to help clients get on services when they were needed. She never dreamed she would one day need to do so herself. Lorraine held a doctorate. Doctors did not need to apply for relief services, she cried out to God at night.

Autumn called social services from college and was told she must go to social services and start the paperwork if her mother was in the hospital. She could do that during her spring break holiday, which was days away. When she arrived at the office, however, the office informed her that her mother, the client, would have to come in and do the initial paperwork herself no matter how sick she was or how hungry her sisters were with their father refusing to give any help. When the social worker told her last year's income disqualified them anyway, Autumn gave up any hope of help. What were they to do?

Lorraine came home from her eighteenth stay in the hospital at last. The hospital would not turn her out, they said, because they were not allowed to cancel her care as a public hospital. They did have to send her home for a few days to see how her body reacted.

Less than twelve hours after arriving home, Lorraine discovered her children had been living on chocolate they had found for the last two weeks. There was no other food in the house. Lorraine was angered beyond belief that Justin would let the children go hungry while he held his new job. He was told he must help provide for his children but failed to comply. Lorraine told Autumn they must try to apply for social services again. Autumn came home from college with Tom and drove the family to the social work office.

Lorraine took a place in a long line, where she waited in a wheel chair for four hours to see a technician. By then she had a sinking feeling that her body was not going to make it through this day. Weak and now feverish, Lorraine felt herself passing out.

A technician finally showed Lorraine into an office. This worker took the forms Lorraine still had from the hospital social worker and began to rant at her. Incomplete forms were inexcusable! Lorraine began to cry softly. They did not allow children to complete forms; so, Lorraine had assumed the worker would help her to complete the necessary paperwork.

Ariana, who now spent more time with her mother and understood her needs better, had come back to the office with her. She told the worker her mother was blind and just out of intensive care. Her mom was going to have to go back to the hospital when they were done, because the long wait in the lobby cost her mom valuable healing and mom was now feverish.

The technician told Ariana she was a smart-mouthed teenager and she must leave the office. The technician put a pencil in Lorraine's hand and told her to complete the form. Lorraine began to cry out loud as the technician continued to attack Ariana, who had refused to leave. "Please, leave her alone," Lorraine begged the technician, "We have never had to do this kind of thing before, so she is not familiar with what is proper etiquette with a social worker." Ariana backed out of the office as Lorraine once again addressed the technician.

"I am so sorry," Lorraine told the worker, "I cannot see to fill in the form. Yes, my papers show I have a PhD. in the helping field, so I understand what the papers probably contain. I cannot see enough, however, to fill them out. Please, please, read them to me and then write down my answers. Then put my finger where I need to sign."

The technician sneered out loud, making Lorraine realize she saw her as a broken-down, useless piece of flesh. She took the pencil from Lorraine's hand. "PhD. my eye," she scowled to herself out loud. "Just probably doesn't know how to write." Turning to the first page of the form, she growled at Lorraine, "I don't believe you, but all right. If that is the way it has to be, I will have to do it."

Thirty minutes later, the technician told Lorraine that it would take six weeks to determine if the family was qualified for services. Lorraine felt the blackness once again overcome her as she slid from her wheel chair and onto the floor. Ariana, who had come back to the office for her mom, let out a scream for help. In seconds the supervising social worker and Autumn flew through the door.

Ariana told the supervisor what had commenced in the technician's office. Autumn helped Ariana to get her mom back into her chair. They would push her back out to the car. The supervisor told Autumn and Ariana to come back as soon as they had their mom in the car. Allison kept an eye on their mother while Autumn and Ariana returned to the office.

Before they left again for the hospital, the supervisor told Ariana they would give the family emergency aid right away. Medicaid would take over her mother's hospital bills and they would help her apply for Social Security Disability. She also gave Ariana a special pass to the local food bank to get a good supply of food for the three days it would take for her to do her paperwork and get her emergency food stamps. The supervisor suggested that the older daughter get a lawyer to write up power of attorney paperwork so that she could act from now on in her mother's behalf on such legal matters. Ariana wrote this idea down, as it made sense.

In addition, fearful a heartless technician may have cost the client's life, or at least a lawsuit against the agency, the technician was fired with Ariana watching. The supervisor had read the cover letter of the paperwork when the technician jeered about that old lady having a PhD. The supervisor recognized her name. Sickened to her stomach, she turned on the technician. "Dr. Hawkins is someone important to our field. I have read her research! Because the worst possible thing that could happen to one of our own happened to her does not mean you treat her worse than a dog! No human being should be treated like that no matter what his or her background! A person with your attitude does not belong in my office. Pack your things and get out!"

Semi-conscious, Lorraine was readmitted to the hospital with a very high temperature as the stress had allowed another infection to begin. Three days later, she was released to go home. In the meantime, Ariana went shopping with emergency food stamps. Lorraine called a church she and the girls had visited on a Sunday when she craved a church service in spite of her weak state. Since Lorraine had been home-bound or in the hospital since their arrival in Denver, she had not been well enough to even ask for the church's help. The minister was shocked to discover what her family and Lorraine were suffering. Someone must do something now!

The pastor rushed to their apartment to help Autumn and Ariana with food shopping. He also informed the girls that the church ran a food pantry. He showed Ariana where it was. "Take all you need," he told Ariana. "There is no need for you and your family to be going hungry. Food stamps are never enough to feed a family for a whole month." Soups and the like for her mom to eat when Lorraine got home from the hospital were once again in the kitchen cabinets. Ariana, stressed beyond belief, sat up alert as sleep evaded her one night after another. She would sleep when she knew they were safe. In reality she would not sleep for months.

The pastor told Ariana that he knew their mom qualified for Social Security Disability benefits. He would see if a Christian lawyer he knew would take the case. The same lawyer could do the power of attorney papers, too, giving overall power and medical power of attorney to Autumn. After this Justin could not, through some quirk of events, sign her life away again.

Once contacted, the lawyer explained that it could take a long time to get Social Security benefits, but at least it would give the family hope if they began the process. He completed the power of attorney papers without charging the family.

Ariana also called her mother's best friend, Rebecca. In hysterical tears, she told Rebecca she and Autumn could not pay the rent on the apartment at all. The utilities were being turned off, too. The manager had told the girls that they planned to evict them the next week. The family now had food because of social services and the church, but they still had no way to provide themselves with housing and money to pay the utilities. What were they to do?

Rebecca realized then just how deathly ill her friend must be and why Lorraine had asked her to take custody of the girls. She had no idea their financial status was so bad that they were at the point of homelessness. If Lorraine became homeless and on the street, doctors told the children that she would die. The street was no place for someone so ill.

In a panic, Rebecca told Ariana she was fast-mailing a check. Out of it, she was to pay the rent, utilities, and whatever else they needed to survive. And for Ariana not to worry. She was Lorraine's closest friend. She and her husband were on the way out to help if she needed them. She would call an airline and get a fast ticket.

A long time ago, Rebecca's sister was murdered and Rebecca went through a long period of distress. In that time Lorraine stayed beside her, helping her, consoling her, giving her any help she could. She would tell Lorraine later that she felt God was telling her that now it was her turn to give!

The lawyer, Mr. Swan, called Lorraine while she was in the hospital again. He wanted to meet with her to see if he could start the Disability Social Security claim. He had already drawn up the Power of Attorney papers and wanted to bring them up for her to sign.

Lorraine had been out of work more than a year now, so the likelihood of her going back any time soon was minimal if at all. The lawyer seemed very kind; as he told her he would do all the work for free if necessary. The pastor had already filled in the lawyer about the family, and he knew they were financially destitute despite her training and education because she was so ill. Later he would tell her she was the sickest person he had ever represented in his long legal career.

Mr. Swan helped Lorraine to complete the lengthy social security paperwork. She was hopeful. Even a little Social Security money at this time would be helpful. She had begun working at the age of thirteen at menial jobs. As an adult, she worked most of her married life, except when she was restricted during her difficult pregnancies and the recovery periods afterwards. Surely, she qualified to get some benefits.

Autumn ran out of spring break time and Tom came to take her back to Kansas. Tearfully she hugged her mother good-bye, fearing she might not see her alive again. After much discussion with Ariana and Allison about being sure they took care of each other and made sure mom was safe, Autumn firmly declared that they were to absolutely prevent dad from coming home. If they ran into more trouble than they could handle with mom's help, they were to call her right away. She would drop out of school despite her scholarship if she had to the next time.

As Tom and Autumn drove off to the east, Ariana became her mom's willing assistant once again. Though very sick and heavily medicated, Lorraine did all she could to care for the children. She especially enjoyed helping Ariana study for her exams and going over homework with Allison. She taught Allison to cook at her request, although she still supervised much of the kitchen work.

It was up to Ariana, though, to do errands, take Allison to school, and make sure her mom took the right doses of her more than thirty prescriptions. Together they slowly became a functional team, but Lorraine would not remember much that happened in the five years that followed. Her brain was so fried by the chemo that it refused to remember much. She was also unconscious in much of those five years.

Lorraine did remember that six months passed without hearing from Social Security. They remained in their apartment as Rebecca continued to pay the rent and utilities. Mr. Swan told her that sometimes it could take up to a year to hear from Social Security. In the meantime, he told her about the Denver Disabilities Office and services they offered. They offered to help her find a lower cost apartment that they would pay the rent and first month's rent for them. Lorraine would, however, have to find someone to move them. That was difficult, with knowing almost no one in Denver. Few people except the pastor of the church knew Loraine and the girls existed because of being home bound. How were they to move?

In that waiting time, Lorraine's vision also improved in what seemed like bizarre steps during her awake times. Her first real vision came back with her only being able to see the world in red and green colors. Jokingly, she had Ariana buy red and green inked pens for the children to write notes to her, because she could read these. The doctors were not encouraged. This was a fluke thing. They did not see how her vision could return because it was the vision center in the brain, first damaged by her stroke, and now by the chemo, that no longer worked normally. Plus her optic nerve was damaged. Eye exams showed that her eye tissue was in perfect condition but brain damage and optic nerve damage was not reversible.

Lorraine had been basically blind for a long time when the red and green colors showed up. In the following weeks, the many other colors within human sight reappeared one at a time. The last to reappear were black and white. What Lorraine did not regain was depth perception, so activities requiring depth perception, such as driving a car, remained impossible.

At first Lorraine could not tell if a curb was six inches away or six feet, or if a wall was a foot high or ten feet high. A car in the distance could jump out at her as if it was going to crash into her. When this problem did not get better over the months, the doctors concluded she would never be able to drive or do many depth-perception dependent activities again. To be told one cannot drive after one has driven for decades is insulting, painful, and unfair! Lorraine ranted and raved at God for giving her eyesight but not enough so she could do many of the things she loved. It was not until she realized she could not understand God's will and should just accept it, that she began to find peace. Lorraine would remain unable to drive. Doctors attempted to give back driving for short distances at limited speeds five years later so that she could drive herself to doctor appointments! Ah!!! Freedom!!! Even a little bit of freedom felt wonderful! Another stroke, however, once again left her unable to drive, this time permanently.

Rebecca's continuation of paying the family's rent and utilities brought feelings of shame. Lorraine had always been dependent on no one but herself, so her friend's help brought Lorraine to tears. She knew Rebecca was a good friend. She also knew no one had a friend who would take care of them this way. How was she ever to pay her back? Rebecca told her she wanted no repayment, that what Lorraine did so long ago to help her was all the payment she needed. This, however, did not lighten the guilt Lorraine felt.

In October, Lorraine finally received a letter from Social Security. Hopeful, she asked Ariana to help her read the letter. In the letter, the government stated that anyone with a PhD. should be able to work no matter their illness. Benefits were completely denied. Plunged into despair, Lorraine slipped back in time to the long ago days of very early childhood when all she had to eat was potatoes. (Before beans and corn bread became a real treat!) There was no one who wanted to take care of her and see that she was fed as a child. Now she could not feed her own children. Lorraine had vowed before having children that she would never allow her children to go as hungry as she had as a child, and here she was doing just that because she became so sick!

Now her health took another turn for the worse. Lorraine began to wonder if her children could survive better without her as she faced another hospital admission. Entering her room, Dr. Berring took her hand and talked gently to her. "Were you thinking about giving up on your fight with your disease?"

Lorraine nodded. "If I die, the girls can get social security survivor's benefits in thirty days. It is the only way left to help them." Lorraine began to sob uncontrollably. "I will not let my children go hungry. I will not. If it costs me my life, so be it. I will not let them go hungry. Rebecca is not made of gold. She cannot continue to care for us.

Tears welled up in Dr. Berring's eyes. She knew Lorraine's fierce maternal instinct would indeed allow her to give up her own life so that her kids could be fed. There had to be a way to care for the children short of that. There had to be. Dr. Berring did not want to lose Lorraine after she fought such a gallant fight. She would help Lorraine make sure the kids got the care they needed, one way or another.

Lorraine signed some confidentiality consent forms that allowed Dr. Berring to begin making phone calls. The call to Social Services proved very frustrating. They required people to work for cash benefits. In Lorraine's case, since she could not work, she had to get on disability. When her disability claim was denied, they questioned whether they could continue to help her without signing up for work retraining. Infuriated, Dr. Berring called the Denver Disability Office. She was told they were aware of Lorraine's plight and had offered cheaper housing, but Lorraine could find no one to move them. As a result, her family had been put on a waiting list that could be two years long before another apartment would be offered to them.

Dr. Berring forcefully reminded the office of the urgency of the situation, and Lorraine's frail health. The caseworker told her she would call back after talking to the supervisor. The nature of Lorraine's situation caused them to agree to come to immediate aide. There was still the problem, however, of manpower to move the family into public housing. The agency was too short-staffed to provide this service.

In the mean time, Ariana, who had turned sixteen and now had a full driver's license, was to be given directions to the disability agency. When she arrived, they loaded the car with food and some warmer clothes, as they could see the children were not properly dressed for the weather.

Next, Dr. Berring called Lorraine's lawyer. Why had she been turned down? His answer was also infuriating. Lorraine had a disease no one had ever heard of, so the government ruled she must not be sick. He was calling their Senator as soon as he got off the phone with Dr. Berring. It was time for political action.

Lorraine spent the next seven days in the hospital. In that time, she came to realize she finally felt safe for the first time in a long time. The children stayed with her during the day with the

Doctor's instructions that the staff were to be sure the girls received three meals a day. Lorraine hated for them to be alone again at night even if Ariana was sixteen. Lorraine was, therefore, very surprised when Justin showed up with the girls for a visit. The disability office tracked him down and told him he had to help care for his kids.

Justin was livid. He told Lorraine that he already called Daniel in Alaska the previous week, because he knew she was back in the hospital. Daniel would be there the next day to take the girls to Alaska. He was getting his kids to Daniel's one way or another. This was the perfect opportunity! Lorraine need never worry about them again!

Horrified, Lorraine begged the nurse to allow the children to stay with her until she could get help. Dr. Berring was called. She advised Lorraine to keep the girls with her and call protective services. In one full sweep Lorraine was told she must charge Justin and Daniel with attempted kidnapping with intent to remove the children from the state, their custodial parent, and needed medical care. Lorraine called Justin at her apartment where he was waiting for the girls to come home. Lorraine informed him of the charges she was willing to lodge against him and his brother. Daniel, unknown to her, was already in the apartment with him.

Justin warned him to turn around and leave or Lorraine would have him arrested. He left. He would try this stunt one more time, but the children would have been trained by Dr. Berring in "how to get away from your kidnapper" by then, and they fled back to the hospital once again to stop this attempt. (Ariana grabbed Allison and took her to class with her to protect her before showing up at the hospital). At that time Lorraine activated the charges against Daniel. Justin told Daniel he had better leave for good after that. He now knew Lorraine would follow through on her threat of arresting him. At last, Daniel went back to Alaska. Justin stayed in Denver but did not threaten to take the children away from Lorraine again. Lorraine would never see Daniel again.

While in the hospital, Lorraine began to search out what God wanted with her wrecked life. Again and again, God reassured her that He intended for Lorraine to finish raising her children. Over and over, He also told her to tell her story. Lorraine must, indeed, tell her story so that others might be helped with the telling. For the first time in a long time, Lorraine began to experience periods of hope, and with it came words of song. How could she sing when life was such a mess? How could she sing when pain did not allow her to sleep more than minutes at a time. She did not know, except that it must have been Jesus giving her His song in her heart and all through the night.

Two weeks after her release from the hospitalization resulting in Daniel finally disappearing, Lorraine received a letter from her Senator. He had looked into her case with her lawyer and was appalled at the miscarriage of justice. He told her he had contacted the local Social Security Court that morning and demanded she be given a hearing right away. The hearing was in two days.

Her lawyer came and picked Lorraine up for the hearing. He told her the hearing was just a formality. He knew the judge, who had already told the lawyer that he, too, was disgusted with how Lorraine had been mistreated. Inside the hearing chamber, a strange man sat down across from Lorraine. The lawyer explained that that was the witness for Social Security. He was supposed to prove she was not disabled.

Lorraine, who could now walk very short distances with a walker, slid into a leather chair next to her lawyer just as the judge came into the small room. As they stood, she pulled herself up by grabbing the edge of the table. A gentle voice came from the judge, "Sit down, dear, you do not need to stand." Gratefully Lorraine slowly lowered herself into her chair with her lawyer's help.

The social security witness tried to speak up after this, only to be met with a scowl from the judge. "We do not need your help today. You are dismissed," he told him. Once that witness left the courtroom, the judge turned to Lorraine. "I cannot tell you today that you have your disability. I have to notify you in writing. That is the law. I do not think it would be worth your time to worry about it anymore, though. Any questions?"

Surprised, Lorraine shook her head. The hearing had taken less than five minutes. Outside in the hall, the lawyer gave her a hug.

"What did he mean?" she asked, confused.

"It means you will be given your disability. And that it will be expedited. This should ease your financial status a little. Also, the state is suing Justin for child support for you. That should start next month. You and your children are going to be OK. You are. It will be hard. Disability does not pay a lot, but I believe God is going to take care of you with these small payments to help. I am so glad you did not give up on yourself, Lorraine. You still have so much to give to your children—to the world."

With God's song in her heart, Lorraine hugged her children and the lawyer. After he dropped them off at their apartment, Lorraine called Rebecca. Rebecca told Lorraine that she has just come from a travel agency. They had booked flights to come to Denver the following day. She could not stand to be so far away anymore when she knew her friend and her children needed her. Her kids were grown and her husband had recently retired. There was no reason why they could not come. They were coming to help move them into the lower rent apartment complex the disability office had arranged. Rebecca laughed as she told Lorraine that she had no say. They were coming.

Rebecca and her husband, Jason, stayed in Denver for several weeks. They thoroughly cleaned the low-income, dirty apartment, including scrubbing the smoke film from the walls. They also took the children shopping and bought them much needed clothing, shoes, and personal items.

Rebecca was appalled when she went through Lorraine's closet. She only found two nightgowns that Lorraine could wear, and those had holes in them. She took Ariana shopping with her, and they picked out several new outfits for Lorraine from a designer store. Perhaps looking nice would help Lorraine to improve, she thought. When she brought the clothes home, Rebecca said her payment was that Lorraine had to model them.

With tears running down her cheeks, Lorraine tried on the outfits one at a time. She had not had any new clothes in the four years she had been at war with her disease in Denver. Yet, these kind people who had already done more than their share, decided to share again. Lorraine and her younger children cried hard the day Rebecca and Jason went home. It had been such a relief to have grown ups that could help with the stressful load for a while. That help disappeared as Jason and Rebecca's plane became a dot in the sky.

A month after Rebecca and Jason left, another long PTSD occurred. The doctor had taught Ariana, however, how to recognize when an episode was beginning so she could help her mother get the help she needed. The doctor had noted a natural counseling gift in Ariana and put it to use. Often, simply a physical touch, such as holding her mom's hand, was all that was needed to help bring her out of the episode. The doctors practiced this skill with Lorraine and Ariana on many occasions. They knew she needed that contact to remember she was safe.

Now that her father, the faceless man, had a face, the power of the actual shooting incident decreased. Lorraine was puzzled, however, about the episode where Eileen, Jenna and she were ordered to the woods by the faceless woman. Why had it kept coming back? She had not quite figured out something about that episode, and her mind would not let her rest with it unsolved.

Night after night, Lorraine woke back in her childhood with Eileen telling her to stay out of the woods. Then Eileen would walk away. After three months without hospitalization, Lorraine woke in a night sweat. Rainee, was in the road again, and Eileen was walking away. Only this time Rainee heard Eileen's low-spoken words and they terrified her. Eileen growled, "I will not let that creep hurt Rainee and try to kill her like he tried to kill me. The bastard can die himself for trying." With chills crawling down her spine, Lorraine saw Eileen take the rifle off safety.

At the click of that safety latch, Lorraine sat bolt upright in bed. A sense of horror overcame her. What Jenna and Eileen knew from experience was that their father intended to rape and kill Rainee. Lorraine now remembered the time when a stranger brought an unconscious Eileen back to the house. Her father had beaten her with a baseball bat and left her in a coma for dead in a motel after raping her. Only she survived. The motel manager found her and called an ambulance. Her parents were called. They told the police that she had run away and must have been the victim of a random crime. No one believed her when she tried to tell them the assailant was her father.

Shaking uncontrollably, Lorraine began to cry as she remembered that terrible childhood day when Eileen walked away with the rifle. She now knew what Eileen intended to do that fateful day in October. She was going to hunt the hunter and end their nightmare forever. And Jenna was joining her.

"No, No, Stop, Stop," Lorraine screamed over and over into the night, until Ariana awoke and came into her room.

"It's just another episode, Momma," She spoke quietly, "Can you tell me something about it?"

Sobbing, Lorraine told Ariana she had figured out another piece. Jenna and Eileen had intended to kill their father that day for his attempt on Rainee's life.

With this realization came the revelation of the faceless woman's face, the woman who ordered them back into the woods. Not surprisingly, this woman was her mother. Had she sent Jenna and Eileen into the woods? Lorraine did not know. She was dead now; so, she could never ask. Lorraine knew her mother did not want her, but would she actually knowingly allow her husband to murder her children? As a child, Lorraine had been continually reminded that she was not wanted; so, in her memories her mother had become that faceless woman. On this night, though, with this episode, she also remembered what her mother looked like. Was her mother an accomplice in the abuse Lorraine and her sisters took over the years, not a helpless bystander, as she had claimed to the police? Nausea consumed Lorraine as she contemplated this idea. There had to be at least some truth or the police charges would not have been filed. Neither parent had wanted Rainee. She knew that even as an adult. She did remember that her mother sought out help after she was grown and spent the rest of her life trying to make up for the past without ever owning her part in it. This ugly piece of her childhood puzzle haunted her nightmares for many months because there was no way to ever know the answers. Her mother had taken those answers with her when she had died several years before Lorraine's illness.

After long talks with her doctor, Lorraine began to understand why she blocked much of her earlier life. It was the only way to survive and remain sane. Lorraine knew her childhood was full of pain and that her pastor's family had become her guardians for her safety. She also remembered that she went into the family-counseling field as a way of giving back the good life those dear people gave her. Many times over, she helped other children and young adults come to peace with their past. Now, she thought, as a middle aged adult, she could finally put her own past to rest. She began to share everything she remembered in prayers to the God her Grandmother shared with her. In so doing, she came to have peace over what she knew of her memories. God had used her terrible illness and chemotherapy for good. It had become an opportunity to heal emotionally.

Would healing old emotional wounds give Lorraine the strength to live longer for her children? The doctors thought so, and so did Lorraine. Her memories, therefore, came more and more to be her friends, her teachers. And the song in her heart grew stronger as she felt her own emotional and spiritual strength returning despite physical weakening because once long ago she had decided to follow Jesus.

Chapter 21:

And Loved Her When She Felt No One Could Love Her

Slowly, through continued medical care, counseling, and physical therapy, Lorraine began to find life bearable. One of her hardest tasks was learning to accept the new person she saw in the mirror. Always physically active even after her first bout with kidney failure, Lorraine felt disgusted by the creature that stared back at her in her mirror. Her face was a contortionist's dream due to the chemo and steroids. She gained almost 200 pounds despite close dieting because all the treatments were steroid based. These pounds seemed to refuse any surrender to the diet and exercise regiment the doctors prescribed. Lorraine felt she was always hungry and forever fat. Somehow, that was not fair in any way, shape, or form, but doctors did not give much hope for losing the weight.

Shortly after her social security pay finally came with two years of back pay, another friend from back east visited. Lorraine knew this friend from days when Lorraine was physically fit and in graduate school. They had often exercised together. On this visit, though, the friend never said anything negative about Lorraine's new looks. When the day came for her to leave, this friend gave her a hug and told her that her eyes were still the window to her soul, and she still had a beautiful soul. It did not matter what the outer self looked like. If anyone judged her by that, they were little people and did not deserve to know the good person inside of Lorraine. Lorraine hugged her friend and thanked her. She wondered if what the friend said was true, but it was nice for her to say such a thing.

Four years after Lorraine's experimental chemo began, she was still alive with fewer and fewer hospital stays. She would continue to have to take many prescription medicines that left her exhausted or sick from side effects, but she had fought all odds and survived. Shortly after her fourth anniversary of beginning chemo, a new social worker asked Lorraine if all she had suffered was kidney damage? To her surprise, Lorraine and Ariana, who still cared for her, burst out laughing.

Humor, you see, came back into the family's lives as they learned to accept their new reality. It helped greatly in coping with their pain. "No," Ariana laughed, "She has one kidney that functions fine now, but she also lost half a lung, the right side of her heart is damaged, some of her brain is missing from multiple strokes, and she developed diabetes, thyroid failure, and adrenal failure from the chemo. Let me see, she sees weird, sometimes her hearing fades and I have to shout at her, and I have to keep an eye on her when I take her shopping or she gets lost. Oh, AND her joints don't work. Other than that, her body works great. Any further questions?"

Ariana and Lorraine continued to laugh at their private joke, as the social worker squirmed, obviously embarrassed by her naive question. "How can such poor health be funny?" she asked.

Lorraine, sensing the worker's discomfort, came to her aide, "Few people understand how devastating so many of the autoimmune diseases are. You are only one of millions who do not understand, and we do not blame you. Just be patient with your questions, because my brain is slow or unable to process questions sometimes. The doctor tells me that is when I run into one of the holes the blood thing caused in my brain when vessels blew up. Sometimes I do not remember the beginning of a question by the time you finish it. Ariana is my right arm and my memory right now. She answers most of the questions. She also has a good sense of humor, which has become a daily blessing for me. Now, what did you ask?" Lorraine asked seriously, while Ariana smirked.

Lorraine doubted the worker would repeat what she said with the knowledge that Lorraine probably really did not remember. The worker did not bother, but moved on to other questions, directing them to Ariana.

Permanent homebound services were provided for Lorraine now. With the help of her doctor, she finally came to accept that she would probably never work again at her profession. For one thing, her memories of how to perform the statistics required for her research were gone. So were many of her memories of clinical models. With no temporary memory, how could she even follow instructions to do something? This left Lorraine frequently frustrated but she continued to trust that God would help her to still do good with her life.

Dr. Berring did not let Lorraine forget her idea, however, that she must tell her story. "You also have all your research you did for years. I bet you could write a self-help book based on that work, too. The research is done, so you wouldn't have to remember how to do it. Your right brain is healthier, so I bet you could write." In sessions, Dr. Berring kept lists of suggestions Lorraine made for her. She then reviewed these with Ariana, who could help to carry out suggestions. When she told Ariana she thought her mother should go back to writing, Ariana was more than enthusiastic. He mom had published a lot in the past. Why not now? Maybe it would be a tool for helping her to get better.

Lorraine began finding her voice once more with the help of a voice-activated computer since her hands remained frozen most of the time. She puzzled over the suggestion of writing her story for weeks. Then one day she broached the subject with her doctor. "Do you think I really could tell my story? It is all so painful. I do not know if I could put all that pain on paper."

"You can. And I think you should," Dr. Berring told her. "Perhaps you should start slowly, and perhaps you could ask the help of another writer, but as your mind continues to heal, you will be able to write. I just know this is a way to help you find yourself once more."

Lorraine broke into tears at the doctor's statement. "Why would anyone want to read my story?" she asked. "My husband did not even love me enough to want to help me when I got sick.

Why would anyone else care enough to want to know about my pain?"

Dr. Berring smiled at Lorraine, "Because I have never met someone with such an indomitable spirit. You have been handed crap in life, and yet you go on hoping, believing there is something out there for you and your children. You have a faith few have. Yes, you give up sometimes—for one moment, but then your spirit takes over again. People need to know your story. Perhaps not for your sake, but you need to tell your story so that many grown up little girls in this country have a better chance at healing, too. There are, after all, so many Rainees in this world who have never had the chance to come home. There are also millions of women with autoimmune disease."

"We know so little about the effects of autoimmune disease on the mind. We know even less of the long-term effects of child abuse. You have a unique story, Lorraine. You have suffered both and yet you sit here today believing in a future. Write your story, write. While you are writing, tell your children your whole story. They need to know. They have been through so much themselves. Yes, you went the hundredth mile to take care of them, but some things you had no power to stop. They need to know your past so they can know themselves better. You have always been willing to give them whatever they need. They need to know about their grandparents. And they need to know how that faith in God shown to you by your Grandmother gave Rainee the strength to overcome impossible odds."

Lorraine swallowed hard. She thought she had worked so earnestly to keep as much of her past as possible away from her children. She thought that was best. The doctor told her the opposite. Could she tell them? Lorraine wondered if she possessed that much courage. Lorraine looked at a paper where Dr. Berring was writing her suggestions. "Write about your past. Tell your children...."

Years after Justin was no longer in Lorraine's life, she

wondered if he ever really loved her. Something in him kept him coming back, but it was not love for her. She knew that now. She cared deeply about him and tried to help him as much as possible, believing somehow he could overcome his past as she rose above hers. The scars he carried from his own childhood, though, kept him from giving that caring back. That would probably never change. He had openly admitted to her a long time ago that he could not love someone the way families were expected to love each other. He also openly admitted he was very self-centered, paranoid, and reactionary in his last conversation with her.

Once child support was ordered by the state, a very small amount of money started coming in from Justin. He was working and the court garnisheed his checks. It was very little, though.

Ariana continued to attend college and worked as much as possible to help pay the bills. Graduating with her associate's at seventeen, she was surprised with a full scholarship to the four-year school for her junior year. It would mean moving to that town. Autumn, who took longer to complete her first two years because of her mother's illness, also transferred to the same four year college. They would go to school together and share mom's care. In addition, Autumn worked two part time jobs to help with bills.

Autumn knew she made the right decision to transfer schools and come home when she arrived home and realized how weak her mother had become. Ariana and Allison continued in care at Children's Hospital in Denver after testing positive for the autoimmune gene. Autumn, however, had left without finishing the testing. Yes, she needed to be put on meds, too, to prevent organ damage. Yes, it was good the doctors could follow her, too. The family needed her—and she needed her family.

In the fall, they moved to the four-year college town of Badger. Finding new part-time jobs, both Autumn and Ariana began classes. Gratefully, Lorraine discovered a lawyer who might be able to help her finally finish divorce papers.

Feelings of complete abandonment and guilt, though, continued to haunt her. How could she have not known about Justin's problems when she was in the psychology field? Why would she will herself to be blinded to his problems for so long? As the months of divorce procedures continued, she wondered if she, a proclaimed Christian, had the right to file for divorce, or was she creating a great sin in spite of the terrible situation?

Lorraine yearned for several essential things in her adult life: a marital relationship where she and her children could feel safe, and the gifts of children doctors never believed she could bear. To their surprise, she gave birth to three children. She loved them more than life itself. Lorraine was glad to have so much love to share to and from her children. She often doubted, however, if she could love herself anymore. What was left of her that anyone, including herself, could love?

Overwhelmed by guilt for ending her "Christian" marriage, Lorraine began meeting with a therapist on staff at their large church. Then one day, the therapist asked the senior pastor to join them. Gently, quietly, he opened the Bible and showed Lorraine that she was not judged by Justin's behaviors and crimes, that she was indeed morally free to divorce him because he turned to evil. The pastor told her God still loved her and was with her. She was not abandoned. He reminded her that her guardians still loved her, and so did her children. She still doubted, though, and felt so very lonely.

Then, alone in the middle of the night a few days later, Lorraine prayed and asked God to take away the guilt if there was no reason for it. An indescribable peace enveloped her as the guilt fled for good.

Lorraine knew her abandonment fears began in early childhood. It was also the time when she came to believe her only real Father was God. She now remembered that day when Pastor Teston had asked her if she had decided to follow Jesus. She knew from that moment that it was God who would be the one to love her. She watched her child self's faith take root as she remembered those days and felt reassurance that she was still wrapped in God's love.

Lorraine came to understand that much of her generalized guilt stemmed from her abusive childhood. As a young child and adolescent, Rainee did not possess the power she needed over her terrifying life. Now, as an adult she had asked Justin if he would join her in marriage counseling to try to heal their relationship. Instead, he told her doctors that her past proved she was really trash even though she showed some good works as an adult. He wanted totally rid of that trash. Devastation enveloped her as Justin spat those words out.—the most hurtful thing he could possibly have said. Lorraine now knew she could heal from the hurts he had caused, too. Lorraine finally understood what he claimed was not true. She was not responsible for the terrible things her parents did to her or her sisters. She was not bad because she had been hurt so badly and was an unwanted child.

In forgiving herself for being unable to stop the abuse, she found freedom to love herself once more. Neither was she responsible for the sick way Justin viewed her. With this thought, she found freedom over much of her adult life's guilt, too. She was no longer a victim, but someone who could, and would, overcome her past in spite of her illness.

Feeling quite at peace with life, Lorraine was very unprepared, therefore, when she received notice that Justin had counter-sued with the divorce and was asking for custody of Allison who was now twelve. Lorraine feared he still might be planning to take Allison to Daniel's commune in Alaska.

A new war for custody of twelve year old Allison began with Justin as the enemy. He did not want Lorraine to have peace. He would not leave the children alone. Lorraine knew it would be a long time before this new battle would end. Ultimately, however, a judge declared sole custody of Allison in favor of Lorraine. Justin could see Allison very infrequently and only with supervision if he would come to Badger every other week from his home out of state. A new era of life had begun for Lorraine and her family.

Chapter 22: How Could Rainee Come Home?

Alone in the living room of their small apartment after their move to Badger, Lorraine sat in the recliner that had become her bed. Hope fluttered in her chest as she gazed at their cozy, new apartment. It was small, but it felt like a home.

That day Lorraine began to write her story using her computer. She had concluded that the doctor was right. It was a work that needed to be told for the sake of others who were dwelling in similar pain—both from disease and from abuse. Too many stories were untold and ignored.

God had given her this gift of time to tell her story. With each completed piece of the story came a new verse to her heart song. Yes, she still struggled to walk. Yes, her temporary memory sometimes made people think she was a lot older than she was. She still took tons of medicine and had to go to physical therapy several times a week to be able to move. She, however, had found purpose in living once more as her faith was renewed. As time progressed, her health issues made temporary memory more and more difficult. Her daughters reminded her, though, that her days were needed to help her almost grown children and her newly adolescent child, Allison, who could not remember "when Mom was not sick, or when Dad was not causing a lot of hurt."

Allison was born with a naturally bubbly nature. Ariana also exhibited a sense of humor that kept the family chuckling. Allison knew indeed that she was a teenager and tested the rules off and on, only to repent later. One thing she said she knew very well—her mother loved her more than anything in this world and had fought to stay alive so she could have a mother. Lorraine wondered if this knowledge limited Allison's rebellion.

Ariana joined Allison in some of her rebellious acts while she attended college, because, as she said, she never really got to have adolescence; so, she had better get it over with before she got out of college. These acts, also, were minimal. Lorraine was secretly glad she took this attitude. It would make a better adulthood for Ariana.

Lorraine's first attempt at writing about her past became a short story that a magazine published. That article came to be been used by agencies to help their clients. This spurred Lorraine on to write more chapters in her life story. She was not free of PTSD episodes but they lost much of their terror; and she knew how important they were to her emotional healing. She began to keep a journal of those she remembered and discovered she could now remember better childhood days, too. She and her children also journaled of daily life as much as they could. Lorraine remembered so little current happenings due temporary memory loss from her strokes . Writing things down helped a great deal with this problem.

Allison took over much of her mom's care in her later teen years as Ariana finished college and began her career. It was during that first year with Ariana gone from home, however, that Lorraine realized how much at peace she was with her past. In that time she found herself before that great metal door in her mind once more. "No, no," she told God as she saw His great Hand attempting to help her open the door. "This time *I must open it by myself.*"

In her mental picture, Lorraine saw herself draw up a footstool as she dropped her four footed cane. Reaching up high, she was able to unlock the door. Then she pulled as hard as she could, but the door would not budge. She leaned to the left and pulled the bolt out of the top hinge to the door. Then, getting off the stool, she removed the lower hinge. Still the door stood fast. "God give me the strength," she prayed. With all her might, Lorraine pulled until the door crashed forward. Expecting it to fall into the abyss, she was surprised to hear a great crashing noise.

Looking down into what had been the abyss, Lorraine saw that the door settled across a wide and turbulent river. On the other side of the river, ridge after ridge of sunlit hills showed splendid spring colors. She stepped cautiously out onto the bridge, and then she knew. The monsters were still with her, but they were now a turbulent river that could be crossed and overcome. The abyss was gone, and in its place was the roaring river.

Glancing over to the other side, Lorraine saw Rainee running among the trees, chasing butterflies and laughing. Deep, deep peace settled over her for the first time in many years. There were also good memories she had forgotten. She was now free to remember those, too.

Suddenly, Lorraine knew why the door failed to just disappear into the abyss. She also knew that she still needed the door in her life—oh, not to protect her anymore as it protected for so many years. No, rather, the door *had become an open bridge*, and in so doing, *it had become a pathway* across the turbulence of her past. Because? Because— and with this Lorraine smiled joyfully to herself—*it was the only way Rainee could finally come safely home. And home she must come.*

Part 2:

Rainee's Journey Home

Chapter 1: Moving Forward

Lorraine sat on the inside aisle of the full Greyhound bus in January, 2007, listening to other passengers chatter. This was her first trip out of the town of Badger since her grave illness began, and the chain of what doctors called miracles. These miracles gave her back enough functioning to feel better although she was not cured. How did she get here? she often asked herself. She could not believe she had survived to see her youngest child graduate from high school and start college.

Five years passed with continued progression of the disease and weakness. Lorraine's children grew up taking care of their mother by themselves to prevent her move to a nursing home. She continually told them she did not want to be a burden on their young adult lives any more than she had to be, but they would not quit. They knew they needed each other as a family.

Lorraine believed that God could answer her prayers and heal her. She also understood some trials were not removed from human lives for good reason. She did not, then, expect the "partial' answers He gave...the series of miracles that allowed that bus ride. Instead of death, he gave her life. Yes, pain continued to plague her, but he gave her the ability and time to raise her children. He also gave her sufficient eyesight and mental ability to go back to her creative pursuits. And she discovered she could have a positive outreach to others facing difficult lives. All of this, though, required one very large miracle.

On Lorraine's 53rd birthday in 2005 the miracle began with a devastating setback in her health. She awoke to severe jaw pain and feeling a little feverish. She wondered if her nerve damage now extended to her jaw, and how it would be unlikely she could even eat without severe pain. She told no one of the severe pain, but dressed as best as she could, as she did not want to worry her children. The girls wanted to have a birthday party for her.

That afternoon, the visiting nurse came while Lorraine was cutting birthday cake. She stayed to visit for a while, enjoying cake with the family. Lorraine noticed her eyes on her off and on in that hour. She finally sat down beside Lorraine. "Where is this awful pain that makes your eyes look haunted?" She asked.

Lorraine tried to deny the pain, but the nurse brushed her bravado off. She relented and told her that her jaw felt like it was falling off. She gave Lorraine a quick check up, and then calmly told the girls their mom needed to go to the hospital.

"For jaw pain?" she asked incredulously.

"I think it is a heart attack," she responded, "Sometimes in women the brain sends pain messages to the jaw when the heart is affected. You have to go to the hospital."

That night doctors informed Lorraine that her heart was shattered from all the steroids and chemo she had faced. She had hours to live. The heart medication would stabilize her enough so they could attempt surgery at five in the morning, but they thought she would die during the surgery if not before.

"This is it, isn't it, God?" she prayed. "I wanted to see Allison graduate from high school this spring. Could you somehow heal me enough to let me do that? Please. I can go if I must, but I think Allison needs me right now because she still struggles with the damage from her car accident."

The girls rushed into her hospital room to pray with their mom. Ariana informed her that she had called the church prayer chain. Others were praying, too. She had called everyone she could think of to pray.

Doctors came in and told the girls their mother needed to rest as much as possible if she had any chance in surgery. In the next few hours of quiet dark, Lorraine wrestled with her fears, her hopes and what God wanted from her. At three in the morning, he gave His answer.

Lorraine felt a touch and looked up to see the angel from her childhood sitting on the edge of her bed. "Rainee, God has heard your prayers," he stated calmly.

In awe Lorraine watched as he reached out his hand and pulled back what appeared to be a large curtain that also seemed to divide the room. Behind that curtain she saw many, many people. Some were people she knew. Others she did not know. All were praying. (A friend would later tell her that God woke her at exactly three to pray for her, something that had never happened to her before).

"God has also heard the prayers of his many followers and now answers their prayers. Today he has given you a new heart." He reached out and touched her chest ever so gently. In that moment Lorraine knew He had indeed given her a new heart, as she felt oxygen coarse through her body for the first time in hours.

"What shall I tell the doctors?" Lorraine asked, "What about the surgery?"

"Go ahead with the surgery. God has reason for you to have the surgery." With these words the angel left and her vision of the curtain and praying people behind it also left. She sat up in bed, wide awake. What had happened to her? Her oxygen tubes were too strong. She wanted to tear them off but calls to the nurses left her with instructions not to touch them.

Two hours later, Lorraine's surgeon told her tests from the evening before showed she was too weak to endure the usual anesthesia for the heart procedure. He would do stage one, angioplasty, with nothing at all as she could not take pain killers either. "OK, God, now what?" she prayed quietly as four nurses took positions to hold her still. As searing pain ripped through her, she prayed aloud.

Time passed when suddenly Lorraine heard the doctor yelling, "You have the wrong heart, you have the wrong heart! This heart belongs to a twenty-year-old athlete! Where did you get this heart?" He cried in disbelief.

Lorraine began to laugh and cry at the same time, as the pain continued. "The people of God prayed and asked God to heal me. He gave me a new heart."

The doctor began sewing Lorraine up. "Today, for the very first time, I have witnessed a miracle!" He stated. He would later proclaim this same statement to those waiting to hear of her outcome in the surgical waiting room, which was full of people praying despite the 5:00 am time.

In the months to follow, Lorraine regained the strength to walk with her cane, her heart pumping strong. Doctors put her in a warm pool to exercise and reduce her pain levels. This was such a relief, joy re-entered her life although pain and chronic fatigue would remain that had to be addressed daily. She told her family that she did not consider herself a victim of life's hardships. God had given her life once again within which to participate fully. She could now revel in that life, laugh, enjoy her loved ones, and continue to share her story. She explained her partial healing to others with a quote from the Bible that a blind man told Jesus: she could "see men as trees walking."

Two years after that miraculous day, Lorraine sat on that large bus.....

The prospect of traveling on the bus frightened Lorraine. Could she take such a trip by herself now? In winter, at that? She shook from head to foot as she approached the bus but she managed to plant herself on the bus like a heavy oak, refusing to give up her seat. She knew it was time to go see her beautiful Colorado world for the first time in ten years.

As Lorraine rode south down I-25, however, a full Colorado blizzard overcame them and blew viciously. As she looked around the bus, she watched other eyes look anxiously out of the large viewing windows. She was not the only nervous one on the bus that morning.

Lorraine chose today to travel because it was the day she finally got up enough courage to walk into the bus terminal after several days of fearful delay. The weather forecast was also for clear, cold weather. Even yesterday the weather was sunny and promising. She had not planned on challenging her newest stretching of her wings in the worst of environmental circumstances! Somehow, she heard God laughing at her, "Might as well really grow your faith!" He chortled.

Looking out, Lorraine realized the snow blew sideways, as well as up and down. Great! A genuine white-out had begun. She glanced up the few seats to their trusty driver and realized he seemed as little interested in the weather as if it was a perfect blue-sky day. She relaxed. If he felt he knew how to drive in this mess, she guessed she should trust him. It was time for her to return.

Return? Yes, this trip was aimed at a return to her family's re-entry point into Colorado—southern Colorado and beyond. She would pass through where her first stroke happened driving down Highway 50 and she lost her memory, her life as she knew it. God, by some sense of His humor and understanding, had chosen to help her move forward by taking her completely backwards.

God had lately impressed upon Lorraine a conviction she needed to share her life with even more people now that she was stronger. What? Yes, she had healed emotionally from her divorce. Her busy life with her girls and "coming to life again" soon found Lorraine not even thinking of Justin anymore. Did God mean for Lorraine to remarry? She doubted that with her health history.

Still, she was lonely. Full of fear and doubts, therefore, she let the girls post her biography on a website with an invitation for others to write to her if they would like to talk as friends. After all, she had a background where she could listen if the person needed someone to talk to now. Lorraine laughed and accused the girls of really setting her up to meet a man… internet dating was for the young, but not for someone her age, especially not with her health record, she told them. As months went by, Lorraine found herself making internet friends with several people, some male. Some were close enough to invite her to join them for dinner or such. A bit paranoid, she agreed to such outings if one of her daughters went with her. Never expecting anything more than friendship, she enjoyed having somewhat of a social life again.

Then one day an email came from southern Colorado. It was a request from a man whose wife had died. He was very lonely and just wanted someone to talk to now. Would Lorraine answer his email? Curious and hoping to be of help, she answered the email. Yes, she had lived not too far from the place he lived. Who are you? she asked. Another email followed. Weeks and months passed with emails, followed by earnest phone calls. His name was Derrick. He was recently retired from the grocery industry and back in college to look at a second career. One day this man called to tell Lorraine that this gentleman would be in her town in the next week. Could they meet in person? Meet? Meet? Would she really want to meet this man?

Lorraine finally agreed that they could meet if her daughters were present. Derrick came to town a few days later in another blizzard like the one she was currently experiencing on the bus. Three feet of snow later that day, Derrick and the family discovered they were all snowed in at Lorraine's rental house, including all of her daughters who were there for the holidays.

It took days for the snow plows to reach them, because the house was not on a main street. Derrick was finally able to struggle out and go home. The week, however, had been full of long talks, hot chocolate, board games with the girls, and a realization that Lorraine had met someone for whom she could care deeply. Would he want to be more than friends? He lived too far away! What was she to do? SHE DID NOT TRAVEL NOW!

That is, Lorraine did not travel, until today…in this new blizzard…Derrick had kept calling and begging her to visit, become better acquainted, and to meet his friends, as his classes did not allow him to come north again for a while. Perhaps she would like where he lived and want to return more permanently? Enough! Lorraine finally protested. He reassured her that she could endure the bus ride…she just had to pray a lot! The doctors had told her she could make the trip. Her daughters had checked Derrick out and agreed a visit would be nice for their mom….bossy children……So, here Lorraine was amidst a blizzard, going back, back, as if in a time loop, only the person waiting for her was kind and gentle…….and wanted to be with her very much in spite of her challenges.

The road, however became so blocked by the blizzard that the highway closed. Lorraine was a prisoner on a Greyhound bus in a white, white world. For some reason the panic she expected never came. Instead a contentment and peace settled down. She had just enough cell phone battery to call Derrick. "We are snowed in at Waltonburg," she sighed into the phone.

The kind voice on the other end prodded her to be sure she was all right. He suggested Lorraine ask the bus driver to drive the block to the restaurant she saw. He knew she needed to eat, and probably so did everyone else on the bus. If they were stuck, they might as well not be hungry, too! There she could recharge her phone, too, he told her, as the restaurant allowed customers to charge their cells in plug ins they provided in this rural area. Reassured that someone cared, Lorraine asked the driver if they could go eat. Grumbling, he turned the bus and swung it out in front of the restaurant.

Fed and recharged, Lorraine reloaded the bus and settled into her seat for the night. The bus was warm and cozy. The other passengers and Lorraine chatted themselves blue in the face, with the four hour trip already turned into a twelve hour trip. Now they settled down to sleep. Who knew when they would arrive in Alameda?

A few hours later Lorraine awoke to discover herself back in the Denver station. The north side of the highway had opened and the bus driver, bored with staying in Waltonburg, and wanting to go home, went back to Denver, taking all of his passengers with him! Spending the rest of the night in the crowded, noisy bus station, Lorraine wondered, "OK, God, I am laughing a bit now, too. I can see this trip to Alameda is to be an adventure in faith for me!"

Morning came and with it a new driver. The passengers reloaded the bus and tried to go south on the highway again. They made it half way to their destination when the driver announced he was going west there instead of going south to Waltonburg where the road was closed again. The way the bus driver chose took them through rough mountains, but she knew the route and this mountain highway. If followed correctly, it would take them to Alameda.

Hmmmmmmmmmmmm. A wrong turn resulted in a very long trip over a dangerous cliff hanger pass in a blizzard without tire chains. Lorraine, who had once again been lulled to sleep, woke up as the bus slid to the edge of the cliff and knew this was not the way to Alameda in south central Colorado. Instead signs showed they were now on the western slope and heading for Utah. High in the highest peaks of Colorado, Lorraine knew they were lost as the bus took that wrong fork, but the bus driver never said a word. Hunched over the steering wheel as they slipped over that icy pass no bus should have been on, the driver refused to listen to her concerns. Once again she asked the Lord, "Exactly what lesson am I learning?"

Lorraine could not call Derrick, for the cell phone would not work in them thar' hills. She could only pray he was not frightened that she had failed to show up…again.

The bus driver finally stopped at a convenience store and discovered the way back to where they belonged without going back over that dangerous pass. They had gone three hours of good highway driving out of the way, and they were driving in a blizzard with icy roads. Late into the night, Lorraine saw the lights of Alameda and the tears finally came. They had been on the road 48 hours to cover a five hour trip. Pulling into the bus station, Lorraine saw Derrick unfolding his muscular body from a small white car, black cowboy hat crowning his receding reddish-brown hair. Dressed for the bitter cold, he looked like a strong lumberjack...just what she needed after such a bizarre ride.

As she appeared out of the bus door, Derrick ran toward her with open arms. Enveloping her in a bear hug, he cried, "I thought you were in a wreck! I thought you were dead!" It was then she realized that he was crying.

"We got lost in the mountains after the driver decided to take the secondary route here. We almost made it to Grand Junction before he realized he was lost and turned around. My phone wouldn't work because we went over the Divide. I'm sorry you were scared! I knew God was with us. I prayed you wouldn't be afraid." she hugged him tight, and then she kissed him. She did not want to ever let him go.

He looked up to see the bus driver staring at them and grinning...those two "Old fogies" were acting like teenagers. Suddenly letting out a deep chuckle, Derrick laughed, "Best we get your bags and let that lost bus driver go home now."

Sliding on solid ice, they approached the gaping bus side where Lorraine's luggage had been dumped. Teeth chattering in the minus thirty degree night, Lorraine took the smaller case while Derrick grabbed her big one and loaded it into the trunk of his little white car.

"Welcome to the Arctic," he laughed, "Coldest day in history for Alameda. My! Did you have to bring the north down with you?"

Lorraine laughed in return and slid into her seat. "Had to have some reason to hold you tight," she grinned back at him.

Thawing her fingers in front of the car heater, Lorraine listened as Derrick chattered about his life in Alameda. Finally warm, she reached over and placed her hand on his knee as he drove. Derrick looked at her and smiled, his eyes shining.

In that moment Lorraine knew. She had to return to her re-entry point to re-enter life. God had sent her on this crazy, wild ride that she might understand His plan to get her here afraid enough to stay long enough to see she belonged somewhere now that Allison was in college!

In the weeks that followed, Lorraine had to wait until the severe weather abated so that the mountain pass could be opened for travel again. She learned more and more how this new chapter of her life was to open....a gentler chapter where her memories would simply slip into the warp and weave of a woven quilt of life....to become a thing of beauty and singing, not something that terrified her in the night. Peace began to settle over her as she remembered a promise God had given her as a teen ager who had never even seen a mountain at that time. The mountains would give her peace. She had found his peace in this mountain place...a peace she had often longed for but never found anywhere else.

The day the pass cleared was sun-sparkling perfect. Lorraine made her journey back to Badger. It was not a time of leaving but of going to prepare. Her children waited there for her, and she must make preparations for leaving them. Most of all, she knew they needed reassurance that she no longer needed their vigilant watching. God had given Lorraine back her life. Yes, it was much different than before, but she was content. He had re-grown her wings, and she knew, she knew, she was ready to fly.

Spring came and with it Lorraine and Derrick's wedding. Derrick and Lorraine decided to stay in Alameda while he finished the schooling he had started upon his retirement. Then they would probably move back to better visiting distance of Badger.

Life was becoming a predictable pattern again. In the mean time visits were carefully orchestrated back and forth to avoid the perilous weather Lorraine had first been caught in while on that bus trip. Derrick and Lorraine began to share joy with Autumn, Ariana and Allison as they learned to coordinate Derrick's crazy schedule and Lorraine's continued medical needs.

A year into the marriage, that joy seemed extra bright. "Girls are coming!" Derrick announced happily as he crawled from the covers into the cold March morning air. Lorraine looked up as he tousled her hair and smiled. Yes, her girls were coming. Her precious girls that she missed so much her heart ached were coming!

Throwing her legs over the edge of the bed, she caught Derrick's sound morning kiss before quoting loudly, "This is the day the Lord has made, let us rejoice and be glad in it!" Then she began singing, "I have decided to follow Jesus," and headed for the kitchen. Soon the aroma of coffee and bacon filled their small, old house. Though a bit weather-beaten, this was her new home where she felt loved and wanted, something she never expected to experience so late in life.

Breakfast dishes were barely done when Lorraine heard tires crunch on the driveway. Magpie voices blended as her daughters' voices always seemed to chatter when they were excited. "My girls!" she cried and almost jumped through the door to greet them.

Allison reached the door first, leaning over her tall frame to swallow her mother in a big hug. "Momma! Momma!" she giggled and kissed Lorraine. Allison's smile crinkled her true almond-shaped eyes, a reminder of her Native American heritage.

Ariana and Autumn followed with hugs and kisses. Then Allison surprised Lorraine by voicing all three's thoughts. "We only have one request while we are here," she stated.

"And what can that be?" Lorraine asked, suspecting a ride

on the local steam engine train as the answer. They had teased about this luxury for months.

Instead Autumn said softly, "Finish your story, Momma, we want to hear the rest of your childhood story. We want to know Rainee better. And we want to finally find out why that door closed in your mind."

Lorraine reached out and hugged her eldest tight. "Of course, honey," she nodded. "I will be glad to tell you as much as I can remember. I am so at peace with my childhood now." Her still dark blonde hair waved recklessly in the strong Colorado breeze. She absently ran her fingers through its mass. Lorraine would finally tell the end of the tale that had haunted her adult life.

"It is really warm today, sweethearts. Tell you what, why don't you all gather under the elms and I will bring out rolls and milk?" Lorraine suggested.

Settled in the cushioned patio chairs, the girls waited expectantly. Derrick came and kissed Lorraine good-bye as he headed into his office to work, a bit of concern on his face. "Don't tell it if it is too hard, honey," he whispered. "I want you to enjoy today."

Lorraine smiled up at him and nodded. "It's Okay. The children know the warp of my story. Now I must tell them the weave." Settling back against her chair cushion, Lorraine looked into the eyes of her daughters, one at a time. Finally, she smiled slowly and began:

"My art teacher and her husband were wonderful to me....My pastor and his wife were so kind to me when I was in high school. They became my family when my father and mother forsook me. I came to call them Dad and Mom over time." Lorraine, however, could hear Rainee itching to be heard in her mind. Ah, her childhood self should tell the story. That is what was needed...

Chapter 2: Never Cry Again, Rainee

It was the end of third grade for Rainee. This tiny blond child had become a favorite for Mrs. Strong. She knew she needed love and gave it freely. The teacher leaned her gray head close to Rainee's to tell her she loved her and looked forward to seeing her again next fall. Tears in her eyes, Rainee reached up and hugged Mrs. Strong. "I don't like summers," she whispered, "Can't I just go to school all year long?"

Mrs. Strong looked at her oddly. "No child hates summer break!" she exclaimed, but Rainee simply looked at her sadly. "I am sorry, Rainee, summer is here and no one goes to school in the summer. Maybe you will get to do something fun or go on vacation to some place fun this summer!"

"What's a vacation?" Rainee wondered as she joined Jenna and her other sisters for the long walk across the small rural town they now lived in somewhere in central Indiana. Her father had gone back to school and now ran a shop where he fixed the outsides of cars. He said it was a body shop, but she had never seen any dead bodies there.....so why call it a body shop?

The shop was actually a run-down shed her dad rented that had two giant front doors you could drive a car into. Inside, to one side, Mama had developed a "living" area with an old couch, an old refrigerator and a stove. They were now living in a condemned, ramshackle house out in the country but never went there before dark. All waking hours were spent at the shop working and helping.

Arriving that day in front of the unpainted dilapidated building, Rainee pulled an ancient bicycle out from behind the one giant door. The bike was adult-size and had no brakes. Rust oozed from every inch of its ancient body, but Rainee did not care. It was a bike! She had learned to ride on this bike and spent most of the daylight hours at the shop cruising up and down the neighborhood streets, shouting for little kids to stay out of the way because she could not stop! Today was no exception. Up and down the street she rode, never seeming to tire. With the wind kissing her face as if with gentle abandonment, Rainee felt totally isolated from her world...and hence, totally at peace.

With darkness coming, she knew Mama would have something to eat on the stove in the shop. Rainee quit peddling so the bike would slow down. Dragging one foot, she slowly brought the bike to a halt in front of the garage that now gleamed with indoor lights.

Suddenly Eileen jumped at her from out of the on-coming gloom while Rainee still straddled the old bike. "Where have you been?" She hissed in a voice that sounded eerily like the hiss of her mother's often-used tone. "I wanted to ride the bike today! Instead I got to do all the work!"

Rainee tipped the bike handles toward Eileen and mumbled, "Sorry." She never crossed Eileen if she could help it because Eileen was mean. Eileen was often beaten beyond recognition and then would find Rainee and beat her up, as she said, so she could feel the pain, too. Today was no exception. Before Rainee could jump off the bike she felt Eileen's hard fist in her stomach.

Gasping as if she would never be able to get air again, Rainee doubled over, the wind knocked completely out of her. Finally, a whistle of air passed through her mouth and the wind returned enough for her to begin to cry as pain enveloped her.

"Stupid baby, shut up!" Eileen cried, her small eyes blazing in the near darkness. She pushed her face up close to Rainee's with a menacing look. Rainee released the old bike then. It clattered to the gravel drive as she ran into the shop, still holding her painful stomach.

"Eileen hurt me," she gasped at her mother, who stood stirring stew on the stove. Her mother, however, never stopped stirring, simply sliding her eyes over to where Rainee stood crumpled over the end of the old olive-green sofa.

"My stomach really hurts," she whimpered, trying once again to get the help she needed.

In that moment Eileen appeared behind her. "Oh, man," she cried, distain dripping like acid from her voice, "Rainee is such a big baby. I didn't touch her. She was hogging the bike, so I told her to get off. She is just crying because I yelled at her!"

Their father, busily sanding the hood of a car with an electric sander, had stopped the awful, teeth shattering, grinding noise just in time to hear Eileen's speech. Suddenly his face twisted into that of a venomous snake as he struck out with his voice at Rainee, "I will teach you not to be such a baby, Rainee! I will teach you not to cry! When we get home, I will teach you not to cry!" He screamed nonsensically until his face looked purple and bloated like a dead fish. He only stopped when the owner of the shop, Mr. Bailey, walked noisily into the shop, asking for a word with him.

Rainee thought she was safe. Mr. Bailey no doubt heard the threats and came to her aid. She was grateful as she forgot dinner and escaped into the darkness outside. She continued walking until she found herself back at the school playground a mile away. There, she sat down on a chain and board swing and began to swing. Rhythmically she pumped and forgot her pain......she forgot about dad, Eileen, and the threats. The rhythm of the swing as it moved through the air gave her calm and a sense of control...she would be OK, she thought, she would be OK. Then she began to pray, something she often did when she was alone because she knew God was with her.

"Dear God, please, keep me alive. I want to grow up and live for you and do whatever it is you have kept me alive to do. Please, let me know you are with me. Just keep me alive."

Soon she heard the chugging of the ancient motor inside

the flat-bed truck her father drove. He pulled into the playground, followed by a shiny-new 1962 Olds green and white sedan. Her uncle and aunt (her mother's brother and his wife) and their children had come to town for a visit. Relieved, Rainee jumped while the swing was at the top of its arch, easily landing on both feet as if she was a cat. Pleased with her jump, she ran to the car and asked if she could ride home with her cousins. Her uncle gladly assented. The two vehicles pulled out onto the road and proceeded down the gravel roads seven miles out into the nothingness where the condemned house stood in the woods, away from everyone in the whole world.

At home, Mama and her aunt started chatting about making popcorn and snacks. Her aunt had brought cherry Jell-O with bananas in it...her favorite. She also had a cake...it was pink...Now Rainee wondered how in the world one made a cake pink but did not have the courage to ask. Her aunt was forever trying to make food look fancy, something Rainee did not understand. She just wanted enough to feel full!

It was a shock, therefore, when the play the cousins instantly began upon arrival was interrupted by her father, once more in his rage. He bore down upon her, looking as if he would devour her with his bulging blue eyes. When he grabbed her arm, she twisted and tried vainly to escape, "No, you don't, little brat!" he cried as if seizing a great prize. "Remember, I told you I would teach you not to cry!"

With that he ordered everyone to leave the house except Rainee. Her aunt, obviously afraid, gave her a worried look but followed her children out of the door, seeming anxious to get her own children out of reach. Alone with her bellowing father, Rainee held her breath until she felt faint. She watched as her father removed his wide leather belt from his waist with his right hand, still grasping her thin arm with his left, as if afraid his prey would escape. She knew she would not escape this beating. For some reason, she must endure it.

Closing her eyes, Rainee began to pray, moving her lips silently as the blows began. The belt buckle cut mercilessly into her back, her bottom, her legs, time and time again, until the marks bled and the pain became unbearable, but she did not cry. Never again would she cry when her father was present. She must be strong and endure....that she might escape.

Perhaps dad had chosen to perform such an exacting beating that day because he had a caged audience. Frozen with the shock of it all, her Aunt and Uncle simply stood in the doorway and watched, their own children peeping in horror from behind their parents. Rainee prayed that they would ask him to stop, but no one moved. Why would they not help her?

Finally exhausted, Rainee's father let the belt fall at his side and released her arm. "Oh, Lord," she prayed as she stumbled from the room, "Just let me live. Just let me live to grow up and get away from here."

Barely looking at her relatives that had failed her; she slid between them and out the door. Rainee made for her safe haven, the woods, bobcats and all. Even bobcats did not scare her tonight. She was safer there. A sympathetic whimper reassured her that her beloved dog, Buttons, was at her side as she ran on bleeding legs, until the woods enclosed her.

Sobbing, she climbed into her safe beechnut tree with its welcoming arms and there cried herself to sleep. Buttons wandered below, keeping her safe. Later Jenna would apply iodine and doctor her so her wounds would heal, leaving scars that would fade over the years. But her father had been right......he had taught her to never cry again while she was a child. She would never cry again in a way that he would find out, because she knew she needed to do this to survive. Jesus wanted her to survive, so she must do what she had to do to survive....and today she knew she was indeed strong enough to do just that...to survive.

Chapter 3: Rainee's First Job

Rainee sat in her new fifth grade classroom, listening to the teacher, Mrs. McMannis, as she talked about President Eisenhower, their current president. The teacher told about his childhood. Rainee absent-mindedly smoothed the sides of her long blonde ponytail. The teacher's story was interesting and old news because Rainee had spent last night reading the President's biography after teacher said she was going to talk about him today.

"Rainee," Mrs. McMannis smiled at her, realizing why she was losing her brightest student, "Can you tell the class how President Eisenhower almost lost his leg when he was a child?"

Rainee grinned back at the teacher. She and the teacher understood each other. "He got hurt on his knee. The cut got blood poisoning that poisoned his whole leg," she answered.

"Very good!" Mrs. McMannis praised her.

Recently when Mrs. McMannis saw how undernourished Rainee was, she got Rainee the job of delivering milk to the classrooms. She was paid fifty cents a week plus all the milk and hot lunch she wanted. The milk delivery man got to know Rainee as she stood by the school door each day waiting for the milk to be delivered, too.

One day as Rainee headed out of the classroom to deliver the milk cartons, Mrs. McMannis handed her a small note. "The principal said I might choose you as one of the children who might benefit from art lessons. We have a new art teacher for a few students. After milk recess, go down the hall next to the library. Your art teacher will be waiting for you. Her name is Mrs. Washington. .

Rainee took the slip of paper and put it in her skirt pocket. She turned and skipped out of the room. Milk…freedom…and art lessons, too. All for Rainee. School was wonderful. In the milk room, Rainee picked up the first graders' milk crate and put it into the red wagon she used for delivery. The little kids got their milk first because teacher said they needed it sooner. After all her deliveries were finished, Rainee replaced the wagon in the blue milk room's far corner.

She turned down the hall toward the library. Stepping into the new classroom, Rainee was surprised to see a very tiny lady with the longest red hair she had ever seen. No other students were present yet. The teacher turned from the drawing she was making with chalk on a pad of paper when she heard Rainee bang into a student desk.

"Hello," the teacher smiled. Gazing intently at Rainee, she finally said, "You must be Rainee. I can tell by that lovely blonde hair." (Never would she humiliate Rainee by pointing out she could tell Rainee was the poor waif of the school by her dirty face and torn, unkempt clothes.) "I am Mrs. Washington, your new art teacher."

"Yes," Rainee swallowed, suddenly as nervous as a cat facing a dog, "My name is Rainee. I am from Mrs. McMannis's class.

"OK, Miss Rainee," Mrs. Washington smiled, "Why don't you open that desk and take out the supplies inside it. Time to get creative!"

Chapter 4:
Finding Hope—Mrs. Washington Becomes Rainee's Friend

Rainee sat in the sun-filled art classroom quietly coloring a picture she had drawn, her little face puckered like a dried orange peel as she concentrated intently. She reached up impatiently to brush wisps of straight, shiny blonde hair that escaped her ponytail, fruitlessly trying to keep the stray strands out of her eyes. Biting her full red upper lip, she grasped the bright green crayon between her index and middle finger, using her thumb to guide it. Then she realized someone was watching her.

"Rainee," the art teacher asked so quietly only Rainee could hear, "Let me show you how to hold the crayon so you can have the prettiest picture in the room!" The art teacher took the green crayon in her petite, freckled hand, and bending her tiny frame over Rainee's desk, she grasped the crayon between her thumb and forefinger.

"See, Lorraine," Mrs. Washington gently coaxed. "This is how to hold your crayon and then color lightly like this." Rainee watched as the teacher moved her wrist back and forth to make smooth, one-direction color strokes.

She whispered to the teacher, "I would like to color like that but I can't hold a crayon, or a pencil, that way. My fingers don't work right."

Mrs. Washington looked in surprise at the child. "Here," she held out the green crayon, "You hold the crayon the way you can, and I will show you how to make the color strokes that way."

Rainee took the crayon and returned it to her right hand, cradling it between her index and middle fingers, balancing it with her thumb. Then Mrs. Washington softly enclosed her hand over Rainee's dirty one. She guided Rainee's hand in single, one-way strokes of color.

"What a beautiful artist you are!" she chortled, as Rainee

finished the picture, using the new strokes. She hugged the frail child and then moved on to another child.

Rainee looked down with eyes wide in wonder at her picture. Indeed, it was the most beautiful she had ever colored. A wide smiled crept across her face until she had to open her mouth to smile, showing her crooked teeth. "See, God, "she prayed, "I can make something beautiful!"

She felt God's smile and love as she stroked the picture with her right hand. Then she startled, for she once more heard the still, small voice of the angel. "She will help you," the voice said, "she will help you to escape."

Rainee looked around to be sure no one else noticed the angel. Finally she whispered, "How?" she asked.

"In God's time," the angel responded and then was gone.

Complete peace enveloped Rainee as she took out a sheet of plain drawing paper and began a new picture. Furtively, as she colored, she watched Mrs. Washington move lovingly, but efficiently, from student to student. Teacher would help her. She would not always be alone anymore.

Rainee looked forward to each new art class. When the classroom teacher would announce it was art day and for the students to transfer to the art class, Rainee would fly to the beginning of the line the motley group of fifth graders were making. She would get to see Mrs. Washington again today! Maybe today she would show her how to get away from the pain and abuse she suffered daily at home. Only the hour would pass, and once again no answers would come.

The year passed, and Rainee was transferred to another school in the district because school boundaries had been changed. Rainee spent the next two years at this new school where there was no art class…and no Mrs. Washington. At first, she held out hope that the art teacher would find her and tell her how to get away from her family. As time passed and Mrs. Washington failed to materialize, Rainee began to forget what the angel said. She never forgot Mrs. Washington, though, because of the love and compassion she had shown her.

In sixth grade her new teacher insisted that Rainee start going by Lorraine. Rainee was a rather silly nickname, she told Rainee. Rainee never liked this teacher but concentrated on her studies. She watched in the broken mirror at home as she began puberty with no explanations from anyone. Hmmm. Maybe she was becoming an adult.

Seventh grade came. She began junior high school where students moved from one class to another and had six different teachers. Rainee soon discovered she knew all the material being taught and became bored. Randomly she began to write…first stories and then poetry. Then one day her English teacher, the short brown-haired Mrs. Baxley, happened to walk by her desk while Rainee was writing a poem. She suddenly stopped and unexpectedly called out in a voice full of joy and excitement, "That poem is wonderful! Who taught you to write poetry?"

Rainee looked up into the wide blue eyes of Mrs. Baxley, a confused look on her face. "God did," she said quietly.

Mrs. Baxley pinched her lips together until they turned an even brighter red than her lipstick, and then finally spoke. "He is a good teacher," she commented matter-of–factly. "May I see your poem?" She reached out her hand, fingers tipped in red nail polish. Rainee, her face turning bright red from her neck to the roots of her still blond hair that was now curled and laid softly on her neck, hesitantly picked up her paper and handed it to the teacher.

"Class," the teacher called out loudly as she strolled to the front of the classroom with Rainee's paper in her right hand, "Class, quiet, please," she called again upon reaching her desk. The feet shuffling stopped and all students' eyes turned expectantly toward the teacher, whose face looked as if she had just won first place in jam making at the county fair.

"Today," Mrs. Baxley said in a warm, happy tone as a smile spread across her pale face, "Today I have discovered we have a genuine writer in our midst! I want you all to listen as I read her poem she just wrote."

Shocked, Rainee looked at her teacher and violently shook her head to try to tell the teacher not to read her poem. Mrs. Baxley ignored her and began her poem called, "The Emerald Green Sea." Here it is:

> I stand beside the lovely endless sea,
>   That sea of sparkling emerald green;
> And wish I could sail eternally
>   To where God's brilliant sunset is seen.
>
> I find myself listening to crashing
>   Waves, and run to dance on the white foam,
> As the waves beat, loudly calling,
>   "Onward, forward, sail eternally home."

"Rainee," Mrs. Baxley waved a hand in Rainee's direction, "You are the best writer I have had the privilege of having in my class. I would like to invite you in front of the whole class to serve as my Creativity Editor for the school paper."

Rainee, mouth gaped open, looked at Mrs. Baxley stunned. No important job ever came to Rainee at school. Her good grades allowed her to be tolerated by her teachers. But her ragged clothes and obviously dirty body always made barriers to being anything except the brunt of many student jokes and pranks. Mrs. Baxley was offering a path across those barriers, and Rainee did not know what to say. Instead, she breathed anxiously for several moments out loud.

"Do it, you ninny," she heard her friend, Peggy, whisper in a loud stage whisper. She looked at her homely, curly-haired friend's broad, friendly face behind glasses too large for her face.

"You think I should?" She asked Peggy out loud.

"Yes, yes," Several other children joined Peggy, chanting the word over and over.

Mrs. Baxley laughed and put up a hand to hush the class. Rainee looked at the teacher and formed, "OK," with her mouth.

Mrs. Baxley laughed again and then said, "Hallelujah! Thank you, Rainee! Please meet with me at lunch today to discuss your new job, OK?"

Rainee nodded and then Mrs. Baxley told the class to return to their work. Rainee, however, had completed the work in a matter of minutes. She took out clean paper and began her new poem, "The Tree." These two poems appeared in the year's first edition of the school paper. Rainee's name was prominently displayed beside them. The title, *Creativity Editor*, stood out in large letters beneath her name. Rainee had brought sunshine to a teacher's heart, and in so doing, she brought joy to her own.

Chapter 5: Mrs. Washington Comes To Help

Rainee stepped onto the noisy school bus a few weeks after becoming creativity editor. Her too-big brown boots made squeaky noises on the bus steps as she went up them. She knew no one wore these kinds of boots anymore, but they were all she had and the snow was deep today. On her bright blond hair she wore an old, European-style scarf in a bright print, the only protection of her head against the bitter Midwest cold. She pulled her brown tweed, too small coat as closed as she could as she passed down the loaded bus seats to the back of the bus. Her best friend waved that she had saved a seat for her.

Mary lived three houses from Rainee, but it was also four miles away. It took an hour to walk when Mary and Rainee would decide to play together....which tended to be every Saturday. Rainee loved Mary fiercely because she played with her even when other kids on the bus called Rainee names and made fun of her. Mary held out blue-mittened hands and pulled Rainee down onto the seat next to her, not caring that Rainee's dirty coat touched her brand new bright blue one.

"I have to tell you what our Sunday School teacher told us yesterday in Sunday School!" She spoke excitedly in a sing-sing voice as Rainee suddenly stared at her unbelievingly.

"You go to Sunday School?" She asked in disbelief, her blond eyebrows coming together in a quizzical look.

"Of course, doesn't everybody? My teacher picks me up because she lives next door." Mary stated, and then, before Rainee could answer, she rushed on breathlessly. "Our teacher is taking all of us to Clear Creek to a real toboggan run on Saturday to toboggan. Isn't that just fabulous???" She giggled.

Rainee, her eyes darting back and forth rapidly, began to think...remembering now her promise to God to return to church. "Do you think she would let me come to Sunday School? Do you think she would pick me up for Sunday School?" She demanded in a nervous, high-pitched voice.

"Sure, I don't know why not. Just call her," Mary said rather bewilderingly, looking at her friend and seeing her for the first time that morning. "Maybe if you call tonight you can go tobogganing, too. But don't you already go to Sunday School somewhere?" She asked unbelievingly.

"No, my mom and dad won't let me go. I went when I was really little for a while. That was when we lived in Florida. Maybe if your teacher will pick me up, they might let me go now, too." Rainee sounded hopeful and doubtful at the same time as tears came to her large gray eyes. Her full lips began to quiver. "What is your teacher's name?" She continued as the tears slipped down her cheeks. Mary patted her back in a chummy way.

"Mrs. Washington....you know, the art teacher...." Mary continued to talk but Rainee heard no more. Instead she heard the quiet voice of the angel, "She will help you. She will help you to escape." Overwhelmed, she hugged herself and closed her eyes so that Mary would not see the light in them. No one must know her secret. God was helping her once more and she felt a warm comfort envelop her.

The day passed too slowly for Rainee, but at last the bus pulled up in front of the condemned yellow house, trimmed in brown, where they now lived. The house only had one window in the front and the door had no screen. As Rainee stepped inside, she could smell the greens Mom was forever cooking.

Although she still did not like greens, she learned to eat them without complaining after her Home Economics teacher told her they would help her stay healthy. Today she could tell by the smell that they would have beet greens for supper. Rainee quickly checked the living room to see if anyone was seated there. Finding no one, she shimmied up to the wall where the only old fashioned dial telephone hung. She took down the receiver and quickly dialed the number Mary gave her.

Two short rings later a familiar, musical voice answered, "Helllllllllllooooooo...."

Rainee, her knees knocking and her voice shaking, started, "Mrs. Washington, Mary Rothersford gave me your number. She said you were her Sunday School teacher and might pick me up for Sunday School." Rainee stopped, all out of breath and waited.

"Well, honey," the sweet voice began, "I will if I can. Who are you and where do you live?"

A long pause followed and then Rainee, once more gaining courage, began, "This is Rainee. Rainee Perkins. I don't know if you remember me, but I had you for fifth grade art and now I am in seventh grade."

"Well, I'll be," the joyful voice responded, "Of course I remember you, Rainee. You are Lorraine. That is your real name, but you like everyone to call you Rainee, like when it rains." Then the musical voice chuckled, "How could I forget my best artist of that year?"

Warmed by her teacher's memory and compliment, Rainee pushed on, "I want to go to Sunday School. I really do. I met Jesus as a small child but my parents took me out of Sunday School. Now that I am big I want to go by myself. I live on Bounty Road, in that yellow house that is broken in two. Can you pick me up there?"

She heard Mrs. Washington catch her breath and mutter, "You poor child!" before catching herself and going back into her positive voice, "I will pick you up at 8:30 on Sunday, OK?"

"OK, I will be all ready!" Rainee accepted excitedly, forgetting all about Saturday's toboggan party, "And thank you! Thank you so much!" A moment of terror seized Rainee as she hung up the phone....now she had to face her parents.

Rainee tiptoed into the kitchen. Her mother stood over the big, cast iron worn sink peeling potatoes with a knife. Her once slim body was now swollen and sickly, and her curly permed brown hair now thin and streaked with gray. Rainee tiptoed over to her mother and touched her arm. "Mom," she said as matter-of-factly as she could with her voice shaking. "Mom, I am going to church on Sunday. My friend and teacher invited me....I am a big girl now...I should be able to choose for myself...and I am going."

Her mother looked up, her thin lips curled in a sneer, showing her toothless mouth, looking like an old hag from one of Grimm's fairy tales. "I suppose you will do that, too. You are just like your grandmother. Well, fine. I can't stop you. Go ahead and go. Just don't expect me to stop your dad from beating you when he finds out."

"I don't care anymore if he does," Rainee lied softly and ran quickly out of the back door before her mother could change her mind. She ran and she ran, through the snow-packed back garden to the one stall, broken down shed where Apache Bill waited for her.

Apache Bill was her small red pinto horse and the love of her life. Her dad had won him in a card game at the race track and had not known what to do with him, because he was not even halter-trained. Rainee and her older sister took care of that with patient hours of training. They had no saddle but taught him to let them ride him bareback. Now every day after school, she rode him no matter how cold it was that day.

"I'm going to Sunday School," she whispered into his soft red mane as she slipped the straight-bit bridle into his mouth and pulled the reins over his head. Apache snorted and pawed the ground, anxious to escape the tiny stall. "Want to run, do you?" Rainee giggled and led him to the block of wood she used to mount him.

The snow was too deep to ride him in the fields today, so

she guided him down the drive and into their almost-always vacant country road. Kicking him with her heels until he was in a full rolling gallop and the cold wind bit her reddened face, Rainee headed in the direction of Mary's house.....she must tell her the news.

In the following weeks and months, Mary and Rainee spent Sundays growing closer as Rainee became used to attending Sunday School once more. Winter turned to spring and soon the school year came to a close. Joy had re-entered Rainee's heart.

It was on this day that Rainee stood next to her favorite beechnut tree, deep in the hardwood forests of central Indiana. She often escaped here these days because home had become one abuse session after another. The constant buzz of a nearby honey bee hive floated to her on the gentle breeze. Smiling, she tossed her book up onto the nearest large, flat branch. She easily pulled her slender self onto its great expanse. Tossing her now waist-length blonde hair out of her face, she picked up her book, so eager to enter the world of her favorite characters that her gray eyes sparkled and a smile tugged at her lips.

Settling against the tree's smooth gray trunk, Rainee picked up her book and opened it to the marked chapter. Sunlight filtered through the beech's vast canopy of two-hundred year old branches that were covered with fresh, June green leaves. Momentarily, she lifted her eyes up to watch the streaks of sun play among these leaves. Then all else forgotten, she entered her book's world.

The sunlight slanted more and more, indicating the end of the afternoon, and the beginning of what Rainee called, "the golden hour;" This was the time just before sunset when the slant of the sun caused vast shadows and brilliant images of light on trees, buildings and the rest of her world—making everything look very 3-D. Rainee closed her book to revel in the rest of the day.

From just outside the woods, Apache nickered, reminding

her that they needed to ride home soon. She called to him, to remind him she was still there. "Just a few more minutes," she called, "We will ride in a few minutes."

Rainee slid down the trunk of the tree, book in hand. Landing with knees bent, she began her ritual dance around the open ground under the tree. Singing to nature's world, she voiced the joy that filled her heart with the coming of golden hour. She patted the tree trunk and told it thank you for a good rest and read. Then she skipped whole-heartedly out of the woods, singing as if she were a tree sprite herself, lost in the world, of gold and green.

Today, you see, was Rainee's last day of seventh grade. Her teachers had all praised her highly, commending her for her straight A's. Rainee had worked diligently for her position on the school paper. School was a good place to be. It was safe. It was warm. And her teachers seemed to love her. Oh, how she had loved school this year. She thought through memory after memory of the last nine months and knew she would always treasure this year in her heart.

This year she had also learned she could be well-liked by others her age. Thanks to her school paper involvement, her academic achievement and her involvement in school activities, she had made several good friends. Some even knew where she really lived and did not seem to care.

They came and played with her in the woods. She also walked the miles she needed to reach their homes, or she rode the bus to their house and their moms brought her home. She more and more felt free to forget life at home and its abuse. Instead, she played, laughed, and deepened her friendships. Some of these friendships would remain even in adulthood.

So Rainee danced from the woods, took up Apache's reins and swung onto his bare back with pure glee. Apache seemed to understand her mood and nickered eagerly as she nudged him into a cantor. Off and over the alfalfa fields they flew, the soft, warm June breeze tugging at Rainee's long hair. Sunset gloriously painted the sky, and yet they ran through the fields. Only when dark finally began to settle did Rainee turn Apache for home. It had been one of the best days of her life. She did not want it to end. But supper waited, and she must not anger Mother too much, or the evening would be too hard to bear.

Chapter 6: Rainee's Breaking Point

Summer was coming to a close and eighth grade loomed ahead. Rainee's Uncle and Aunt (her mother's brother and wife) called asking to come and play cards as one last summer get-together before school schedules made life too hectic. Rainee usually enjoyed these visits. The boy cousins now had a baby sister, whom Rainee was expected to entertain, but she enjoyed this task and did not complain. These were the only relatives Dad let come and visit them now. Rainee thought something odd that no one else could come, but they could.

Maple trees were just beginning to turn their brilliant reds, yellows and oranges the day the relatives arrived at the condemned house. This day was no different than many others for Rainee. She had spent the day riding Apache Bill in the meadows and visiting neighbor friends. All the neighbors knew her. The adults often supplied her with food and water as she roamed miles from home with no thought that children simply did not do this. She lived to be out-of-doors, to be as far away as possible. (One day she counted and realized she was fourteen miles from home. No matter. Apache Bill knew the way home).

Today Rainee set Apache Bill to run in a dead heat. The saddle-less rider grabbed a hand full of mane and plastered her body against that of her horse. Fly. She must fly! On and on they ran until the road ended abruptly at a fence and Apache Bill pulled up short, almost throwing her. Whinnying as if to say he was sorry, he turned at her touch and followed the fence west. She urged him once more into a cantor as they crested a long hill.

Snorting and shaking his head, Apache stopped at the top of the hill, knowing Rainee always wanted to stop at the top of hills. "Good boy, good sweetheart," Rainee crooned as she stroked his neck. Leaning fully forward, she hugged him around his sweaty neck. Apache gave her a reason to get up each day; joy in each afternoon, a friend she could always confide in, and a love she knew he shared. In a world where Rainee only knew pain, Apache was her real world.

Rainee drew a long draught of the acrid fall air into her lungs. Gazing around from her vantage point at the top of the hill, she felt a prayer come to her lips. Here was her chapel, her place to be close to God, Grandma's God.

In the time she had not darkened a church door, she still doggedly recited the Bible verses she had learned in Sunday School as a small child. And here in the wide open spaces, she sang her little Sunday School songs at the top of her lungs with only Apache and God to hear… "I have decided to follow Jesus…..no turning back, no turning back."

"I can tell you are here today, Jesus," she prayed out loud. Apache nickered as if in agreement, making Rainee smile. "Yes, God, I can feel you with me. Will you please find a way for me? "

Almost audibly she heard these words, "Be strong and of courage."

Rainee nodded, accepting the message. "I love you, Jesus," she shouted, and took a deep breath. "Isn't he wonderful, wonderful, wonderful? Isn't Jesus my Lord wonderful? Eyes have seen, ears have heard, 'tis recorded in God's Word, isn't Jesus my Lord wonderful!" She sang full of joy.

"Thank you, Lord, for meeting me here this day," she smiled up to heaven as her benediction. Reluctantly she turned towards home, for she knew the relatives would arrive any minute. Taking the road back, she arrived just as her kin folk pulled into the driveway.

Back at the shed, Rainee pulled Apache's bridle off and began brushing him. After she fed and watered him, she kissed him goodnight. Just as she finished her chores, she heard her boy cousins approach the shed.

"We want a ride. Uncle Peter says we can have a ride,"

they whined.

"Not tonight, Billy and Gene," she said patiently. "Apache had a long day today and is too tired to go out again. She carefully closed the door to Apache's stall, clicking the padlock behind her to discourage intrusion. She locked the stall door on purpose, because Dad beat Apache when she was not home if the lock was not in place. Now she locked it against this intrusion.

With the cousins still whining, she promised to play tag with them in the last light of the day. They finally agreed and moved toward the front yard, which was really a small field of uncut grass and weeds.

"Freeze tag, freeze tag!" Marta, one year younger then Rainee, called. She began to organize the game. Soon all but the new baby cousin were involved in a rollicking game that left children scrambling and giggling on the ground more often than not. Crystal, now eight, tagged Gene and everyone ran for the next round. And so darkness fell as the children's laughter echoed to neighboring farms.

Finally, Mother called that dinner was ready. Her Aunt had brought Jell-O and a pink cake again. Tired after a hard day of riding and playing, Rainee combed her fingers through her tousled long hair and pulled it into a pony tail. She then corralled the younger kids into the house. Last one in, she was just opening the screen door when she felt someone reach out and grab her by her right breast.

Dad pulled her back into the darkness faster than she could catch herself. "Let's see just how grown up you are," he snarled in a sinister voice as he grabbed both her breasts now.

Horror becoming pure anger brought instant strength into Rainee's usually small arms. She reached up and pummeled her father in his face. "Don't you ever grab me like that again!" She growled at him through gritted teeth. "And don't you ever touch me again," she added as he let go of her in surprise. "I will kill you the next time you touch me." Her voice was cold and menacing, not that of a child's. And she knew in her heart that childhood had taken its last breath in that moment. God had told her to be strong, and now He had given her the strength to fight. The battle for her very life had begun.

Lorraine startled as she finished this story and looked up at her children, for she realized that indeed this moment had marked a dreadful beginning to the next couple of years.

"I don't think I can go on," she began to cry as Ariana hugged her.

"Someday you will. Someday you will," Ariana said softly, "Until then, thank you for your story. You were a brave little girl, Momma."

Lorraine hugged each of her girls and went into the house for lunch preparations. Derrick joined them for sandwiches and lemonade. Then she and the girls returned to the lawn chairs. "I want to finish this today," She told her girls. "I think I need to finish my story now, while I still have the courage."

With this statement, Lorraine looked inward once more, asking her childhood self to take over the story telling. Rainee needed to know that others knew her story. She should tell it.

Chapter 7: Help Arrives For Rainee

Sitting in the broken down brown recliner, Rainee listened to the crash of canning jars from the kitchen amidst cursing and shouting. She knew why her mother and father were fighting so viciously. She had told them of her promise to go to Sunday School with Mrs. Washington tomorrow.

Her father was obviously opposed to Rainee's new habit of attending Sunday School with Mrs. Washington. His face held distain and contempt as he spat words at her mother. "Just you wait," he screamed, "She'll act like your other religious relatives and be holier than thou in no time! Or they will try to tell her we are bad people."

Rainee looked at the now guilty look on his face and wondered just how bad her father really was. She knew she was terrified of him because he hurt her a lot. How deep did the bad go? Her mother screamed back at her father that she saw no harm in Rainee going to church now that she was old enough to want to go alone. No one else had to go. (It was only as an adult that Rainee came to realize that somewhere deep down inside her mother did love her enough to stand up for her this one time. This realization would give her comfort.)

While her parents fought, Rainee sat embroidering a small table cloth imprinted with a wheat shaft pattern. She enjoyed creating things and had recently discovered how to transfer embroidery patterns onto cloth through lessons from her Aunt. Mother had also embroidered as a child and recently she had showed her how to make the stitches, giving her some much needed rare attention. Rainee realized this new activity together was probably why her mother defended her today. She found a way to reach her mother on a very small scale by insisting on going to Sunday School.

Mother finally walked determinedly into the living room, the broken floor beam groaning under her weight. "You are twelve.

You are old enough to know your own mind now. If you go to church, we don't want to hear anything about it or God or anything around here. Do you understand?"

Her mother had no idea that Rainee still secretly read the Bible she had won in Sunday School in Florida, or that she prayed when she was on her long walks or pony rides. No one knew. She was well aware this part of her life had to be kept secret.

Rainee told her mother she could keep quiet, and began a herringbone stitch. She heard the back door slam as her Dad left the kitchen incensed. That alone left her shaking inside like a leaf in the wind. She gritted her teeth, though, resolving to carry through on this chance to return to church. Five long years had passed since she'd attended church and heard people talk about God's love. She hungered to hear it once more.

Picking up the old black wall phone next to her chair, Rainee called Mrs. Washington to tell her she would be ready in the morning to once again go to church. Her teacher, obviously pleased with Rainee's message, reminded her to be ready by eight thirty. Rainee was a good addition to her Sunday School class, and she enjoyed her company on the ride there.

Sunday came bright and sunny into the uncurtained window beside Rainee's cot in the attic. She carefully dressed the best she could in her old dress, making as little noise as possible so as not to waken anyone.

Leaving her shoes off, she tiptoed down the stairs. Grabbing a piece of cheese and bread, she slipped out of the sleeping house by the old kitchen door, careful to close it slowly so that it would not creak. Slipping her shoes and the old rubber boots on, for it was cold, and then her old tweed coat; she quietly skirted the old yellow house that leaned into its middle.

Taking a seat on a concrete slab in the front "yard," Rainee ate her bread and cheese. She had no idea what time it was, but the sun sent diamonds over the snow banks all around the house.

When finished eating, Rainee pulled on her thick woolen mittens, for her hands were beginning to get very cold.

Shivering, she stood and began to walk down their long driveway to the road to warm up better. Her father plowed the long driveway with a fifty year old tractor a neighbor gave him. She was especially glad today that he had plowed yesterday, because she could stay dry while scooting to the road's edge.

The plowing had left several feet of snow piled high on either side of the driveway. The road itself was plowed down to the icy glare that always covered the dirt surface in January. The ice glowed in sunlight's yellow, making Rainee smirk. This afternoon she would get to ice skate on the road. It was only smooth enough to do this a few times a year. Eileen and Jenna would no doubt join her in the skating. Whooping up and down the mile-long expanse, the afternoon would be full of fun.

Thoughts of her older sisters brought a troubled look to Rainee's face. Both girls had changed a lot lately. Neither smiled much anymore. Both looked frightened all the time. Jenna was sixteen and Eileen fifteen, and Mother said they were just being teen-agers. But none of their friends seemed so scared and solemn. Eileen did not even talk anymore. Instead she shook constantly with eyes darting as if they would leave her head.

Once Rainee asked her what was wrong and Eileen had slugged her hard in the head. "Don't ask me! I can't tell you!" she screamed and walked away.

Rainee kept her silent counsel today as every day, simply pondering what must be wrong with Eileen and Jenna. Instead, she began to watch down the icy road for a car that would come and take her to church.

Chapter 8: Rainee in God's House

Today, Rainee thought, was the most important day of her recent life, but it filled her with fear. After years of being alone in her faith in God, she had returned to Sunday School. And today she would stay for worship service for the very first time. Would they accept her? Had it been too long?

At the sound of the purr of a nice car engine, Rainee pulled her coat tighter and looked down the road. "Hi, Rainee," her teacher called as she opened the car door to let Rainee in out of the freezing weather. "Room for you in the back seat!" Rainee climbed into the crowded back seat where several other girls her age were sitting, talking and giggling. One was her best friend, Mary.

God had finally answered Rainee's years of petitions that somehow he would return her to church, where she might get some support for her walk of faith. As the weeks passed, Rainee and Mrs. Washington became very close. This teacher, who did not seem to fear her parents, became her rescuer, her hero, and someone to love her once more. Rainee came to rededicate herself to Christ in that little country church. She knew God had always been close to her, but now she felt stronger in her faith as she learned more about Him.

As time passed, Mrs. Washington and her husband would take her on outings with their own family, and she would spend weeks with them. The following two summers she joined them at Christian camps at Mrs. Washington's expense. Rainee happily soaked up the love and attention that Mrs. Washington and Dell Washington offered her.

Sometimes when things were really bad at home, Rainee walked the four miles to Mrs. Washington's house and found peace. No one ever told her to go home. On one such a jaunt, she found only Dell home, as Mrs. Washington had a work commitment. He simply opened the door and told her he was making grilled cheese. Would she like a grilled cheese?

Delighted, Rainee nodded her head and watched the huge, clumsy farmer carefully put together the sandwich for her. Sandwich and a glass of milk for each, he seated her at a table surrounded by paintings that Mrs. Washington had done. As they ate, he told her about each picture, much to Rainee's fascination. Rainee asked him what kind of a farmer he was, and he explained he had a large dairy herd. The kids helped now that they were teen-agers, but it kept them busy every daylight hour! Sometimes the work even lasted all night.

Dell was a kind, gentle man, as different from her Dad as she could imagine. She knew he loved her as his own, and that she was safe when she was with him. He never criticized her, but he would tell her he was glad God loved her, and he loved her too….just like Grandma used to say.

Mrs. Washington and Dell had five children of their own. Three were grown and away from home. Terry was a senior in high school and loved to tease her in a pleasant, loving way. Connie was one year older than Rainee but went out of her way to let her know she was her friend. One son was going to Bible school to become a preacher. He went on to pastor very successfully and become a leader in the denomination. God had made sure Rainee was mentored by a family who loved Him, and had great big hearts to love her, too.

It was not until many years later when Rainee attended Mrs. Washington and Dell's 50th wedding anniversary party that she really understood how much reaching out to her had cost this family. "You were such a wild thing when you came into our lives," Dell told her. "Almost like a little animal with no idea what humanity was really about. At times I wondered if all our love and attention would really help you. Your family was really scary, too. But I look at you now and praise God! In my humanness I never dreamed God would take that little wild child and make her into this beautiful lady serving God today. You certainly were worth every drop of love and energy God asked us to put into you, Our Little Wild Child."

Jarred back to the present for a moment, Lorraine smiled while thinking of her sweet mentors, Mrs. Washington and Dell. As tears filled her eyes, she dwelled on that now remembered anniversary day and thanked them for never giving up on her. Lorraine still loved them so much even though she had grown children and the Washingtons were now in heaven. Few people exist who can give the way they gave to little Rainee. Few people would want to even get involved in such terrifying circumstances.

Chapter 9: Rainee's School Dance

Rainee stood nervously in front of the old cracked mirror in the attic. With slightly shaking hands she pulled at the collar of her heavy lavender dress. She had found it in a box of clothes a church gave them recently. The dress fit and was lovely, but it was made of wool. And today was a very warm May 28th. But it did not matter. She had no other dress to wear, and she was determined to attend the eighth grade graduation dance. She needed to at least not look shabby, and this dress looked new.

Patting her well-curled shoulder length blonde hair, she started down the stairs when she heard Jenna start her "new" car...a 1958 Olds. It, too, looked like it belonged in a throw-away bag, but it gave them transportation without having to ride on the back of that open farm truck.

Slamming the screen door behind her, Rainee climbed into the back seat of the car. "Got your lipstick on?" Jenna joked, for she had loaned Rainee her lipstick to wear for the first time. Then she turned around and looked at Rainee. "Hmmmm. A bit too bright for you, but oh, well!"

Rainee self-consciously touched her lips as Jenna laughed. The lipstick did seem a bit too much!

Arriving at the junior high school gym, Jenna let Rainee out and told her she would be back at nine o'clock, when the dance ended. Rainee made her way through the crowds and into the gym, her eyes searching for anyone she knew.

Music ripped through the room as a teacher put records on a hi-fi. Everyone seemed to be laughing and giggling. Finding two friends, she was soon talking and giggling, too.

The principal stood up at the front of the gym to make announcements when the first song ended. Then he spoke loudly into the squeaky mike. "OK, kids, let's get this dance started! Line up for the grand march!"

He looked around a bit apprehensively. Then suddenly his eyes fell on Rainee. "Ah, yes, Miss Perkins, you will head the girl's line as school paper editor." Rainee began to look faint but his eyes had wandered on to where the boys were grouped.

"Yes, yes," the principal huffed happily, "Mike, you are here. Mike, as class president you will head the boy's line. So let's line up!"

Mike glanced Rainee's way with a curl on his lip. At the top of his lungs he shouted, "I can't be her partner!"

"Why ever not?" the principal challenged him.

"You want me to be a laughing stock?" he asked derisively.

Totally embarrassed, Rainee blushed and looked at her feet. Then anger took over, and finally a cold resolve. She walked across the gym floor and took her place at the head of the girl's line. She was school paper editor. She had been good at it. She was an excellent student. No one was going to make her feel ashamed.

Several girls began to twitter and ask her where she got the rag she wore, but Rainee stood firm. Some girl called out that her grandmother had that dress years ago and the crowd whooped. Still, Rainee stood firm.

The principal pulled at his stiff collar, not quite knowing what to do. Looking at Rainee's face, he realized she was resolved to follow through on his instructions. The principal turned to Mike, and said, "I guess she is a bigger person than you are."

The insult worked. Chagrined, Mike stepped forward and lined up next to Rainee. "We will see about that!" he shouted at the crowd.

Sliding his eyes sideways, he looked at Rainee's face.

Tears were creeping down her rosy cheeks, but she stared straight ahead. He took her hand and led her across the entire gym floor, beginning to wonder if his cruelty had been necessary.

As they heard hoots from his supposed friends, he felt the tension in Rainee's fingers. "I'm sorry," he whispered so only she could hear. "I thought you didn't care that people hurt you. Now I know you do. I don't want to be one of them anymore."

Rainee turned to look at the almost frightened face of Mike. In a firm but caring voice, she began speaking to the most popular boy in her class for the first time, "I am a good person, Mike. I respect others. I work hard and get straight A's. I am proud of my work on the paper. After school I tutor younger homeless kids. I know how hard it will be for them to move forward, because it has been hard for me. I want to give them hope. I know I will go to college no matter what anyone says. I will make something good of myself. These things you do not know because you have never bothered to even talk to me. Yes, you hurt me a lot. I never get used to being the brunt of kids' jokes around here. I am just glad you seem to have a heart. Thank you for your apology. I accept. That took a lot of courage."

They danced on making small talk until the grand march music ended. Then taking her hand from Mike's, Rainee escaped outdoors. Leaning against an ancient oak tree beside the school, she gave in to the pain inside her. As wave after wave of sobs rolled over her, she finally wore herself out.

Returning to the school, Rainee went into the gym locker room to wash her face and comb her hair. Several girls stood at the sinks staring at her. Finally one came forward. "That was a brave thing to do," she said and then slipped out the door.

Her time to be brave was over for now, she thought. She would relax and enjoy time with her friends. What she did not know was that her time for being the butt of jokes was also over. She had gained a hero-worshipper in Mike. He would begin to weave tales of her bravery, her kindness; her caring that changed the children's outlook on her for good. In so doing, he, too, became her hero.

Chapter 10: Returning to the Hunt

Gathering her courage, Lorraine finally let Rainee tell her daughters about that terrible day in the swamp.

It was late fall just before Rainee turned fourteen. Rainee followed her father out the front door of their house at his order. He had announced to the family that he was going deer hunting today. Usually he took Jenna or Eileen, but he thought it was time for Rainee to find out what it was like to hunt deer.

Having gone on bird hunts before, Rainee was not scared of the prospect of deer hunting. She was, therefore, surprised when Jenna and Eileen gave her frightened glances and then begged their father to take one of them. "No," he snarled, "It is Rainee's turn."

Rainee followed her father deep into the cedar swamp shaking her cold hands and stomping her cold feet. Deep in the woods he put out a hand and told her to sit beneath a large tree. He sat down in front of her, telling her the deer came here and he would find his prey. Rainee looked around curiously. "How could one accurately shoot one's prey with trees so thick?" she asked. Her father told her to be quiet and do as she was told.

Rainee sat very still, staring between the two trees that flanked them. She was getting very cold sitting on the dry leaves under the tree. Just when she thought she had to move, her father reached over and touched her face in an odd way. She looked up startled. The look in his face was strange and frightened her. She shook him off and told him not to touch her. Suddenly he sat up straight and pointed his gun between the trees, firing a shot.

"Did you see the deer?" he asked?

Rainee shook her head. She knew there was no deer between the trees. She looked at him and asked what he wanted? He shook his head as if in a trance. "Run," he said,

"Just run as fast as you can! I need Jenna and Eileen. They will do as they are told. You don't, so just run!"

Rainee stood quickly and began backing away from her father as she watched him reload his two shot rifle. She turned her back and started to run as fast as she could between the large trees. Run, she must run toward the house, she thought. She must run and get help.

Lorraine shook her shoulders and felt the present settle around her. Looking at her daughters, she thought to herself that she finally understood part of her sisters' fear. He had not planned to teach her to hunt. Her father had planned to sexually abuse her as he had them. When she resisted, he had decided to shoot her. She wondered what the rest of her sisters' stories were from their hunting trips? Too much pain and damage had happened for them to ever talk to her of their own pasts. When she attempted to reconnect with her family and called Eileen, she told her sister that she was beginning to remember things. Eileen confirmed the events of that day in the woods, but no, no one would help put their father in jail now that the statute of limitations was removed. They were still too terrified to want him to know where they lived. Lorraine was to stop contact and not look into that action further. The police had said because she protected herself, she needed her sisters' collaboration for action against their father at that late date to be taken. It never happened. It was no wonder she had buried her past and followed directions to disappear as a young adult. She had not been safe as a child or young adult. It was no wonder no family member of her past really knew who she was or where she was as an adult. This incident also explained her extreme fear of fire arms.

Rainee reasserted herself into Lorraine's thoughts and she went on to tell more of her story to her children.

Chapter 11: Rainee's Skating Party

In January Rainee slipped out the front door. Snow crunched under Rainee's brown farm boots. Her ragged brown tweed coat she had worn for several years now flapped in the wind, held together only by two large brown buttons. She tightened the knot of the red cotton scarf she had pulled over her head and then pulled on heavy woolen mittens. Picking up her ice skates, a gift from a church in town, and a full grocery sack, she flung her items onto the flat bed of the large green farm truck behind the cab, crawling onto the bed after them as their Dad had gone somewhere in Jenna's car and not been home in weeks.

"Come on girls!" she called excitedly to her sisters. It was Christmas break of ninth grade, and she and a neighbor had decided to plan a skating party for the country neighborhood. The neighbor had a frozen pond and would provide a bonfire and hot chocolate. The grocery sack contained dozens of homemade cookies Rainee had made for the event. "We are going to be late if we don't get going!" She called toward the broken down house again.

Her four sisters poured from the house, placing their skates on the flat bed with Rainee's. Buttons, their cocker spaniel, piled in with the girls. The sisters poured into the green cab with Jenna behind the wheel, leaving Rainee alone to watch the skates and cookies on the back of the truck. Rainee braced against the cold steel cab as Jenna started the truck and ground the gears, shifting into first to maneuver out of the rutted icy dirt driveway.

Chattering erupted, and then Eileen broke into, "Over the river and through the woods." The other girls joined her in song. Rainee from behind, heard their loud singing and joined in joyfully. This was the first party she had ever helped to plan...the first party she was a part of since her birthday party with Grandma. She was excited. It did not matter that temperatures were well-below freezing. The bonfire would help the children keep warm.

A mile away, Jenna pulled into the neighbor's barnyard and slid to a stop on the north side of the barn where a large frozen pond had been newly plowed out. The elderly neighbor man was tending a large fire, while his wife stirred hot chocolate over a gas grill. Pouring from the truck cab, the girls sat on the flat bed's edge to put on their skates. Then with whoops they slid out onto the pond. Only a couple of children had arrived so far, so Rainee took over as hostess. Soon everyone she knew for miles around was sliding on the pond, even kids she did not remember to invite. Obviously the tale of the pond party had made its route around the farms. She was glad. She was also glad she had made so many cookies.

When Rainee approached the farmer and his wife, she realized they also had set out the makings for a hot dog roast over the open fire. She giggled and told them she was so glad they wanted to help her have a good party. They simply smiled and told her they were glad to see so many of the neighborhood children happy, including their grandchildren from the next farm over.

A neighbor boy came flying over on his skates and asked Rainee to skate with him. Kids at school said he had a crush on her, but she could not believe it. At thirteen, this was a new idea to her. But she took his offered hand and off they went around and around the pond. Someone had brought a transistor radio and turned it on for music. On and on Bobby and Rainee skated until the farmer's wife called for treat time.

Thoroughly frozen, Rainee accepted a hot dog on a stick and stood next to the fire, more to get warm than to roast a hot dog. Bobby soon joined her. He surprised her by asking her if she believed in God. She told him yes, and soon disclosed the stories of the kumquat people and grandma. Bobby seemed intensely interested.

Having had their fill of hot dogs, hot chocolate and cookies, Bobby took her hand once more and led her out onto the ice. The other children whooped and joined them. Skating continued until sunset painted the sky in coral and pink. Helping the farmer and his wife to clean up, the children removed their skates and began scattering to their parents' cars that pulled in to take them home.

Jenna and Rainee headed toward their truck with the other three girls after once more thanking the farmer and his wife. Penny, a girl from the school bus who said she detested Rainee, came up behind her. Penny's older brother had once beaten Rainee up badly on the bus, so she was afraid of the entire family.

Penny touched her arm. "I am glad I got to come. I know you did not invite me, but Mr. Nickerbocker said it might be good if I came. I am sorry I have been so mean to you. My brother shouldn't pick on you so much. Can't we just be friends?"

Rainee turned to look at the plain, be-speckled faced girl in surprise, "You want to be my friend?" She asked incredulously. "I still live in that shack, you know." (Penny was the daughter of the wealthiest farmer in the area, and had told Rainee before that she was scum).

Penny actually started to cry. "I am sorry. I have treated you badly. You can't help where you live. You obviously are a nice person who loves people. I don't care where you live. Can't we just be friends?"

Rainee looked into Penny's eyes and realized she was telling the truth. Sighing, she put her hand on Penny's shoulder. "I don't believe God discriminates against people, no matter where they are from, or who they are. He wants us to love each other. Yes, I would like to be friends with you."

Rainee stepped onto the bed of the truck as Jenna started the motor. Smiling broadly at Penny, she waved and told her she had better stand back, because Jenna had only been driving for a few months. Penny laughed and backed away.

Arriving home, the other four girls went quickly into the

house to cuddle around the pot belly wood stove in the living room. Rainee escaped to the shed out back where Apache nickered a welcome.

Curling up in the straw beside her best friend, she told Apache all about the party, Penny wanting to be friends, the kind neighbors, and Bobby, the boy who had told her she had hair like sunlight.

Chapter 12: If Rainee Could Fly

February of ninth grade came and with it extra heavy snows. Rainee loved the snow. A farmer-neighbor had given her a pair of old wooden skis in January. She practiced going up and down the small hills around the country-side as part of her daily routine with Apache.

The old apple orchard, as broken down as the house, moaned under the heaviest new snow. Morning, however, had broken clear and crisp, setting the world aglitter with stars shining in the snow.

Rainee awoke on her army cot, pulling the heavy old quilts around her to block out the frigid air. Snow sifted through the ancient window pane next to her cot. With no heat in this attic room at all, the cold air seemed to penetrate even the heavy quilts. She finally pulled the covers over her head, as she often did on such cold days. Curled in her quilt igloo, she found some warmth.

"Get up, you lazy bums," she heard her mother call from below. "I only cook breakfast once, and it is hot now! It is Saturday, so you have to get your chores done now!"

Rainee moaned and crawled out of her igloo. Placing her socked feet on the cold floor, she shivered visibly. Grabbing her clothes and shoes she raced the other girls to the stairs to descend to the warm pot belly stove. The old stove could be heard roaring when the stair door opened. Mother also had the oven door open to allow the hot air to fill the kitchen area.

Dad came out of the one bedroom of the house just as Rainee finished dressing. He leered at her and then watched the other girls dress. Disgusted, she turned to block his view of the younger two girls. Something about Dad was not right…it was downright evil. Why did he look at them like that? Jenna just gave him a dirty look and continued dressing. Rainee helped Crystal to button her blouse and then went to help put breakfast on the table.

Grabbing bowls and spoons for the oatmeal, Mother placed breakfast on the old oak table that once belonged to Grandma. Then she filled each bowl before scattering them around its round width. The girls sat down and began gulping the hot food.

"So," Dad said, "I have to cut wood today. We are getting low. Eileen and Jenna can help. Rainee, you feed the animals. You young 'uns help your Ma in the house." With that he went back into his room to pull on his outdoor clothes.

Rainee was secretly glad she would not have to help cut wood. She had plans for the day. And she needed to do them alone.

Rainee looked up to see fear come across Jenna and Eileen's faces. Why were they afraid? Cutting wood was dangerous but all of them had learned how to stay safe. What were they so obviously afraid of then?

Rainee watched as Jenna stared hard at her father's door. A sinking feeling went into Rainee's stomach...the fear had something to do with Dad...What, she wondered, did he do on these trips that made her sisters so afraid? She said nothing, fearing all she could do was make whatever it was a lot worse. Dad was a bad person. He hurt everyone a lot all the time. Often Eileen came home from such outings with cuts all over her body. Rainee wondered how she could stop all the pain. How?

Animals fed, Rainee pulled her antique snow skis out of Apache's shed, telling him she would see him later. "Tell Mom I have gone skiing," she told Crystal. I am out in the old oat field, if anyone needs me."

Her sister hollered back that she heard her from the kitchen door. Rainee headed out into the fields and freedom.

Trudging through the heavy drifts of snow in her rubber farm boots, she listened to the peculiar squeaky crunch they made on the snow. Finally arriving at her pre-determined destination, Rainee leaned over to strap her feet into the old skis. She stood up to enjoy the view from the top of the hill. This hill was gently sloped on one side going down to the orchard, but the other side ended in a sharp cliff that was covered in snow. It was this side Rainee faced today.

This was Rainee's secret challenge. She had watched the winter Olympics this month on their tiny new black and white TV. The ski jumping fascinated her, so she studied each jump carefully. She watched how the skiers leaned into the jumps, and how they landed with totally bent knees. She knew she wanted to jump, too. Today the snow was very deep, so she figured if she fell; the drifts would cushion her fall. She did not think of how far she might actually end up jumping from the top of the cliff.

Inching up to the edge of the cliff, Rainee looked over at the mounds of snow below her. Giggling, she backed up a few feet to give herself a start. Push, push, crunch, crunch, she went down to the cliff's mouth. Bending forward straight as an arrow, she shouted in glee as her skis and body lifted into the air above the cliff.

The brisk air whipped her frozen cheeks, but she paid no mind. She could fly! She could fly. On and on she flew, clearing the field below, and then with knees greatly bent, she landed neatly on the snow covering the hay field. Yes, she thought, she was born to fly! Setting her skis as the Olympians had, she came to a halt. Then she began the long, hard journey through the drifts and back to the top. She felt exhilarated and sweaty beneath her old clothes. Today, today, she had learned to fly.

Jumping for most of the morning, Rainee set off through the apple orchard toward home. This was a day she would not forget.

Her father was back with a load of wood and the older girls. Both looked haggard. They had unloaded the wood and were cutting it into burnable pieces with a chain saw. When Dad looked up and saw Rainee coming, he turned the saw off. He stared at her angrily and she ran for the house. Rainee sighed and began hauling in wood from the pile out back.

As she returned for another load, Dad grabbed her arm. "I know what you did all day," he growled. "What are you, daft? Want me to go to jail if the neighbors see you? That hill can be seen for miles! How dare you embarrass me!" With that he began hitting her over and over, each time echoing in sharp, bone-breaking sounds.

Withdrawing, Dad went back to cutting up wood. Rainee touched her face gingerly and realized her nose was broken again. Her jaw was also swollen and felt like it was where it did not belong.

Her little sister sidled up to her, crying, "I'm sorry. I'm sorry. I told. I thought you looked cute up there. I didn't mean him to hurt you!"

Rainee turned to numbly pat her sister on the head before running into the house. She must get the bleeding stopped. Her mother met her in the kitchen with an ice pack.

"I think I need a doctor," Rainee looked pleadingly into her mother's face. "My nose is broken and I can hardly move my jaw," she whispered through her teeth.

Mother shoved the ice pack into her hands and glared at her angrily. "Ice is all you need. We don't use doctors!" With that she turned back to the stove, shoving things around angrily.

"Momma," Rainee sobbed through her teeth, "I need a doctor."

Mother turned back to her, a strange look on her face. "I

made you a lemon cake. Now get that bleeding stopped so we can eat."

Rainee went into the living room and applied the ice to her face as she lay down on the old sofa, now ratted and smelly. Pinching her sore nose shut, she finally was able to stop it from bleeding. She put the ice pack on her mangled jaw. Gradually the pain decreased and her sobs slowed.

A cake! Momma had made her a cake. And she had flown today. She could get through the pain. She could get through the sadness. Then she remembered. Today was her birthday, and Momma had remembered enough to make her a cake. She was now fourteen. Only four more years before she could really fly.....away from home.

Lorraine looked at her attentive daughters. "Do you remember when you were little I had to wear that weird wire stuff on my head? My jaw that had been broken by my Dad never worked right after that. Then when you were little I got so I couldn't open or close my mouth to eat. It took a lot of medical work to dislodge my jaw from my skull. I wore that wire contraption to hold it in place for several years as the skull bone re-grew. I had to do that so that the jaw would not slip back into my skull."

Rainee began speaking once more.

Chapter 13: Rainee Faces Hard Facts

Chaos erupted in the house just as Rainee stepped through the screen door, letting in the warm late April breeze. The screen closed with a snap as if it was an alligator closing its mouth. Across the room, mother stood facing Rainee beside the old, round, pedestal oak table. Her hand rested on its edge. Her face was red and her eyes snapped as angry words spew from her almost toothless mouth. Rainee stood transfixed where she stood at the door, listening to an argument that she was obviously the center of between her mother and father.

"*You* tell Rainee she can't go to church with them thar Washingtons! You tell her!" Mother screamed in an almost animal-like pitch.

"Tell me what?" Rainee asked as she turned to her father.

He turned to her, eyes smoldering as if a furnace had been awakened in them.

"You are not to go to church with that family anymore! Last Sunday was the last time. Tomorrow you cannot go. Do you understand me? If that woman ever steps foot on this property again, I will shoot her, understand? She is making a lot of trouble for me because of you!"

Shock caused Rainee's thin body to begin shaking as if a gust of wind had hit it. "You said I was old enough to make up my own mind," she cried in pain, "And I have decided I want to go to church. I want to go to church with Mrs. Washington. You can't stop me. You can't!"

Angered even more by Rainee's denial, Father moved forward like an enraged panther. "You won't disobey me this time. Understand? If you do, you will die, and so will your friends. Understand?" With this snarl he reached out and pulled the old fashioned telephone cord out of the wall. "And you won't call and warn them either!"

Sudden unexplainable peace descended on Rainee as she stood her ground, her mind rapidly forming a prayer for God to be with her and tell her what to do. As calm as if she were talking to a friend, Rainee looked her father in the eye as he raised his hand over his head to strike her.

"Do as you please," she said softly, "I know God is with me." She closed her eyes to accept the blow but it did not come. Instead she heard the screen slam as her father left the house. Afraid for her friends after her own recent life-threatening experience, Rainee ran to the door. She followed her father into the yard, "You can hurt me but leave my friends alone!" she begged him.

"You will see. You will see what I can do!" he chortled as if in glee, for she could tell he had gone completely mad. "Might be fun killing those stuffed shirts. I'm not done with you either!"

Rainee ran out through the ancient apple orchard and across last year's corn field that had not been plowed. The old stalks tore at her legs, but on she ran. Over the open alfalfa field and into her precious woods she ran before she slowed down. Throwing herself against her beechnut tree, she gave in to the wave of sobs that threatened to crash over her like a title wave. Slowly her breathing came back to normal and her heart quit racing.

She was so afraid. Memory of her father's recent attempt to shoot her with his .308 rifle now left her feeling frozen. She could not let her friends die with her. Never! Never!

She felt a gentle touch on her shoulder, but when she turned around, no one was there. "Hush, little one, hush," a quiet voice spoke, "I am here. I am here. I won't leave you. Remember my promise? You are my child. I will care for you."

Tears of relief now slowly etched their way through the stains on her smudged face. "What am I going to do?" she asked her Heavenly Father. "I know he is capable of killing my friends.

He tried to kill me already. He stole Apache and sold him when I wasn't here last week. If I try to go over to the Washingtons, he will just follow and then it will happen for sure. What do I do?"

"Be patient and watch what I shall do," the quiet voice answered. "Just trust me."

"God, I am so tired. It has been so hard to stay alive. I am fourteen now and I need to get away from dad if I am to stay alive. Can you help me do that, too?"

"Just wait and watch, dear one. My answer comes," the quiet voice responded.

Calmed, Rainee brushed the leaves from her ragged pants. A longing filled her as she looked around, for she was looking toward the hill where she and Apache had often spent hours in prayer. "At least you are safe," she spoke to her pony friend, "I hear the man who bought you loves you and takes good care of you. I am glad."

Rainee turned back toward the house, praying constantly as terror once more tried to fill her throat. As she approached the apple orchard, she stopped to gather a few stray flowers under the trees. If she brought her Mom some flowers, at least she would not be angry. One less enemy tonight would be good.

Just as she reached under a bramble for a very pretty white flower, she heard her father's truck start up with a rumble. She darted behind the tree to avoid detection. The last time he had found her alone, he had tried to molest her again. That day she had fought him off successfully. Today, she did not know if she had the strength to fight back. She was sure that was why he tried to kill her…because she refused to do what he asked.

She listened as the truck banged on down the dirt road until she could hear it no more. She finished picking her flowers. Now would be a good time to take Momma flowers.

Rainee smiled to herself as she watched the sunset behind the apple trees from her bare attic window. The cot she slept on moaned as she wriggled down into the old quilt to warm herself. Spring nights without heat could be chilly.

The bribe had worked…at least for now. Momma told her to go ahead and go to church in the morning if she liked. Dad had taken off and she did not know when he would return. Besides, there was no phone to tell Mrs. Washington to not show up come morning since dad destroyed it.

Rainee pulled on her heavy winter pajamas while still under her quilt. Reaching for her brush, she brushed her long hair. Far away she heard the motor of a truck. Maybe she heard wrong. Maybe it was another truck, she prayed. She squeezed her eyes shut to concentrate on her prayer.

The clatter of the truck, however, roared as it pulled into the driveway. She was not wrong. Dad had come home despite threatening not to come back.

Rainee dove beneath the quilt, head and all, forgetting her half-finished hair. The old truck door slammed with a creak and bang. Perhaps he was drunk, she thought, and he had forgotten their earlier disagreement.

Moments later the war downstairs began louder than ever…almost eerily as if it had never ended. Mother told him she had told Rainee she could go to church, and for him to leave her alone. Something soft started in Rainee's heart when she heard her mother's demand. Did Momma love her after all, she wondered?

A loud crash followed by something hitting the wall, and then the obvious sound of pieces of glass hitting the floor echoed up the stairs.

"Oh, God," Rainee prayed, "What is going to happen? What shall I do?"

"Go," a soft hand touched Rainee, "Go talk to him."

Rainee pulled back the quilt and looked around. "I am too afraid!" She cried with sobs caught in her throat.

"Do not fear. I will go with you. Now, go," the voice continued firmly.

Rainee pulled back the quilt and placed her small feet on the floor that felt as cold as steel. She slowly moved through the old boxes of junk that made up her attic room, pausing at the head of the wooden, rickety stairs. Crash after crash resounded from below. Her sisters, who had also been asleep in the attic, now slipped up behind Rainee and whispered in fear that she had better stay put.

"Sounds like they will kill each other this time for sure," Eileen sneered, "More power to them."

Crystal cried out in a whimper and Jenna told her to be quiet. No need to turn the venom onto themselves.

"I am going down," Rainee said quietly, with resolve she could not feel.

"Yeah, right," Eileen hoarsely laughed, "Then you will be dead, too."

"Then I shall see Grandma in Heaven," Rainee said with conviction she did not feel. The other girls stepped away from the stairs as Rainee stepped down the first creaky step. Slowly, she went, bracing herself against the wall to stop as much creaking as possible.

At the bottom of the stairs was an old door with an oval metal handle. Her parents sounded as if they were fighting just on the other side of that door. Rainee shuttered as she cracked the door open. Seeing they were backed away toward the cold stove, Rainee slipped out the door and into the sagging living room.

Both parents stood with their backs to her. Her dad had his arms raised, his fist clenched as he held a hot coffee pot.

At the sound of the creaking attic door, he whirled around, leaving a stream of hot coffee to circle and hit Rainee in the arms and face. Rainee screamed like an injured animal and jumped back. In horror, the coffee pot dropped from her father's hand as more hot coffee slithered onto Rainee's legs and bare feet. Crying now, she turned to the haggard face of her mother.

"Go away, Momma, get safe," She said to the unbelieving eyes, "I will fight my own battle now. I am big enough." With that, Rainee stepped between her father and her mother, her painful hands clenched in fists.

Turning to face her father, Rainee pulled up to her full height of five feet six to meet the gaze of her father who stood almost six feet tall. Surprised by the steel she heard in her own voice, Rainee began to talk, "Worker of the devil," her voice spoke, from where she knew not, "God has commanded that you cease your evil ways. Mrs. Washington has done nothing but care for me and love me. You will not harm her. If you must harm someone, kill me now. I am ready to meet Jesus. I want to go where you can not touch me anymore. I will see Jesus. I will see Grandma. They are the ones who love me. So go ahead. Finish your job! I am not afraid anymore. *I am not afraid!"*

It was her father's face that now looked terrified. "You. You!" he screamed. "God told me He would protect you from me! And now there is an angel behind you. I see an angel!" Her father's scream was one so eerie Rainee was to hear it in her sleep for many years and not be able to tell where it came from until she wrote this story. It was often how her PTSD episodes began…with the scream of someone evil who looked death in the face.

"God is my life, my joy, my all," Rainee said firmly, "His angels do watch over me."

Cursing, her father began to back away from Rainee, screeching shrilly. When he had backed to the front door, he reached behind himself to open it and slipped into the night as if a shadow had taken him.

"You," mother said unbelievingly, "You stood up to him. He won't come back now, so long as you are here." Then suddenly she also began to scream irrationally, "You have destroyed my marriage," she cried and reached out and slapped Rainee's face.

"But he wanted to kill you!" Rainee cried to her mother.

"No, he didn't," mother denied emphatically, "He just blows off steam. Tomorrow he would have been fine. He never hurts anyone really!"

Shocked, Rainee dodged up to the safety of the attic. She was not ready to face mother as assailant tonight. She needed to feel God's arms wrapped around her now. Dad did hurt others. So did mother. The scars on her body and her sisters told the tale all too clearly.

The coffee burns on Rainee's body throbbed but she crawled under the quilt anyway. Mother never came up here. She would be safe. In the morning, she thought, I will go to church with Mrs. Washington. She will tell me what I must do.

The early morning sunshine woke Rainee long before church time. She dressed quietly in her everyday work clothes and combed her hair. Descending to the first floor with the idea of getting chores out of the way, she realized mother was up and making bacon.

"You will have to feed the chickens and calves before you go to church. The other girls will sleep till noon," Momma said quietly. She handed Rainee a plate of bacon and eggs, "The pie you made yesterday is good," she awkwardly complimented Rainee as if to say she was sorry but never said it.

Rainee mumbled her thanks as she ate the food. She was hungrier than one of those big alligators she used to watch! Skipping out into the back lot, Rainee scattered corn for the chickens. The chickens pecked happily as she mixed up the milk substitute for the two little calves that now lived in the shed where Apache once lived. She listened for a moment as the calves slurped up their meal and then turned toward the house, joy in her heart.

"I have decided to follow Jesus," rang from her lips as she banged the kitchen screen door behind her. The sun-splattered morning had raised her spirits. Somehow she was coming to realize in that moment that something had changed in her life. It was a good change.

Shortly after dressing, Rainee heard Mrs., Washington's car approaching. Her motor always purred like an old, lazy cat. Rainee ran downstairs to find Jenna dressed.

"I am going to church with you," Jenna said off-handedly.

"Really?" Rainee sounded surprised.

"Yes. If you can stand up to Dad, I can go to church.

Moments later Rainee introduced Mrs. Washington to Jenna as they joined the other children in the back of the station wagon. Soon dust flowed out behind the car as they skittered down the road toward town.

"So, how is my best student?" Mrs. Washington asked as she opened the Sunday School room to let Rainee in after showing Jenna to the high school room. Concern immediately made wrinkles in her small forehead below her deep red hair when her words brought Rainee to tears. Startled, Mrs. Washington put her arm around Rainee, "What is it, child?" she asked gently.

Rainee proceeded to tell Mrs. Washington the whole ugly

tale of the day before, leaving nothing out. She told her how sorry she was that she had put Mrs. Washington's life in danger. Mrs. Washington listened without interrupting until Rainee stopped with a sob and a gulp. Then she told her of that day with her dad in the cedar swamp.

Stunned, Mrs. Washington simply pulled Rainee closer to her. Rainee loved the way Mrs. Washington smelled…always of lilacs or roses… "He can't be trusted," she continued, "If he tried to shoot me, he will try again. And he will try to shoot you, too." Mrs. Washington stroked Rainee's soft hair, horrified and yet glad this child had finally been brave enough to open up to her. She knew Rainee had been hurt a lot at home. Teachers have a way of figuring these things out….there were always bruises and pains that went unexplained on Rainee.

"I know, I know," she crooned to this child she had come to love, "but it is over now. I won't ever let him hurt you again."

Rainee stepped back and looked into the tiny lady's face, wonder beginning to fill her eyes. She knew Mrs. Washington was telling the truth. She was finally safe. She had come to rescue her just as the angel had told her years before.

"What shall I do?" She asked in confusion.

"We must tell the pastor. He will know what to do," Mrs. Washington told her with a smile of encouragement. "You must get away somehow."

"We can get away?" Rainee asked in disbelief, "Mother won't like that. She will be mad if we get away. She will be mad if I get dad in trouble. She worships the ground he walks on."

After church, Mrs. Washington stopped her husband in the hall and told him they must stay after church to talk to the pastor. Her husband skirted around others and found the pastor by the door. Telling him there was an emergency and to meet in the office, he returned to Mrs. Washington and Rainee.

Together the three proceeded into the church office. Sitting in a soft brown leather chair, Rainee listened. The Pastor came rumbling into the office. He was a large man with slicked back black hair. He always seemed to be rumbling, she thought. Rainee liked to listen to the conversation he was forever carrying on with himself. Or was he praying? He reminded her of a powerful waterfall she once saw when she was young.....

"Well, well, missy," Pastor began. "Dell tells me you need my help. That you are in danger. Take your time now, but tell me everything. I want to know everything. I won't hurt you. And I will believe you. Just tell me what you know needs to be told."

Between chokes and sobs over the next few hours, Rainee spilled out the years of torture and abuse for the first time in her life. As she told it, she knew for the first time, too, that what she had been through was very wrong. She did not deserve all that pain from the abuse no matter what her parents had said. The sexual abuse of her sisters and her dad's attempts on her were just plain ugly evil.

Pastor, Mrs. Washington and Dell listened intently, love and concern showing on their faces. Sometimes just plain horror flitted across one of their faces, too. For the story Rainee had to tell was one few children lived to tell. All three knew Rainee's life was in much more danger than even she realized. They also knew that what they needed to do could endanger them, too, but they must rescue her.

Exhausted, Rainee sat back in the leather chair, placing her small hands in her lap. "Can anything really be done?" she asked hopefully.

Pastor picked up the black, rotary dial phone as he nodded, "Yes, my dear. It is going to be done now."

All three people had come to realize how dangerous Rainee's father was in the telling of the tale. None realized, however, that her mother also caused a lot of pain. Right now they knew she needed protection from her father.

Minutes later, Mr. Smith, a policeman who belonged to the church, walked into the office door. He soon had details of the assaults on Rainee on paper. And she was able to tell him how she knew he had sexually assaulted her sisters. She told him everything she could remember, even when her father tried to kill her with the 308 rifle. She ended with how he had threatened her and the Washingtons yesterday.

Mr. Smith told her he was glad she was so honest and tousled her hair. He proceeded to make a few phone calls while asking Rainee to sign some papers. What she didn't realize is that in that moment Mr. Smith had her sign a request for her father to be arrested on rape and attempted murder charges. There were few child abuse laws in those days, so these were the charges that were brought forward.

Hours later, police discovered that her dad had fled the state. He was nowhere to be found. He had seemed to know he had crossed a line he could never go back on and so had fled. Rainee feared facing her mother, but Mrs. Washington reassured her that she would make sure she was safe before leaving her at home. The police had Rainee's phone re-installed for Rainee's safety, too. If there was any trouble at all, she was to call their fast number.

The house was surprisingly quiet when Mrs. Washington drove Rainee up the bumpy driveway. Mr. Smith, the policeman, followed close behind. The door stood askew, and chickens had gone into the living room. Inside she found mother sitting in the broken down recliner, her face ashen gray.

Mr. Smith walked into the house and stood before mother. "Mrs. Perkins, we need to talk," he told her in a directive manner.

"I did not know about any of it," mother stated flatly before Mr. Smith could begin to talk. "He hurt the kids. I didn't. I did not even know about it..." She seemed to be in another world.

Rainee shuttered. She knew what mother said was not true, but how could she contradict her? Unbothered by her mother's statements, Mr. Smith began asking questions. The questions would continue off and on for the next year. Charges were filed against her dad first, and then accomplice was charged against her mother. She was able to get probation in court when she agreed she would testify against dad when he was caught. He never was caught. Mother never spent a day in jail.

Rainee would be asked by the courts to remain with her mother until she was eighteen. She asked to be put in the state foster care system, but the court told her that families did not take fourteen year old adolescents. The court would appoint her pastor and his wife as her guardians; so, she would have someone to help her stay safe.

Rainee never felt safe until she left home. In those high school years she spent as much time away from home as she could. When home, she began to sleep with a kitchen knife beneath her pillow and an escape plan in her head. The police continued to keep an eye on her due to death threats from her father that came in the mail from all over the country. Even at school she was told the authorities were keeping an eye out. They needed to catch this man. They needed to keep her safe.

(Finally the authorities told her that as soon as she could she needed to go away. Her mother had promised to not reveal Rainee's whereabouts to her father if he contacted her mother. Rainee, they thought, would be safer if she planned to attend college out of state. It would not hurt to change her name either. Could she do that? Could she just walk away from the only family she knew? If she left she would never know if her mother loved her. She would never know if her sisters had stopped hating her. Going away was just too hard. It was just too hard.)

Chapter 14: Rainee Under His Wings

Rainee sat nervously on the front seat of their 1958 Olds sedan. Jenna, now 17, was driving. Marta and Eileen sat in the back seat. Their mother had hurriedly moved them to this big city after their father disappeared. Rainee anxiously peered out the car window and gazed at the tall buildings they were passing. She felt so lost, so very lost.

Jenna looked upset as she turned onto a nearly vacant street, only to realize she was going the wrong way. Yanking at the steering wheel, she pulled over and did a U-turn. "Are you sure these are the directions mother gave you?" she asked Rainee.

"Yes, she said to take Saguache all the way across town to Watertown Road. We have to pass the skyscrapers. That is the half-way mark. Saguache ends on Watertown Road. Go left on Watertown to Green Street. The church is on Green Street."

Jenna shook her head and looked around, realizing she needed the street that went the other way. It must be a block over. Turning onto a side street, she slowly progressed north and was surprised to see the new one way street not only went the right way, but it was Saguache Avenue. Making a left to go west, Jenna relaxed a little and began to sing. Soon the other girls joined her. Old songs from their early childhood when the kumquat people took them to Sunday School were sung with gusto one after another.

Turning left on Watertown Road, Jenna told the other girls to look for a street sign that said Green Street. Try as they might, though, none could spot this sign. In frustration Jenna finally turned around and returned to the one way street that was opposite to Saguache. "Mom will just have to come with us next time and show us. I can't find it. I am sorry, Rainee, but we can't go to that church this morning that Pastor Davis told you about. I'm sorry."

Rainee felt a catch in her throat, then a drowning sensation. Her one hope in this move was to find the church her old pastor recommended, because he said the pastor there was looking for her and would continue to help her. Almost sobbing, Rainee stared out the window as they once again passed the skyscrapers. Her eyes ached for the open valleys and woodlands. Closing her eyes tight she pretended she was on Apache again, riding through the alfalfa field with the wind in her hair. A smile returned to her face as her new world disappeared and her home came back to her.

Arriving at the house their Uncle had rented for them, Rainee was the first out of the car. Slamming through the screen door she announced, "We looked and looked and could not find it. We have church tonight and we want to know if you will take us."

Mother appeared from the kitchen, a dish towel in her hand, "Oh, no, not me. I don't go to church. I don't have anything more to do with God. God belonged to my mother, not me. No, no, no....if you can't find that church, you can go to the one we saw down this street. What is the difference, anyway?"

Rainee began to cry, "You don't understand! My pastor told the new pastor about me. He has been appointed my guardian. They are expecting me. I need to find the church so they can know I am here. Please. Just go with us. You can sit in the car while we go to church. Please!!!"

Jenna came in and joined in the pleading. After several minutes, mother muttered, "Oh, all right, but just to ride in the car. I will never darken the door of a church again!"

Happy again, Rainee ascended the stairs and passed through the small bedroom Marta had claimed. At the other end was another staircase. She also ascended these stairs to the single room attic she called her bedroom. She went to the front end of this room where a dormer window overlooked the street. A large maple tree spread its branches clear over the porch's roof, providing Rainee a quick escape if she needed it. For she always made sure she had an escape now.

Rainee's Dad had called her Mother the day before they left the country. He had a plan to kill Rainee yet, he told her, and Rainee had better never sleep! Rainee went over to her bed and felt under her pillow. (Her Uncle had given her a real bed for the first time and was it nice to sleep in!) Carefully Rainee removed a long kitchen knife from under her pillow. If God protected her, why did she feel the need to stay armed? She did not know except fear seemed to overcome her so much these days, and the knife made her less fearful.

Rainee's Mother told her she had told dad where they lived because she loved him and wanted him back. Surely the police would let him come back. Rainee could not understand this. How could you love someone who hurt you so bad? And so she prayed and asked God to keep her safe, and hid the knife just in case she needed to protect herself.

Evening came after Rainee spent the day reading a book she had checked out of the new city's library. Rainee descended to the second floor. Anxiously she combed her hair and brushed her teeth. Would mother back out of her agreement to take them? She wondered.

A bit surprised, Rainee found mother dressed and at the door when she landed on the first floor, "Well, if I must do this, we need to go now. I have not been over in that neighborhood in thirty years. Things could have changed. Who all is going?" This time all five of the girls loaded into their old white car.

Jenna slipped behind the wheel again (Mom did not drive. When she drove them places, Jenna drove, and Mom gave directions). Soon everyone was loaded and Jenna began the trek down their main street to Saguache again. This time she remembered the correct turn and was soon heading past the skyscrapers. At this time of day traffic had picked up, so Rainee was glad they somewhat knew the way.

Arriving on Watertown Road, Mom soon picked out Green Street, and they headed back east two blocks to a tiny white church on a corner. A black and white sign in front announced this was Green Street Wesleyan Church. Singing already came from inside the building. Jenna pulled into a parking place and the girls disembarked, but mother stayed put. "No one will get me into that church," she said with hostility.

"OK, no big deal," Rainee said quietly and skipped hopefully to the church's front door. Pulling a heavy door open, Rainee entered the little church and the sanctuary. There, seated at the piano, sat her new pastor, playing hymns heartily while also leading the small congregation in singing. Rainee slipped into a pew, followed by her sisters. She removed a hymnbook from the rack in front of her and easily found the page of the hymn the pastor was leading. It was the same hymnbook her old church used. Somehow that gave her some small comfort.

Soon Rainee was joining her voice in full force with the rest of the congregation.

The hymn ended. The pastor asked everyone to sit down stating, "That is all but the young people on the back pew. Would you remain standing? I don't believe you have been here before. Would you like to introduce yourselves?"

Embarrassed, the other girls shook their heads and sat down. Rainee, however, grinned, because she realized in meeting his eyes that he knew who she was. "Pastor Stevens," she began, "I am Rainee. These are my sisters. We moved here two weeks ago. Pastor Davis told me to come to your church, so here we are!"

Pastor Stevens grinned and said, "And so you are. And we are glad you came!" The congregation agreed with a series of Amens. "Now," Pastor Stevens continued, "Sunday nights we just have singing many times because we like singing so much. Do you like singing, Rainee?"

"Oh, yes," Rainee answered brightly, "Can you sing *Under His Wings*? It's on page seventy-one."

"Certainly," Pastor Stevens smiled, "but first can you give us your testimony? Why is this song so important to you?"

Rainee startled. Testimony? She was a child of fourteen. No one had ever asked her to talk about her walk with Jesus before. Still, she would like to tell.

"I love this song because I can tell that is just where Jesus keeps me, under his wings. In his protection I am safe and loved." Rainee smiled with tears in her eyes, remembering the angel's admonition to tell no one of his visit to her when she was eight and Grandma died. She could sense even now that it was not the time to tell that story.

Pastor Stevens began playing the song jubilantly and then the congregation joined in the singing. Under Jesus' wings she did safely abide and knew He would continue to watch over her.

As time passed the Stevens would indeed take over as guardians for Rainee. Their mother descended into a mental breakdown for the remainder of Rainee's childhood that Rainee could not understand until much later in life. What little chance they had of finally becoming a family disappeared. Jenna and Eileen were now grown and left home. Mother finished raising the two younger children by herself because they chose to stay with her, but she never could really mother them. She was too lost in her own world of pain. Meanwhile, the Stevens became the mainstay of Rainee's adolescent world. Oh, how she longed for her mother's love. She could tell her mother was trying to get better as Rainee finished high school, but she did not seem to want to include Rainee in her life.

Chapter 15: Rainee & Mr. Berlington's Prophecy

Rainee sat at the back of the noisy eleventh grade U.S. History class. Mr. Berlington, her teacher, stood at the front, leading a ripping discussion of how people impacted history. Rainee listened, engrossed in the subject. Then, without thinking, she raised her hand.

"Yes, Rainee?" Mr. Berlington acknowledged her hand.

"I am going to influence history. When I am an adult, I am going to be somebody and make a difference in this life," Rainee said the full conviction of her thought written within her deep gray eyes.

Her complete faith in her statement did not prepare her for her teacher's reaction or words, for in the next moment she was humiliated more than she could ever recall. Mr. Berlington began with a roaring laugh, pointing his finger at her, "You? You?" He laughed, "Why, you are a good for nothing from the wrong side of the tracks. People like you don't change history. In fact, they don't do much of anything!"

Angrily, Rainee retorted, "How would you know? You don't know me! Not really!"

"Oh, I know you enough," Mr. Berlington rebutted. "You live in a ghetto. Your single parent mother isn't even allowed to really finish parenting her children because she is such a loser. You are the dregs of society. You are what gives other people fear for their lives. Why, you are only good for dropping out of school, getting pregnant and becoming a hardened drug addict. That's what you are good for! Change history, my eye!" he was now shouting.

The class had become unusually quiet in only a moment. Rainee stood facing her new enemy, tears streaming down her face. "And you can go to Hates!" She shouted back, gathering her books from her desk.

"Yes, get out, you little monster, you!" The teacher shouted to her back as she ran from the classroom.

Sobbing, Rainee ran the long second floor hallway to the stairs that led to the counselors' offices. In the stairwell, Rainee was alone and likely to remain alone, because classes were only half over. She sat down at the top of the stairs and sobbed until her throat hurt. How could he? He was a teacher. How could he say such terrible things to her? Was he right? Could she ever pull herself out of her social situation and make a difference? Was she just fooling herself?

When she could cry no more, Rainee pulled her books to her chest and descended the stairs. She turned into the counselors' office suite just as the bell rang to change classes. She would have to get a note to miss Mrs. Jennings's English class, she sighed to herself. Mrs. Jennings was a tough teacher, but at least she didn't make fun of her in front of the whole class.

In the office, Rainee asked the student in charge to see if Mr. Houston, the eleventh grade guidance counselor, could see her. The student nodded and went back to Mr. Houston's office. To her surprise, Mr. Houston himself came into the waiting area.

"Come on back, Rainee, I was just thinking about you!" he called cheerily, dismissing the student aide with his left hand.

Rainee followed Mr. Houston into his office. He ushered her into a chair and then sat across the desk from her. "Now, tell me what is wrong," he said kindly.

Rainee burst into tears once more and relayed the events of the last class hour. Mr. Houston sat quietly, running his right hand through his hair. When Rainee had exhausted her speech and sat quietly, Mr. Houston patted her hand. "That was awful mean of your teacher," he consoled the weeping adolescent. "That teacher has no idea who you are, your gifts, your talents, and your drive. Don't listen to what he says, Rainee, please. I know differently. *You are_*going to make a difference in this world,

Rainee. I already know that. I consider it a privilege to have been allowed to work with you while you are still in school. Someday I expect to hear you have made an impact in this life that few can. Do you hear me?"

Rainee gulped and looked into the eyes of her counselor, a feeling of trust and hope billowing up inside her. She nodded. "I will need to go to college, Mr. Houston. No one in my family has ever gone to college…most just drop out of high school. Mr. Berlington is right about my family…we have been a sore on society's side, but I don't want to continue that history. I want to go to college. I want to be able to take care of myself and others, too. I want to make life better, even if it is just for one other person. My pastor and his wife, and Mrs. Washington and Dell have done that for me. Don't you think I can do it for another child?"

Mr. Houston smiled, continuing to pat her hand, "I already have a plan in place to help you, Rainee. That is why I was just about to call your teacher and ask for you to be sent down here!"

Mr. Houston sat back in his chair and opened the lower drawer of his desk. From the drawer he took out a fat file folder, "This," he said, "Is the beginning of your history-changing future, Rainee," he opened the folder and began to read, "On this 23rd day of April, 1969, I recommend Lorraine Perkins, as a candidate for your program, Upward Bound. Lorraine, or Rainee, as she prefers to be called, is a bright, inquisitive student who belongs in college classes. Her social history, however, has blocked such opportunities from her. I understand Upward Bound is a program designed to help such students to see they are college material and give them college-level learning experiences to show they can handle a class load. I am applying for the Upward Bound program commencing in June, 1969, at Indiana State University for Rainee.

I understand Rainee will be expected to spend the summer living in a dorm and participating in college classes specially selected by the Upward Bound directors that can give her a glimpse into the field for which she holds most promise.

Thank you for asking for one of my students to be one of the candidates for this program. I know Rainee will do your program proud. I know, because she already makes me proud with the accomplishments she has achieved while I have served as her high school counselor. Sincerely, Mr. John Houston, guidance counselor, Western High School, South Bend, Indiana.

Rainee sat in semi-shock mixed with glee, listening to Mr. Houston's words. A whole summer at a college totally free? For her? They would help her reach for her stars, as Daddy Stevens called it?

"When will I know if I get in?" she asked in awe.

"You are already in, Rainee. I got the phone call today. I didn't want to tell you until I was sure. The program starts in two weeks. I would say, go home, sweet young lady, pack your bags, and I will let you know when someone will pick you up to take you to the college. OK?"

"I have nothing to wear to college," Rainee sighed, "I have three dresses, all two years old. I got them when I came here from a mission box. What does one wear to college?"

Mr. Houston chuckled, "Smart kid, and yet a lady, huh? Tell you what; I know a program that can help with that, too. Now go on. I have work to do!" He handed Rainee a hall pass so she could get into English without getting into trouble. "You tell Mrs. Jennings you just got into college classes a year early, and let her put that in her pipe and smoke it for a day!" He laughed out loud, then he escorted her to the counseling suite's door.

Rainee almost skipped her way to her next class. College...college...she was going to college! All her fears melted away as she tackled English Composition.

The semester ended a few days later, following the end of

the semester exams. Mr. Berlington angrily told her after her history exam that he had been fired. She was the reason. Who had she talked to? "No one," she lied, and turning her back, she walked away jubilantly. Already, she thought, she had changed another child's future, for no other child would have to be hurt the way he had hurt her. Inspired by her own impact, Rainee finished the eleventh grade with flying grades. God had sent another angel to help her, she thought, only he had a human face.

Chapter 16: So Rainee Could Come Home

Rainee stood in the door of the freshman dorm of the college her guardians had helped her to get into in the spring. It was hundreds of miles from her home. A full financial scholarship in hand, she looked forward to the new life this college represented. Her pastor and his wife, her guardians, had encouraged her to apply for admission and the scholarships offered through different programs. Surprising herself, she had scored at the top of competitive scholarship tests and landed the full scholarship to any school of her choice.

Rainee chose this college because her guardians wanted her to go to a Christian college and a friend would be going here. (Rainee would transfer the next year, however, to a state school in Colorado upon discovering that they would also take her scholarship. This further opportunity allowed her to finally lose herself far from home, ensuring her safety).

But now there were new friends to make, new things to learn, new experiences to encounter. She could not contain the excitement that welled up in her as she looked across campus to the white stoned academic buildings. Her vast imagination saw students pouring into the buildings, books in hand and looking expectant.

Fall had not yet arrived to this southern Illinois campus. Rather, a warm breeze gently buffed the many hardwood trees that dotted the green between her and the academic buildings, erasing her imaginary people. Smiling, she turned to enter the dorm and started toward the stairs.

Returning from her room, she found her older sister, Eileen, bringing the next box of her things through the door. "You could at least help unload your own things!" her sister complained.

Rainee took the heavy box from Eileen and skipped down the half case of stairs to the garden level dorm room. Dumping the box on a student desk, she checked out the room more carefully. A set of tall bunk beds rose in one corner. Two chests of drawers stood next to the beds and under the wide window. A second desk was arranged to face the desk she had dropped the box on just now. The room was painted pale blue with a black linoleum floor. A wide closet took up half of one wall.

Passing back through the hall, she noted a communal bathroom with many showers and sinks. Home. She smiled. This would be her new home. Her guardians had taken a new church far away this fall; so, they were no longer able to act as her guardians. Eileen and her mother brought her to college at her request. She had hoped a reconciliation would happen with her family, for she feared she would have nowhere else to go when classes were not being conducted if she thought she might have the courage to go home.

Rainee returned to the old turquoise and rust-colored Ford for her suitcases, "All done," she chirped as she pulled the suitcases from the trunk. "Shall we have lunch before you head back? It is an awful long drive." Rainee looked expectantly at her mother and sister.

Her sister snorted out loud as her mother shook her head. "This was a favor," mother stated, "We are leaving now. It is hours of driving before we get home, and I want to get there before dark. I don't see why those goody friends of yours couldn't have brought you. They are the ones who claim to be closest to you!" A snarl had entered her low-toned voice as she swung her heavy body toward the car.

Rainee cringed and sat the suitcase down. "My pastor and his wife were hoping the trip would give us time to sort some of the stuff out from our past," Rainee barely spoke aloud. "Maybe a quick sandwich before you leave would be good," She added more loudly with hope.

Eileen then looked her in the eye with a snarl also on her face, "We are leaving," She stated in menacing tones. "You chose to come here. You chose to disconnect from us. Live with it. We never want to see you again! I brought you here to get rid of you!" With that Eileen got into the driver's seat and started the car.

Rainee turned to her mother with tears on her cheeks, "So I am never to really have a mother?" She choked.

"Goodbye, Rainee," Her mother said in her low growly voice, "I never want to see you again." With that she also got into the car quickly, slamming the door behind herself.

Rainee stood in shock as the car pulled away from the front of the dorm and disappeared down the street. Other students passed her, jostling their way into the dorm, but she felt nothing. Finally, Rainee leaned slowly over to pick up her suitcases. It was then that she suddenly felt a heavy metal door slam across her mind. It was too large to see around…and silver-gray in color…and cold.

Lorraine, stood, squared her shoulders and turned her back to the lovely campus outside as if turning her back to her past. It would be Lorraine who lived her life now. Rainee stood forgotten behind that cold metal door. It would be many years before Lorraine would be able to pry it open again, never remembering her old name of Rainee.

It was Lorraine who grew up, completed a B.S., a Master's Degree and a PhD., all with highest honors. It would be Lorraine who went on to help many other troubled children and students, drawing from a strength she could not yet understand that made her work so successful and beautiful.

It would be Lorraine who would reach out to her mother late in her mother's life and try to establish some kind of bond, too. Her mother would agree to get to know her three grandchildren on a small scale. She told Rainee she did not want an emotional involvement with them, but she should acknowledge them as her grandchildren.

It would be later, after her mother's death, when Lorraine could finally remove that door in her mind. It was then that she knew that her real strength came from the pain she, as Rainee, suffered and survived. And it would be that journey back to herself that would mark the beginning of her story. It would be the finding of the joy in life God had always intended for her. And it would be her way of finally making sense of adult life choices, too. In order to understand herself, Lorraine now knew, she had to know Rainee. It had been a long, painful journey triggered by an illness that still haunted and crippled her. She did not regret that illness, though, because it had given back her past and healed her in more important ways.

Lorraine smiled as she looked toward the worn adobe house she shared with her second husband, Derrick. An old song from her childhood had formed on her lips and she began to sing softly, "I have decided to follow Jesus, no turning back, no turning back....."

Derrick strolled out of the house with a smile on his face. Lorraine stood up, shaking the kinks from her bones. It had been a long day of storytelling and lemonade with her daughters. Lorraine stepped off the patio to meet her husband. At fifty-six and with her medical history and joint pain, her bones needed careful adjusting whenever she moved. Derrick reached out, touching her still long blond hair.

He kissed her forehead as they stood in the doorway., "Are the girls staying for supper?" he asked in a friendly voice.

"I didn't ask them!" she suddenly realized her entire afternoon had passed without thinking of dinner. "How about if you shower, and then we all can go out to dinner as a family?" Lorraine smiled bewitchingly up at her husband, lovingly caressing the thinning gray part of his hair.

Derrick gave Lorraine a loose hug and then agreed.

"What? You don't want me to smell after tilling the garden this morning? A shower it is, then!" He grinned. "Hey, you all are invited out for dinner on me!" He called to the girls on the weather-beaten patio. Then he entered the adobe style home through the sliding glass door.

"Does this mean our story hour is over?" Allison, her baby, now a beautiful tall blonde college student, pouted.

"I think," Lorraine smiled, "I have finally come to the end of my story. Maybe it is time for yours to begin. Maybe you should tell the story of those years I was in darkness because I was too sick to stay conscious for long and you, my dear children, continued *our* lives." With this statement, Lorraine turned as if to follow Derrick into the house.

The girls smiled at each other and mutually agreed eating dinner out would be wonderful. It was good to see Mom the happiest they could remember even if they still worried about her health. She had lived to see all three in college and was continuing to enjoy living. Their lives, too, were growing into things of beauty. "After all this time, and all our pain," Autumn said to sum up their day with their mother, "Mom has found peace." She looped an arm through each of her sisters' elbows. "Come on, girls. Let's go order the most expensive dinner on the menu. Tonight we all deserve to celebrate!"

"Autumn, Ariana, and Allison," Lorraine, mused to herself as the girls entered the house in front of her, "My over-comers...my heroes...walking into my and Derrick's house together, smiles playing on their faces. It is so lovely to watch them." Lorraine turned toward the garden with tears on her cheeks, as she thought she heard singing there.

As Lorraine continued to watch her precious daughters out of the corner of her eye, she could see Rainee skipping in the flowers in her summer garden. She was singing, "I have decided to follow Jesus...." Laughing, Lorraine motioned for her to come in, too. Not only could she remember Rainee now, her heart shouted, but Rainee was a full part of herself. That big metal door was gone. It was no longer even a bridge. Rather, it was totally gone…forever gone, because Rainee had finally, finally come safely home.

Epilogue

This book is based on a true story. Because the main character's illness caused temporary memories problems, though, it was decided that the book should be written as a work of fiction. Thus there is no claim that all the details of the story are true, but the author attempted to stay as close to the truth as she could. The main character was raised in such an abusive homeless family that her teachers and pastor felt compelled to rescue her when her father attempted to rape and murder her. Their heroic acts can never be repaid, because they risked even their own lives to ensure her safety.

In addition, most names and places have been changed to protect some people. The one name left as in real life is Pastor Teston of the Citrus Park Baptist Church in Florida, to whom this book is partially dedicated. The author decided to leave his name in place, because she thought that if Pastor Teston was still alive, or perhaps members of his family, he/they might want to know what a gift he handed Rainee in 1958 when he taught her, "I have decided to Follow Jesus." In addition, the University of Colorado Hospital information is accurate, as others may need their services.

In the autumn of 2008, the government contacted the main character to tell her that her father had passed away at the age of 87. He avoided arrest his entire life despite his numerous atrocities through staying hidden and moving from state to state. His death gave her beleaguered family a peace she cannot explain. Finally, she told her children, she feels it is time to tell her story. She prays that her father found peace with God before he died.

It was also later determined that her mother died of the same illness she battles. The sister called Jenna in the story is still her childhood hero, although no contact exists between the siblings. They have informed her that the past is just too full of pain to have physical reminders by keeping in touch. She prays that one day they, too, will find God's peace and healing. She also hopes that some day one of her children will be able to finish the tale by writing their part of the story. Lorraine's first husband wrote recently. He told her he wanted to ask her forgiveness and make things right from their past. He was in the process of getting his life right with God and trying to spend his life doing good. That, too, gave the author peace as she returned a letter sharing both her deep belief in God's love and forgiveness and her forgiveness for the past. Lorraine and her second husband have been married for five years.

Although she continues to struggle with physical challenges as a result of her illness, she knows God allows her to continue living far beyond expectations for several reasons. She is thrilled to have been able to see all three of her girls to adulthood. She now looks forward to one day meeting her grandchildren and continuing to tell others of God's love. She tells people that there are many things God has taught her along her difficult journey. First, God holds out a hand of love and says, "Just come, come and follow me...I know the way, and I will turn your ashes into a thing of beauty." Second, He does not promise a rose garden, for this life is full of trouble. Finally, she has learned from her life that no matter how great the pain, no matter how ugly the scars, God loves and accepts unconditionally, broken pieces and all, and willingly goes with his children even through the darkest nights.

Author's Note

Lexi Pierce, a retired college professor and counselor, has spent many years as a researcher and writer. She has published in a wide range of formats from articles to books beginning with the publication of her first poem when she was fifteen years old. Her writing and work have gained her many awards. She decided to write her new fiction works under a pen name when she felt she needed to protect the real persons that the characters in this book depict. She, her husband, and adult children live in northern Colorado.

I hope that this story was not just a good read, but may have helped in some manner. I especially hope that other women who suffer from autoimmune disorders or PTSD might find encouragement through reading this story. I would enjoy hearing from you, my readers. Please feel free to write to me at Rainee's World, P.O. Box 81, Milliken, CO 80543, or email me at rememberrainee@gmail.com. Thank you for reading *Remember Rainee.*

www.ingramcontent.com/pod-product-compliance
Lightning Source LLC
Chambersburg PA
CBHW070834250626
47159CB00003B/778